QUEEN OF CHARADES

DONNA BENEDICT

ISBN **978-1-7376303-1-9** (Paperback)

ISBN **978-1-7376303-0-2** (eBook)

Cover Artist: Karen Phillips - Phillipscovers

Tarra Thomas Indie Publishing Services:
Project Manager/Interior Design/Formatting/ Editing (Tarra Thomas with Dänna Wilberg)

To Dänna Wilberg
who wouldn't allow me to quit.

Acknowledgments

This book would not exist without the following support: my faithful critique group authors Suzanne Shephard, Cathy McGreevy and Dänna Wilberg. They drove many miles and spent many hours meeting with me to support my dream of finishing Queen of Charades. Nor would this novel exist without the computer savvy of Kathryn Querry and my daughters Erin Cormier, and Donna Stenberg. Special thanks to my son, Dennis Cormier, for a place to write—my lovely office/sitting room.

Of course, it's one thing to write a book and another to have the courage to publish it. If Dänna Wilberg hadn't insisted I publish it and put me in touch with my editor, Tarra Thomas, along with my cover artist Karen Phillips, this book would have remained where it was: in a binder on my desk.

Also, I'm convinced no one with a family can write without their trusting support. And so, to my children, Kurt Stenberg, Richard Johnson, Shauna Ezell, Lanei

Moore, Donna Stenberg, Erin Cormier, and not forgetting their brother, James Stenberg, who has gone on that final "cruise" we all must take much sooner then we'd like, thank you.

Donna Benedict
August 2021

Prologue

A long Southern California's beaches, beginning in late April, spring played hide and seek, peeked out now and then over the Pacific, impatient for the earth to turn its face to the sun.

On the veranda of her house overlooking a beach near Malibu, the modest share of sea Samantha Pryce enjoyed never limited her vision. Instead, it represented an endless river circling the globe, bringing life to the planet. Well aware that same sea lapped at shores thousands of miles from where she stood, it carried her thoughts back to a past still dear to her.

Samantha had lived in the tiny village of Kenmare, Ireland from the morning she was born until two days before Christmas, the year she turned seventeen. Winter arrived impatiently that year. The restless Atlantic pummeled much of the island, sinking boats up and down the West and Northwest coast from Cork to Donegal, leaving grieving widows and fatherless children in its wake.

Despite the savage weather and The Great Depression, tourists still came to Kenmare—and their presence kept many of the locals in business during the spring and summer months. That winter the natives sat, as they had for centuries, by their peat fires and told their children and grandchildren myths of the little people, of Leprechauns and gold, and of the great heroes who once populated the land.

Most years, throughout summer and fall, Samantha's father, Timothy O'Sullivan made a meager living renting out a tiny fleet of boats to visiting tourists and sports fishermen who came to Kenmare Bay in County Kerry. He also supplemented the family income, like his father before him, by working year around as caretaker of a manor house situated on a tiny Island in Kenmare Bay. After marrying, his wife helped him maintain the manor house until they started their family.

The first four children born to Hannah and Timothy O'Sullivan were girls, a fact Timothy privately considered unfortunate except for his eldest daughter. Before she turned ten, Samantha helped her mother Hannah at home. When Deidre, their second daughter, was old enough to replace her, Timothy began to take Samantha with him to work. Gradually, Sam, as she was called, learned to care for the boats her father owned. At twelve, she could maintain and handle any craft in Timothy's small fleet. Eventually, he taught her to act as a guide to the best fishing spots for the tourists and fishermen who came to Kenmare.

When she reached her teens, her father delegated her "to clean and air out the Island House," as it was known. This pleased Samantha. She called the house "a modern wonder." Instead of the inadequate fireplaces at home, heat came from a great coal furnace in the basement and warmed the entire building. The kitchen she considered a "miracle." It contained a green enameled electric cooker with an oven on top, as well as a machine for washing dishes. A machine, Timothy assured her, "rare, even in America."

Her friends at school considered her description of the house highly exaggerated. And as they were not allowed to visit the Island, her school friends accused her of telling tall tales with her stories of these wonders. Until Samantha's sixteen-year-old cousin Maeve, who worked in Killarney, a few miles from Kenmare, convinced Samantha's friends the Island House was indeed a manor because of its size.

"It has to be," she said, "because it looks like Muckross House," which was a famous Victorian manor.

Once, a guest of the Island's frequently absentee owners explained to Samantha that unlike the famous 1893 mansion, Muckross House, the "Island House" reminded him more of newer mansions wealthy American industrialists built on the New England Coast. Samantha, whose exposure to geography was sorely limited, did not admit to the guest that she knew nothing of a place called New England, except it was part of America. But the visitor's descriptions of these distant mansions reinforced her pride to be in charge of such a similar house.

She was too shy to ask if the mansions in America also

contained what she suspected were museum-like collections of the art in the Island House—rare, she believed, because she had only seen others like them in church. Instead, she turned to her favorite teacher, Sister Bridget, and told her of the treasures she had seen. Sister Bridget, well acquainted with the owners of the house, suggested the works she described were likely French Impressionist and possibly Italian original oils, porcelains or copies of original masterpieces collected during the family's travels in Europe.

~

Chapter One

Anxiety did a step dance in Angela's nervous system. Her red, three-inch-heels beat out a staccato drum roll on the marble-floored lobby housing KCBT's television network. Today was her last chance, she'd either win First Prize and gamble for the Grand Prize or lose everything. At the elevator she stood tapping her foot, willing it to come. When it arrived she stepped in and moved to the back. The elevator rose slowly, stopping at every floor to allow passengers to board or leave. At each stop, Angela dug her fingernails into her palms.

Breathe, she ordered herself when the elevator slid to a stop on the fourth floor. It will all be over soon. The door opened. She pulled in a deep breath and stepped out of the elevator.

"Good morning." The smiling studio receptionist handed her a clipboard with a sign-in sheet. "Don't forget to put in the time of arrival."

She scribbled in her name, the date, and the time of

arrival on the form. As if I could forget today's date. Must they ask for the same information every time?

Cool it Angela, be patient, let her do her job. She forced a smile and handed over the clipboard.

The receptionist glanced at the information. "Why don't you take a seat?"

But before she could sit down the telephone rang.

"That was production," the receptionist said. "Someone will be here in a minute to take you to the studio."

Aptly named for the color of its walls, the Green Room was empty. Assorted magazines on coffee tables rose in orderly stacks. The dull brown industrial carpet must have been vacuumed, Angela noticed, as it no longer wore a layer of yesterday's food crumbs. Clean makeup tables gleamed at the back of the room. A large television screen mounted in one corner was silent.

Angela's nose followed a heavenly scent, the promise of freshly brewed coffee. She poured herself a cup, silently blessed its maker, and sank down on one of the sofas. She rolled her shoulders in a vain attempt to relax the tension in her neck, and then with a sigh, she lifted the paper cup to her lips.

The door opened before she could take the first sip. A gnome-like little man with over-large ears and a smile the width of an Arizona canyon walked into the room.

Angela set down the cup of coffee, almost spilling it.

She was staring at the man and was ashamed when she realized it.

He didn't seem to notice. He smiled, stepped forward, stopped on the other side of the low table and bowed.

"You are early, oui? I am Monsieur Jean Jacque," he said, pointing to the iridescent green badge pinned to his orange smock.

His bald head and shorter than average arms reminded Angela of a dwarf. No, she concluded,-too tall for a dwarf. It was his head. His head was so large she wondered how he kept his balance.

What was wrong with her? A physical therapist, she'd seen all kinds of bodily distortions. Mankind was wondrously diverse, and for her, usually delightful.

"You are ready for the makeup, Mademoiselle?"

Angela hesitated—then read the badge he'd pointed to. Under his name and employee number it read, Makeup Department.

"Where's Louise?" she asked. "She's done my makeup for the past two shows."

The words were no sooner out of her mouth than she regretted them. She'd probably hurt his feelings.

"Louise, she is ill," he said. He didn't look hurt. "You are ready now, oui?"

Angela cast one longing look at the steaming cup of coffee and rose to follow the little man to a makeup station, wondering once more, why makeup? All the contestants wore masks.

"Such magnificent cheek bones," he said, the moment he'd seated Angela in front of the illuminated Hollywood vanity mirror.

He cupped her chin with his small hand and turned her face first right and then left, studying it closely in the rosy glow cast by the mirror lights.

"Mademoiselle, with your face and my talent, I can only create the masterpiece," he announced. "Magnificent cheekbones," he repeated.

Angela's face registered her surprise. Her former fiancé, Edward Fournier III, M.D., would not have agreed. "Your cheekbones are a bit too prominent for real beauty," he'd said, too often.

Only now did she allow herself to recognize how much Edward's remark hurt.

As if he had read her mind, Monsieur Jacque said, "All things, Mademoiselle, they are relative. Beauty, ugliness, these are not real. We see what we choose to see. Oui? We believe what we choose to believe."

He spoke as if he knew Edward Fournier, knew what he'd done to her. Ridiculous. She'd have to stop reading fantasy novels. The man wasn't a mind reader. He was a makeup artist—at least, she hoped he was.

"And now, Mademoiselle, we begin a masterpiece." Without further comment, he turned the chair away from the mirror, but not before she caught the twinkle in his luminous brown eyes.

Beside her Angela saw a small table, its surface crowded with jars, brushes and what appeared to be tiny pallets of luminous colors. Eye shadow she decided. Then she watched when he dipped his long, slender fingers into the luminescent contents of one of the jars on the table, and then felt his fingers moving deftly across her face. With a delicate but certain touch, he applied the white substance under her eyes, above her cheekbones and across her broad forehead.

Then he reached for another small jar, this one full of what appeared to be a brown, viscous substance. Angela felt him draw a crescent in the hollows below her cheekbones. Apparently satisfied with his choice, he blended the creams, then stepping back one pace, he clapped his hands. "Bon!" he exclaimed, his affirmation full of enthusiasm. Without a mirror, she could not see the results, and could only hope his lopsided smile meant he was pleased, when once more he stepped forward and selected yet another jar from the table.

When Monsieur Jacque applied several more layers from the numerous jars on the table, she allowed her thoughts to drift. Time? Where did it go? When the show ended she'd race back to Santa Monica and hopefully arrive in time to supervise the packing and transportation of the equipment she'd be storing near her apartment in Venice. At least, she'd be on her way if she lost, and if she won, what then?

"Tres bon!" The little man interrupted Angela's thoughts, and after dropping his hands to his sides, he stepped back.

Angela tightened her hold on the arms of the chair. What did French for "very good" mean to a Frenchman?

"Fini!" he said, with a toss of his head. Then stepping away, he spun her chair, and gestured to the mirror.

Angela's eyes widened.

"Oh!" She gasped.

A satisfied smile lit Monsieur Jacque's face; he bowed, "I'm beautiful."

"But of course," he said, "We spend our days masquerading before the world, but seldom do we see the beauty we are meant to be. Oui?" Then without waiting for a response, he reached beneath his makeup counter and pulled out a jeweled half mask layered with sparkling rhinestones.

"For me? It's stunning," Angela said. "So much prettier than yesterday's," she added indicating the black satin mask on the makeup counter she'd worn the past two days.

Still holding the mask, he stepped closer. "Today awaits your future. A future with a mask." His face darkened. "Soon, Mademoiselle," he lowered his voice to almost a whisper, "you will need this mask. The jewels, they are not real, but the colors, the colors, each radiates a truth of who you are meant to be."

Angela shifted in her chair. "It is lovely," she said.

He continued. "Many faces are beautiful But evil, too, he hides behind le beau face." He paused, seemed to study her in the mirror. "The mind of courage, it lifts the mask, looks beneath to see the true face."

Angela dropped her gaze. Evil with a beautiful face? He wasn't making sense.

Seemingly unaware of her discomfort, he continued. "Le Grand Prize, she is alluring. Oui? Consider before you accept to compete for such a prize, Mademoiselle. You believe perhaps for you it brings riches...and amour."

He leaned closer. "But no, it brings perhaps danger." He shrugged. "Who can know? Only les masques know what they hide. Les masques, Mademoiselle, do not trust what you think you see. Look behind les masques for truth."

With a sweeping bow, he held out a jeweled half mask.

Beauty, danger, love? Laughter bubbled up inside Angela. But before it escaped, she met his eyes, and swallowed. He was serious.

Ridiculous. The last thing she needed was romance and what danger could there possibly be in winning a game show contest? Charades wasn't that kind of beat-them-up dump-them reality show. No, today was her last chance. If she lost today, she would lose everything she'd worked for. If she won First Prize, she could go for the Grand Prize. She reached out her hand, her fingers closed on the mask.

As for "amour," she'd unmasked her "prince" six months ago. His betrayal was still raw. There would be no amour in her life, not now, not soon, not if she could help it.

Angela nodded at the little man reflected in the mirror before her. He looks solemn, sincere. He may be a bit odd, but he's no fortune teller, she decided. And she swiveled her chair away from the mirror to face him.

"You are talented Monsieur. As for the uses of money, I agree. It is always wise to watch out for danger where money is involved. I'll certainly watch out for danger," she paused, "and especially for amour!" Her voice echoed her conviction.

Jacque shook his head and looked beyond Angela into the mirror just as the stage manager opened the door to the Green Room

"It is time." Then again with a bow, he added, "If I have been, as you say in English, of service, then the future is good, bon."

When they'd reached the studio the stage manager warned, "Eight minutes, Ms. Hamilton. If you'll take the first seat at the right of the platform."

Near the edge of the set, he watched while she picked her way across the stage stepping gingerly over thick electric cables taped to the floor of KCBT's Studio Two. It was her third day as a contestant on the game show Charades, and win or lose, he knew, her last day. He'd seen plenty of contestants in the four years he'd worked the show, but few he chose to remember. He knew she would be one of the few.

Her name was Angela, and her name matched her face. With long blonde hair, a slim athletic body, and quick mind, she was any man's dream. She also had a way of making the people around her feel good about themselves. She had it all. And he realized she didn't have any idea of how others saw her or what she could do to a man.

Intent on avoiding the cables, Angela didn't notice the stage manager hadn't moved. If she had, she would have assumed he was simply doing his job by making sure she didn't trip. Without looking back, she climbed onto the circular platform at the right of the stage and sat down in the fire-engine-red swivel chair he'd indicated. She put on the jeweled half mask she carried, tugged at her skirt and tucked it under her to keep it from riding up around her hips. Then she checked her watch—almost seven minutes to show time. It couldn't be over soon enough for her.

Off to her right, a camera moved in and she checked

her watch again—six minutes to go. On the other side of the screen shielding the set, she could hear the audience taking their seats. During the taping of the first two segments of the contest, she'd managed to block them out while she concentrated on the game. Today, however, she felt uneasy. Concentrate, she ordered her restless mind. Leaning back in her chair she closed her eyes and mentally recited the names and biographies of the six Oscar winners she'd read about the night before.

A minute later she heard the stage manager directing the other two contestants to their places on the dais. She opened her eyes. Mindy and Letticia appeared in the wings and skillfully avoided the cables without looking down while crossing the floor. They mounted the platform without a pause in what was obviously a heated discussion.

"It's him, I know it's him," Leticia insisted. "I saw him on Extra last week."

"I didn't see anyone in the wings. Who'd you say?" Mindy asked.

"I told you, Pryce, Jeremy Pryce. The millionaire—Monica Thorne's latest."

"Where?" Mindy demanded looking around the set.

"Right there! What do you want me to do, point at him? He's standing right there, where I said he was, at the other side of the set."

"Oh my, that boy is choice."

"You sound like you're talking about a steak," Letticia said.

"A steak? Yeah, he's rare alright." Mindy licked her

lips. "Hey Angela, take a look. Then tell me you wouldn't like a bite."

"He's CEO of Pryce Cruise Line," Letticia interrupted. "You know, the corporation sponsoring this show. I saw him on one of those late night talk shows last year— said he's a Rhodes Scholar, went to Oxford, played polo with Prince Harry."

Letticia, clearly star-struck, dropped dozens of names the entire week they'd been on the show, Angela recalled. She couldn't hide her amusement and turned her head away, but not before Letticia saw her smile.

"You think I'm trippin'?" she said, "Ever seen a picture of him?"

"Once. Maybe. Wasn't it on the cover of *Time* last fall?"

"Uh, hello, have a look. Tell me he's not Pryce," Letticia insisted.

"I'm looking." Angela swiveled her chair, faced the wings and inhaled sharply.

The photograph on the cover of Time paled by comparison. This was Pryce, all three dimensions of him. Jeremy Pryce. Tall, with heavy sun-streaked brows that matched the color of his hair. Blue eyes? No, she couldn't really tell this far away. Not blue, maybe, but blue-green, perhaps translucent the exact color of a tidal pool on a summer day late in August.-The portrait on the cover of Time was believable, looking at him now. But a poor imitation of the man in the wings. And his mouth? No photograph could capture the reality. Delicious, turned up at the corners slightly, as it was now in a smile of...?

She caught her breath. He was staring at her with a look of...No! Impossible! Recognition?

Could they have met? She certainly would have remembered him if they had. Yet strangely, there was something familiar about him. Something that had led her to study the photo, had made her heart beat a little faster, the way it was beating now.

On the opposite side of the stage, at the entrance to the set, Jeremy's gaze traveled from the three inch high, red sandals, above her delicately turned ankles and followed tanned legs that went on forever. His exploration continued above the short skirt tucked tightly under the curve of her hip, continued to her belly and narrow waist, then paused abruptly, lingering on her breasts. She wore a pale green, scoop-necked sweater designed to enhance her upper body. It hugged her breasts, exposing the shadowed cleft between them—a vision to please any healthy male. He couldn't see her eyes. She wore a 'jeweled' half-mask similar to those of the other two women, except hers sparkled beneath the set lights.

The stage lights backlit her head, outlining a small straight nose and a confused expression. Her long, honey-blonde hair was pulled back from her face and anchored with a black velvet ribbon. A few tendrils escaped. They clung shimmering to her cheeks. He pulled in a ragged breath. He had to see her eyes. He'd bet himself they were blue. But he couldn't make out their color with the mask shading them. Jeremy looked up at the digital clock above the set. Four minutes to show time. The commercial would begin running any second. Four minutes were enough for him to approach the dais, pretend to ask all the contestants a few questions about their impressions of the show, and of the emcee in particular.

Across the set on the dais, Letticia turned to Angela. "I thought you didn't know him," she demanded.

"I don't." Angela felt her face flame. "I don't know him."

"He seems to know you," Mindy nodded her head in agreement. "If you don't want him, he can put his number twelves under my bed any ole time."

"It won't be too soon, Mindy," Letticia said. "It looks to me like he's about to head this way to put them under Angela's."

But before Angela could protest, Mindy whispered, "Too bad, too late. Here comes the competition. Isn't that Monica Thorne?"

The three contestants watched the famous soap opera heroine sweep down the corridor.

She stopped behind Jeremy, threw her arms around his neck and covered his eyes with her hands.

On the dais they heard her croon, "Darling Jeremy. Guess who?"

Who else? Jeremy reached behind him, removed her hands from his eyes. She doesn't wear Gucci, she baths in it, he thought.

"Some women have all the luck," Mindy said.

"Yeah." Letticia sighed. "Not only is he gorgeous, I read that he and his sister will inherit Pryce Cruise Line when their grandmother dies."

Angela stiffened and shut her eyes. She didn't see Jeremy turn, close his hands around Monica Thorne's wrists and back her away from the entrance to the set.

You don't even know him. And if you did, the last thing you need in your life right now is another man, especially another wealthy one.

Not attracted—not even a little bit? her inner voice challenged. *Nope. No way. Never.*

Seconds later the curtain rose. The dais where the three contestants were seated rotated slowly to face the audience.

"Here we go," Mindy mouthed the words.

Applause swept up over the stage and the game began.

"Ladies and Gentlemen, at home and in our studio audience, welcome to America's favorite game show, Charades, the game where everyone can win.

"Today, one of our three remaining contestants will compete for first prize, fifty thousand dollars and an all-expense paid trip for two to an exotic location.

"The winner may accept the money and take the trip with no strings attached. But, Ladies and Gentlemen," he paused, his stern gaze swept the contestants, "if the winner chooses to compete for the one million dollar Grand Prize, she must agree to take her trip incognito, impersonating a minor celebrity without being identified as an imposter within ten days, by you or our television audience."

Again, he paused, glanced at the three contestants and smiled. Then turning his attention back to the audience, he faced the cameras

"During each of the ten days," he said, "you, our studio audience and our home audience, will be offered a clue to the identity of the celebrity being impersonated.

Correctly identify that person, and the contestant will forfeit the fifty thousand dollars they've gambled to the first person to recognize which celebrity our contestant is masquerading."

Another pause. "And now, Ladies and Gentlemen, before the game begins, a word from our sponsor, Pryce Cruise Lines. Luxury on the High Seas."

Angela didn't have to see the faces behind the masks of the other two contestants to understand how they felt. In a few short minutes one of them would win first prize and be offered the opportunity to become a millionaire. If she won, would she have the courage to risk it? She didn't know.

Less than eight minutes after the commercial ended, the second game began and Angela felt desperate. She trailed by fifty points. Mindy, a first-year UCLA film major recognized all the old black and white, silent films being projected on the studio screen. Letticia recognized the titles and actors of every horror, and almost every sci-fi film, from the nineteen twenties to the twenty-first century.

Angela loved movies, she also knew the names of some of the old black and whites Mindy identified, but she didn't press the button on the arm of her chair fast enough. As for science fiction films, she didn't try to identify most of them or the horror films. She disliked horror films.

If I don't answer two of the next three questions, she thought, I won't have enough points to try for the last scene. If I don't have enough points for the final scene, I won't be eligible to answer the final question.

The final question, always a live pantomime acted out by a popular star, allowed the contestant with the most points to gamble for the Grand Prize.

Angela felt certain today's pantomime would be acted out by Thorne, since they'd seen her with Pryce in the wings of the set.

When she caught herself wondering if Jeremy Pryce was still in the studio, Angela commanded herself to focus. There were other categories still available. She read the numbered electronic board next to the huge wheel. Twentieth century to twenty-first century Oscar-winning performances, legitimate theater, Greek classics.

After the commercial, Mad Martin addressed the audience. Angela watched his lips move. But panic overcame her. The words seemed incomprehensible, only sounds, why couldn't she comprehend the words? She smothered a self-pitying whimper of rising panic. Then she blinked, turned to the two women beside her. Neither looked particularly stressed.

"What makes you so special you have to lose?" She heard the words as clearly as if he was standing beside her. Not Martin's words, her father's words. The same words he repeated on the way to every swimming meet, before every swimming competition. Since the first one when she was only eight. She always recited those and other words her father taught her when she stepped up onto the block and looked into the water below.

"Before you dive, check your form: hips high, eyes looking down, arms loaded, rear foot behind your hips. Focus, and above all remember, somebody has to win, why not you?"

Why not win? It's only another competition, she thought. She couldn't afford to feel sorry for herself. She couldn't afford to lose. A new clinic? It had taken years to refine the methods she used to successfully help her patients. Working in another clinic, one not hers, she might be prevented by the owner from utilizing her own methods. There were therapists who did not see the significant value of water therapy. She didn't want that. Didn't her patients deserve the best she could offer, individualized treatment, any and all treatments needed? Hadn't she just seen an example of what could be done? Was it only yesterday she watched while Merry swam the length of the pool. The Merry who could not walk when she first arrived at the clinic almost a year ago?

Angela lifted her chin, sat up straight.

Across the stage, Mad Martin signaled his assistant to spin the giant wheel while Angela focused, shut out the whispers, the rustling noises, shuffling feet and barely subdued coughs coming from the studio audience.

She held her breath while the glittering ball of light bounced in and out of several categories: cartoons, fantasy, science fiction, romance, horror, famous stars, academy award winners, actors. Beside her, she could sense the increasing tension in her two fellow contestants, Mindy and Letticia.

Gradually the wheel slowed, the ball dropped into number four, science fiction movies.

"Good." Angela heard Letticia whisper the word.

No! Angela's mind demanded. The ball hesitated, and while she watched, it magically bounced again to settle into Oscar Award Winning Performances.

Angela slid her hand along the arm of the chair and placed her finger just above the buzzer. She could do this.

The buzzer sounded. "Dr. Jekyll and Mr. Hyde, Fredric March, 1931," Letticia said.

Damn. A little faster, Angela chided herself. You knew that one. Come on. Come on.

The wheel spun, her heart stuttered. The wheel stopped.

"And our next category," Mad Martin announced. "Oscar Winning Actors. Before the twenty-first century. Nine actors have won Best Actor in a Leading Role twice," he said. "You must name two films and name the actor in those films who won Best Actor in a Leading Role twice."

The buzzer sounded. "Spencer Tracy, in Boys Town, 1938, and Captains Courageous 1937," Angela answered. She looked at the board—fifty points to her. She'd caught up with Mindy, she smiled.

"Oh, hell," Mindy whispered again under her breath.

Across the stage Mad Martin gestured. Once more the show's assistant spun the giant electronic wheel. The wheel slowed, stopped at paranormal films. But before the ball could settle, the wheel spun again, the ball teetered, the wheel stopped. This time, the glittering ball rolled gently into another Oscar question, "Second Best at the Oscars."

Angela blinked. Odd she thought. Three questions in the same category, Oscar winners? She didn't see any unusual reaction from Mad Martin. Maybe three questions in one category was common. She mentally added the points to her score. Please, she thought, no more sci-fi or horror films. She needed thirty more points to beat Letticia. She crossed the fingers of her left hand in her lap.

"This scene, from the film Chicago," Mad Martin narrated, "starred Renee Zellweger and Catherine Zeta-Jones. These two actors shared almost equal time on screen, one of them won Best Actress in a Leading Role, the other only Best Supporting Actress. Who came in second best?"

Before Angela could react, a buzzer sounded. "Catherine Zeta Jones won Best Supporting Role," Letticia said.

"Sorry," Mad Martin said, "Best Actress went to Renee Zellweger, while Best Actress in a Supporting Role went to Catherine-Zeta-Jones"

Angela could almost feel Letticia weep. *Oops!* That was tough on her, she thought.

The emcee nodded to his assistant. She spun the giant electronic wheel. The glittering green ball bounced in an out of several categories, Oscar winners, vampire sagas, westerns. The wheel slowed, stopped at paranormal films. Letticia leaned forward. Angela sighed. Then, miraculously, before the ball could settle, the wheel picked up speed, spun again, stopped. This time, the ball dropped into Best Actress in a Leading Role.

Across the stage, Mad Martin blinked, stared at the wheel in obvious disbelief while the studio audience roared. This was the fourth time for Oscar winners. The film clip rolled. A slender, blonde woman appeared on the screen behind the emcee.

A flush of adrenaline raced through Angela. Her

finger was on the buzzer instantly, "Meryl Streep, 1981, Oscar winner, Best Actress Award for Sophie's Choice."

Letticia curled her fingers and grimaced. Mindy, who hadn't answered any of the Oscar questions, shook her head.

Applause erupted from the audience.

Mad Martin signaled for silence. The applause ended and he turned to Angela. "Ms. Hamilton, if you answer the final question correctly you will win fifty thousand dollars and an all-expense-paid, exotic vacation for two. And if you do identify the next scene, you may also choose to gamble the fifty thousand you've won for a chance to win the Grand Prize. Do you understand, Ms. Hamilton?"

She reviewed her options: Get the next question right and walk away with 50 grand and a nice trip. Or...get the next question right, use the 50 grand to qualify for the incognito trip, win a Million if no one figures out who she is—or lose the 50 grand if they do and get a great trip but no prize money.

"Yes," Angela said, "I understand."

When the applause ended, Mad Martin smiled at Angela. "Are you ready for the final question?"

Angela tightened her hold on the chair arms. "Yes," she said, in a clear voice.

"Our final charade," Mad Martin said, enunciating each word in his sonorous voice "will be a pantomime of a riveting scene from an award winning play, a great, classic Greek tragedy. Because the performance is as usual a pantomime, I respectfully expect the audience to be especially quiet."

A Greek play. Angela almost laughed with relief. She'd loved those plays as an undergraduate.

"It will be performed by a star we all know and love, the beautiful and talented Monica Thorne." He smiled his best toothy smile and added. "But first, a word from our sponsor."

Behind the dais a scene featuring a cruise ship sailing through crystal blue waters blossomed onto a huge screen hung like a curtain behind the contestants. The sonorous voice of an unseen narrator listed the joys of cruising on a Pryce Line cruise ship to several impossibly lovely places.

Angela didn't turn to look at the screen. If she wanted to answer the final question, she knew she had to relax, and she began counting backwards the way her Yoga instructor, Deanna, had taught her to calm her mind when she still swam competitions. Ninety-nine, ninety-eight, ninety-seven, ninety six. On each count she imagined stepping down an elegant, circular staircase. Far below she could hear music, people were dancing, laughter floated up to her. If she could just reach the final step and enter the ballroom...?

The commercial ended. Angela opened her eyes.

Mad Martin looked at Angela. "Ms. Hamilton, you know the rules. You have thirty seconds to press the buzzer on the arm of your chair."

Then he turned to face the wings. Monica Thorne, robed in a flowing white toga, swept onto the stage to a delighted round of applause. She did a low curtsy to the audience, raised her arm in a salute to Mad Martin, ignored the contestants, and advancing center stage, began to pantomime her scene.

Oh that one, Angela thought. The Greek dramatists could be brutal. What was it Letticia had said about women and luck? Some women seemed to be born with it. They grew up in happy families fell in love with the hunk next door, married, had children and lived happily ever after. Did the ancient Greek women believe in luck? Angela doubted it. Certainly not according to the ancient Greek playwright Euripides who wrote the scene Monica Thorne was competently pantomiming of a woman crazed by the betrayal of her powerful husband.

It was a short scene, and when it ended applause for Monica Thorne's performance erupted from the audience. Once more she gave a low curtsy. She smiled for the audience, for Martin, and finally, as if suddenly seeing them for the first time, she nodded in the direction of the three contestants before exiting in a swirling cloud of white silk.

Martin signaled the audience. When they'd quieted he turned to face Angela and asked, "Your answer please, Ms. Hamilton."

Angela looked toward the wings of the set. The corridor was empty.

"Your answer, please," Martin prompted.

She moistened her lips and in a strong clear voice said, "Medea, a famous tragedy written by the Greek playwright Euripides. The slaughter scene."

In apparent surprise the emcee's eyebrows rose. "Exactly," he said.

The audience applauded enthusiastically, until he stepped out from behind his podium and signaled for silence. The audience stilled.

"And now for the million-dollar question, Ms. Hamilton."

"Will you take the fifty thousand you've won, or try for the Grand Prize?"

Angela stared at the emcee.

"Are you ready to answer the question, Ms. Hamilton?"

The voices from the audience were deafening.

"Don't be a fool, fifty thou...!"

"Five hundred Benjamins, lady, fifty thousand dollars, you can't..."

"You're a winner, go for it!"

"A million dollars. Take a chance!"

Her senses battered by the sound surging across the stage, Angela recoiled.

"Don't do it," Letticia whispered.

"The last two who tried lost," Mindy chimed in.

Mad Martin said, "If the audience will please be patient!"

The audience stilled, waited. Mad Martin crossed the stage to Angela and took her hand.

Dazed, she rose from the chair and stepped from the dais. With her hand held securely in his, Martin led Angela to the center of the stage.

"And your decision?" he asked again.

Angela felt the cameras close in on her. Their glassy eyes stared, moved closer, demanded an answer.

Beads of perspiration broke out on her forehead. She felt the audience rustle, advance. Numb, her eyes fixed on some elusive horizon, and she fought the urge to step back, to run. Someone coughed. Mad Martin's toothy smile remained fixed. How long had it been since he asked for her answer, seconds, minutes...?

Does it matter? her mind mocked. *Open your mouth, Angela. You know the answer. You have no choice.*

She swallowed. Her voice hoarse, she whispered, "I'll chance it."

The emcee's smile unfolded, spread across his face. "Would you please repeat your response a little louder Ms. Hamilton?"

Angela straightened and lifted her chin. "I'll gamble the fifty thousand for a million dollars."

The audience roared.

~

Chapter Two

Moisture coated the tiled walls. A warm mist rose from the Olympic-size pool, condensed and dripped from an oversized, chrome-rimmed clock on the far wall. Angela Hamilton felt the water pulse at her ankles, heard rather than saw it rhythmically drumming against the walls. Thrilled, she watched five-year-old Merry Johnson cut through the water as if she'd grown fins. She refused to answer the question poised on the rim of her consciousness. *What would she do if Merry stopped swimming?*

Clenching and unclenching her hands, she forced her mind to shut out the question, to remain focused on the physical skills of the girl in the water until Charlie cracked the door open.

"Hey Boss, that woman is still outside."

Angela bit back a need to demand, *What do you want from me? What do you expect with only seven hours left? I can't fix everybody!*

Without taking her eyes from the child in the pool, she forced a smile and said, "Thanks, Charlie, I'm on it. Please close the door, quietly"

Intent on analyzing the way the girl used her body, Angela had forgotten the child's mother standing at her side until she heard her whispering, "Please, please, please." Whatever deity the child's mother was begging, Angela knew the success or failure of nine months of physical therapy would be determined here and now within the next few minutes.

At the far end of the pool, Merry reached out, touched the wall, made a perfect underwater turn and began to swim back to where the two women waited. Tremors of excitement raced up Angela's spine. "Yes!" Her fist shot into the air. Once more the gods of pain had been bested, a child snatched from a wheelchair. Beside her, Merry's mother wept.

Minutes later Angela lifted the laughing child out of the water, wrapped her in a towel, and placed her in her mother's arms. Tears threatened. She turned away from the pair and headed for her office.

Over the months of treatment, she'd grown fond of the child. Not the most objective behavior for a physical therapist, Angela recognized, but difficult to repress with many of her hapless patients.

Someday, were she lucky, she would have a child of her own, boy or girl, it didn't matter. And now she needed to rein in her emotions. At her office computer she opened Merry's log, reread her *Subjective-Objective-Assessment-Plan* notes, the carefully compiled record of the child's condition at intake, the biweekly treatment and progress to date. An essential tool, the *SOAP* was one Merry's new therapist Pete could refer to for future treatment.

After saving the log, and before moving on to the next file, she checked the time at the bottom of her computer screen. Six hours and seventeen minutes left before she closed the doors of her clinic to patients for the last time. In three months, or maybe only two, the building it housed would cease to exist. Yet another upscale condominium overlooking Santa Monica's share of the Pacific Coast Highway would rise on its lot near Third Street, a prime location in an upscale shopping area.

Angela refused to feel victimized. She could hardly blame her landlord for selling the property. According to him, the money his real estate manager said he'd been offered "would fund the infrastructure of a third world country." Recalling the cliché, Angela might have laughed except for the lump in her throat.

The screen's cursor winked a warning. Six hours and fifteen minutes left. She brushed away the tears, checked, saved, closed another file, shut down her computer and picked up a felt marker. But, before she could fill in the label on one of the file boxes stacked beside her desk, Charlie poked his head in the door once more.

"Hey boss, that chauffeur's in the waiting room again. He says his employer is still sitting outside in her car. He insists she must see you."

Angela's pen hovered in mid-air over the box. "If it's about treatment," she said without turning around to face him, "I assume you told him she'd have to go somewhere else."

"Sure, I referred him to Pete over in Metro clinic, but..."

Angela laid down the pen, and with more force than necessary, rotated her desk chair.

"And?"

Charlie leaned his long body against the doorframe, crossed his arms and grinned at Angela, a slow grin that took up most of his narrow face.

"Yes, Ma'am. I told him, Boss. I all but ordered him out the door. Even if he is the size of a small gorilla."

Well aware of her intern's quirky sense of humor, Angela ignored the description Charlie supplied.

"And he said...?"

Charlie straightened his back, squared his shoulders, glowered at Angela and growled. "'Hey, Dude, you must be hard of hearing. This message is for your boss.'"

Angela couldn't hide the smile. "Dude, huh? And you said?"

"Faced with King Kong, I knew enough not to arm wrestle him out the door."

"My hero. But why doesn't she just come into the waiting room?"

"Message boy says it's difficult for her to walk."

"Oh, got it."

Angela studied the clock over the doorway above Charley's mop of unruly black hair. She blinked. *It couldn't be...almost noon.* Only recently she'd become aware of a new, unwanted compulsion, keeping track of minutes, jealously watching them slink away as if they were fearful she might catch them, cage them.

"Mrs. Brinsky is due in ten minutes," she said.

Charlie's grin widened, again. "Yeah," he said. "Ten minutes plus another ten or fifteen. When has the dragon-lady ever been on time?"

"Point taken. But, how would you behave if you didn't like yourself? You have to admit she's doing better."

"Yeah, well you're leaving and..." Charlie looked past Angela to the stack of files on her desk. His mouth tightened, flattened. "Last day, and all that..." She nodded at the stack of boxes on the floor. "Fed Ex will be here in a just a few to pick up the last of the files. As soon as..."

Charlie sobered. "Look, Angela, I know I'm bugging you about that woman. But, I hate to tell our boy you can't see her. She's waited over an hour." Charlie paused, looked at Angela, "You can quit grinning at me. It's not because I don't want to explain to gorilla-man what's keeping you. I'm betting on you, you'll win the big money, build that new clinic. You'll want patients. You're good. They need you. And—well, damn it!" Charlie shrugged, looked down at the floor, and said, "You know I'll be certified soon. I might want to work with you again. If you'd have me, that is."

Angela knew the speech cost Charlie, knew he didn't want to suggest she was dreaming, that she would be working for another therapist soon, in their clinic, not her own, perhaps with a colleague she disliked. She'd only agreed to compete on the game show after the banks refused to consider a loan. And now, she couldn't pass up a chance to compete for a million dollars, a final try to raise the money to open a new clinic.

"Okay," she said. "Tell the messenger, I'm on my

way." She paused just long enough to step into a pair of Levis and pull on a tee shirt over her swimming suit.

Outside the limousine, a dark blue Mercedes stood directly in front of the building with the passenger door open. The woman seated inside obviously belonged in a limousine. At first glance, she reminded Angela of a delicate, ivory sculpture she'd recently admired in the Los Angeles County Museum of Art.

She was seventy if she was a day, a lovely seventy.

"Do come in and sit down, my dear." The woman patted the seat beside her.

Angela slid inside. She'd seen hundreds, if not thousands of limousines in movies, magazines, on television, and cruising the streets of Santa Monica, but she'd never been inside one. No media image could capture the luxury of the interior. The deep leather seats closed around her and the scent of leather and some mysterious and memorable perfume filled Angela's senses. Clair de Lune played softly through hidden speakers. And there it was, just like in the movies: beside a darkened television screen, a single white orchid in a vase attached to the back of the chauffeur's seat. For the first time in her life she understood the term *opulent*.

"I'm Samantha," the woman said, holding out one narrow, blue-veined hand. "I understand you are expecting a patient. I won't keep you long."

Angela smiled, but quickly withdrew her hand. She'd never seen a ring with a diamond the size of the one on

Samantha's right ring finger. The stone, she guessed, probably cost more than the limousine. Aware she'd been staring, she shifted her gaze to the woman's face.

If Samantha noticed Angela's fascination with the ring, she was too polite to let it show. "And I must apologize for not making an appointment," she said. "But there simply wasn't time to do so after I'd been advised last night you would be closing your clinic today." She paused as if expecting some comment, then continued when Angela only nodded. "I do hope it isn't too much of an imposition on your time."

It was. Surely, Angela thought, whatever this woman wanted she could buy. Right now, money, the absence of it, ruled her own life. And she doubted there was a need for her to be listening to a stranger who hadn't even revealed her surname. *Why not? Who is this woman?* But, she had picked up a note of anxiety in Samantha's voice, and after all, she had waited over an hour to speak with her. Clinic or no clinic she was a caregiver. Maybe the woman really did need help. She felt annoyed with herself for her lack of patience.

"If you're here to schedule an appointment, I can recommend. . ."

"Oh no, my dear, not at the moment, that is. I am seeing a very capable physical therapist where I normally reside." The woman's hands fluttered, as if to discard the idea. "She's set in her ways," she added. "Unfortunately while competent, she lacks imagination."

Angela bit back the impatient question that sprang to her tongue. *What does your therapist's lack of imagination have to do with me, or my clinic?* She still had so much to do before the day ended.

As if she'd overheard her thoughts, Samantha said, "I know you must wonder why the skills my therapist has, or does not have, should matter to you."

Busted.

Angela hoped the heat she felt rising wasn't coloring her face. "I don't mean to be rude..."

Samantha smiled, "Nevertheless, the question must certainly have occurred to you. To be frank, it isn't your concern. If you will bear with me a moment, I will explain. You know Angela, may I call you Angela?" She continued without waiting for an answer, "We have met before today."

"Have we?"

Surely she would have remembered this woman if they'd met. "No offense but I'm afraid I don't recall meeting you."

"No offense taken, Angela. I hope you don't mind if I call you Angela?" Samantha repeated.

"Of course not." Impatience made her want to demand, *Get to the point.*

If Samantha noticed the clipped response, she didn't indicate she was aware of Angela's growing frustration. "Good. I didn't expect you to remember me. Perhaps if I'd mentioned we met on a beach in Malibu. . ."

Angela frowned. Malibu, a hazy picture teased her memory.

"We had a nice chat once. My, doesn't time roll on?" she added absently. "It has been more than seven years."

A beach in Malibu? Angela couldn't remember the last time she'd been on that beach.

"You were younger then, a life guard."

Bingo.

How could she have forgotten? The ink was still wet on her high-school diploma. A wonderful summer. The summer before she left for Yale, the summer before she met Edward Fournier.

"Oh, yes," Angela said, her voice lightened. "My first responsible job. I was petrified."

Samantha nodded. "You did seem nervous. Nevertheless, I was quite impressed with you. I fully intended to keep in touch."

Keep in touch? Angela stared, but if Samantha noticed her confusion, she did not address it.

"I lost track of you shortly after you graduated from college," Samantha continued. "Then yesterday, quite by accident, I encountered an acquaintance who attended the same meeting I did, several years ago. You spoke to the board of directors of Santa Monica General that day. Your subject was aquatic physical therapy and its benefits. You may remember Dr. Cohen?"

Of course she remembered, Angela thought. *How could I forget? I'd just opened my clinic.* "He was the Director of Santa Monica General, wasn't he?"

"Yes, and the person who invited you."

"He had a reputation for encouraging young people just entering the medical community."

"Yes. A fine man—a dedicated physician. We met quite unexpectedly last night, at a dinner party of a mutual friend. Recalling the meeting we attended a few years ago, he happened to mention your clinic was closing. You'll be pleased to know he was sorry to hear the news. I gather he referred several patients to you before he retired."

Angela's smile was genuine. "He did. That's true."

"Meeting him was a happy coincidence. Only a few days ago I'd been wondering how to find you."

Once again, confusion clouded Angela's face. What did she miss, why would Samantha be concerned about her closing the clinic if she planned to stay with her own therapist?

"You're not asking me for a therapist recommendation?"

"Oh no, my dear," she said, patting Angela's hand. "No, no. But, it occurred to me recently your approach to physical therapy would be ideal for a new project I have in mind. Yes, a new project." Samantha paused and seemed to review what she'd said. "I am the president of the board of. . ." She hesitated, then added, "A service company."

"A service company?"

"Yes." Ignoring Angela's implied question, she continued talking. "At this time, we do not have the facilities for any extensive physical therapy. However our CEO suggested adding a program for our clients with severe physical disabilities."

"What kind of disabilities?"

"A good question, my dear, those requiring uninterrupted treatment."

Angela had noticed the swollen knuckles of Samantha's hand when she'd admired the ring. It frequently indicated an especially painful, debilitating form of arthritis. Could she be asking advice about establishing a program specializing in therapy for arthritic patients? Unlikely, Angela thought, any good clinical therapy program would include treatment for arthritis. As a former hospital board member surely Samantha would be aware of the availability of such treatment.

"You mentioned a new business."

"Yes, I'm thinking of building a spa for those of us who are somewhat disabled. And, I'm not quite certain how to go about it. That's when I remembered meeting you, and listening to your little presentation."

"A spa?"

"Yes. As your clinic is about to close, it occurred to me you might like to use your skills in such an endeavor. I can assure you, you'd have free rein to develop any program you felt was best, and a salary appropriate to such an executive position would be fairly negotiated.

Who is this woman? Angela thought. She appeared out of nowhere like some fairytale godmother. She looked away from the woman beside her and into her empty hands open in her lap. Part of her, she admitted, was almost desperate enough to consider Samantha's offer. Ashamed of the thought, of the nagging voice inside her that insisted she would be a fool to ignore such an opportunity, she looked up at the serene face of the woman beside her and fought back an unjustifiable anger.

She's only offering you a job. She hadn't suggested you'll never open another clinic. She stifled the urge to challenge her. *How dare you come here and tempt me to give up.* Guilt washed over her. She shook her head.

"Sorry, you caught me off guard." She shook her head again. "I'm flattered. Thank you, but no."

Samantha's eyes danced, sparkled.

She almost seems pleased, Angela thought.

"Ah, yes. I can't say I'm surprised by your answer. I did believe however, I had to ask."

"Why? I would think managing a spa, even one catering to women with disabilities would require a person more in tune with the beauty industry."

"That is certainly standard, " Samantha agreed. "However, what I'm talking about is a bit more complicated," she added, and appeared to be considering how to explain why.

Angela saw a large shadow fall across the car window beside her. Mrs. Brinsky. She recognized the grossly overweight, middle-aged woman lumbering toward the clinic doors, and reached for the car door handle.

"Please excuse me, Samantha. I see my next patient has arrived."

She was already part way out the door when Samantha said, "You don't remember meeting me several years before your presentation at the hospital, do you?"

Angela paused, looked back over her shoulder at the woman. "I'm sorry. I'm afraid I don't."

"I'm not surprised. No doubt what you did then must have seemed almost routine for a life guard. That summer in Malibu, you saved my only granddaughter's life."

Chapter Three

The morning after her visit to Angela Hamilton's therapy clinic, Samantha Pryce, president of Pryce Cruise and Shipping Lines, sat at work in her study. Across the room from her desk, a Today Show host muttered softly on a small television. Only dimly aware of the sound coming from the set, Samantha moved some personal letters aside and opened a bound copy of the cruise line's quarterly profit and loss statement. While reading, she ignored the television program, only reaching for the remote when a raucous advertisement for used cars interrupted her concentration. But then, a familiar scene filled the screen. She increased the volume and watched a picture of a dock and a two story gray concrete-block terminal at Florida's Fort Lauderdale harbor appear. Behind the terminal a huge white cruise ship rose out of the water. Even before a television camera focused on the eight-foot high letters across the ship's hull, Samantha recognized The Lyre.

On the dock in front of the terminal, a television reporter stood with his back to the scene and addressed the camera in front of him.

"Greek officials in Athens announced late last night they have completed their investigation of Margret Kopinski's murder," the reporter said. "Lorraine Campbell, Vice President of Communications for Pryce Cruise Lines, was on hand this morning when The Lyre, carrying Mrs. Kopinski's body, docked at Fort Lauderdale. Questioned by this reporter, Ms. Campbell refused to comment on what the Greek police found when they investigated the murder scene on board the famous cruise ship. She admitted to this reporter it could be relevant to a congressional investigation scheduled in March to determine the level of security afforded passengers sailing on ships that call at U.S. ports." The camera cut to Campbell.

"Naturally all cruise lines take steps to insure the safety of their passengers," she said. "Pryce Cruise Line like other cruise lines based in American ports is a member of the U.S. travel industry. While all cruise ships are required to report any suspected criminal instances to the local authorities of any port where one of their ships dock, American based ships, on returning to the United States, must also file a report of any suspected criminal activity with several stateside agencies, including Homeland Security, the F.B.I. and the Coast Guard. Until all reports are filed, there will be no further comments on behalf of Pryce Cruise Line."

In Malibu, Samantha Pryce nodded at the screen. "Good for Lorraine." After the report, the advertisements began again. Samantha sat staring at the screen for a moment before turning off the set.

Samantha knew her grandson Jeremy, the CEO of Pryce Lines, planned to be in Los Angeles later that afternoon to meet Burt Chaney, his friend and Director of Pryce security. Burt would be returning from Athens where he cooperated with the Greek authorities investigating the murder on the Lyre, but Jeremy had alerted her earlier to the results. In spite of the investigation in Athens, the Kopinski murder remained unsolved.

Jeremy also divulged that Burt had gleaned information in Athens that led him to suspect something equally as confounding: the Kopinski death might be related to an earlier death on one of their other ships.

The obvious question was unsettling. Were there other murders, either among missing passengers or among so-called accidental deaths? If Burt was correct, could a serial killer be at work—a passenger or possibly an employee who worked for the line moving from ship to ship, stalking and killing single women? Samantha shuddered at the thought.

Jeremy, as CEO and Burt, Director of Security, would testify before a congressional committee on cruise line security practices in March. After the hearings Burt would fly to Florida and board the newest ship in the line, The Queen of Charades, to observe current security protocols and possibly make changes. Jeremy would join him for a working vacation.

The results of the contest could potentially set into motion a plan for her Jeremy's future she'd only shared with her closest friend. Samantha was determined to set her plans for Jeremy in motion before he left. But, she could only do so much. The rest would be up to fate, luck, Divine intervention or all three. Samantha was suitably familiar with each to know the outcome was more *out* of her hands than *in*.

The sun barely lit the horizon when she reached for the telephone.

A slight breeze off the Pacific danced in the tops of the trees. In late November early December the weather in Santa Barbara turned cold. When he became CEO of Pryce Cruise Line, Jeremy Pryce built his west coast hideaway in the hills above the beach at Santa Barbara. Located on a wooded bluff overlooking the Pacific, it was an ideal location, not more than two hours driving distance from L.A., beautiful and secluded enough to avoid bumping into business associates on the streets. Perfect for Jeremy, now in his late twenties.

From his second story bedroom with its floor-to-ceiling windows and wrap-around decks, he had an unobstructed view of the mountains behind his home and the beach below. On clear mornings, he would circle the deck to watch the sun creep up over the mountains behind his house and spill down the hills. Then he'd circle to the front to watch it ignite the tips of the waves several hundred feet below his bedroom window. Jeremy loved the beaches of the world and especially his home in California.

When he was five his parents died in an automobile

accident. He and his sister Heather left the high rise apartment that had been their home in New York and went to live with their grandparents at Malibu Beach, California. It was a dramatic change for two children who had known only a sky that could be seen above and between the city streets. It didn't take them long to adapt to the more leisurely pace of living their grandparents preferred.

As they grew, one of their favorite things was to follow their grandmother to the beach on her "hopeful dawn walks." With their grandmother "Sam," they searched for shells and exotic objects, precious or at times worthless, deposited on the shore, gifts endless waves offered up for enchanted children. On school leave many years later, he and Heather talked about those morning walks and confessed that even as teens they might have preferred to sleep late, but Sam rarely allowed that to happen. With the early wisdom of young adults, they finally recognized that their Grandmother, who rarely did anything consistently or without a purpose, contrived the "hopeful walks" to teach them that each new sunrise brought its share of unexpected gifts.

When he was at home, Jeremy didn't need an alarm clock. Through un-curtained windows, he would wake to the sun and the birds' dawn chorus. Hundreds of birds—Finches, Sparrows, Mockingbirds, Bluejays and many others he could not name—chattered in the trees behind his home.

In December, before either the dawn or the birds were awake, Jeremy awoke abruptly and completely.

"Damn dream!" Wide awake, he set up straight in

bed, wrestled two feather pillows from beneath his head, and propped them on the mahogany headboard behind him. Right out of Dickens, he thought, one of those ghostly kind with a one major difference, no Marley. No figures at all—only a disembodied voice, a lilting, haunting voice calling him, telling him to hurry, hurry but, never a destination. Throughout the dream Jeremy recognized the distant voice calling him, or, once awake now, he thought he should recognize it. He searched but never found it.

"Monica?" Not quite awake he scanned the room, shook his head. No, not Monica. Not her voice. He'd been with her just before he left Los Angeles, taken her to dinner, more out of guilt than pleasure. For the past several weeks she'd left little doubt she expected their intimate six month relationship to lead to marriage. It proved an uncomfortable evening for him.

When they first began seeing each other, he believed Monica might be the one. She'd been married and had a child, a disabled boy he enjoyed. The child's existence wasn't the problem. Monica, beautiful, charming and successful fit the criteria for a wife he'd settled on. Any woman he married, he'd decided while still in college, must be financially and socially his equal, or nearly equal, at least. Apparently she was. He could not think of a rational reason for not proposing to her—he only knew it wasn't going to happen.

In a week, Monica would be leaving L.A. for Puerto Rico, the site of her latest film. She'd suggested he meet her there during the Mardi Gras. He probably would, he'd decided, if not for her sake, for the child's. The least he could do was face her. He would meet her in Puerto Rico in March, if everything went as planned during the Hearing in D.C., he'd fly from to Fort Lauderdale, and board the Queen of Charades when it docked there to take on passengers for its ten day Caribbean cruise. Scheduled to reach Puerto Rico during Carnival, San Juan would be the last place the Q.C. docked before returning to the States.

But that wouldn't be until March. Too restless to remain in bed, he reached for the heavy robe he'd thrown over the footboard the night before. Yes, he'd tell her then, he decided. He swung his feet to the floor and shrugged into his robe. In the bathroom he turned on the gold plated faucets of the shower.

He was still in the shower when the telephone rang. Only one person would call him on his private line before nine. He grabbed an oversized towel from the heated rack on the wall and wrapped it around his waist before reaching for the receiver on the bathroom wall.

"Good morning, Sam. How's my favorite grandmother?"

"Humph! Your only grandmother," came the response.

She was okay. Relieved, Jeremy could almost see the twinkle in Samantha's bright blue eyes. He hadn't heard from her during the two days he'd been hiding out in Santa Barbara. And he seldom allowed himself to think of a day he wouldn't hear her voice on the other end of the line.

He punched the button for the speaker phone and still wrapped in the bath towel, he returned to the bedroom.

"Do I need more than one?" He crossed the bedroom to the door of his dressing room and began sorting through his business wardrobe. His day would be busy.

"No, you don't. However this morning like every morning since you achieved your majority, I find it quite disturbing that a seventy-one-year-old woman is the only one on the planet who gets you out of bed before dawn."

Jeremy grinned. Here it comes, the "You need a wife," lecture.

"...and your little sister is likely to marry before you do." Samantha was wrapping up her lecture with the money shot.

"Obviously, you haven't been reading the Enquirer this week," he said. "It seems I'm engaged to several of the planets most desirable..."

Samantha cut him off. "That rag."

She was not only okay, he thought. She was feeling good.

"Let me guess, you've been mesmerized by the erudite questions and scintillating testimony televised during this week's congressional hearings."

"As well I should have been, Jeremy Pryce. Someone in this family has to pay attention to business."

"And, you learned?"

"The same thing the congressional committee members did, nothing. But, I did hear an interview with Lorraine Campbell this morning."

"Yes?" Jeremy stopped looking through the shirts in his closet and listened.

"The usual questions from the media. She's a good girl. Gave all the right answers."

"Good, that should keep the media at bay for a couple of weeks. Since I'll be in D.C. for the hearings late March, there's not much more we can do on this end before I leave." He paused. "Unless you've thought of something we've overlooked."

"No, I think the board agrees we've covered everything we can."

Jeremy removed a shirt from its hanger.

"What about Burt? Were you able to reach him?"

"We spoke last night. He flew into Boston from Athens. There was some delay in Boston. I didn't get the details, something wrong with the plane he'd chartered. He's in the air now. He'll bring his report with him to the office later today."

"Did he say when?"

"He should land in Burbank around one. I'll pick him up there."

"Good, and then I'd like to hear about your visit to the game show. The advertising agency wants to know if we will continue to sponsor the show. I've only met the M.C. once—the guy with the ridiculous name of Mad Martin."

"I've seen the show. And?"

"I understand the point of the show—it isn't simply a game show, it's one of those new reality shows. The agency seems to think this Martin might not be the best choice for M.C. I'd like to discuss your opinion of him and of the producer Evelyn Carstairs. Carstairs work seems quite acceptable to me, but I'd like your input."

"I understand the ratings have been good."

"There is that," Samantha agreed. "I'll see you at dinner."

Chapter Four

On the first Monday following her final day as a contestant on the game show, Charades, the producer's secretary telephoned Angela with a message. She was instructed to meet the producer, Evelyn Carstairs, at Two Rodeo drive in Beverly Hills at precisely 1:00 pm. Furthermore, she should plan to spend most of the afternoon and possibly part of the evening with the producer while an appropriate wardrobe to wear during the second phase of the contest was selected.

Until the telephone call, it hadn't occurred to Angela that she didn't own the kind of wardrobe required to compete in the final phase of the contest. Obviously Carstairs had known. When the call ended, she checked the clock on the kitchen wall, nine, on the dot. She hadn't had breakfast and had just returned from her morning run, a daily exercise routine she'd established when she discovered she could no longer swim.

Charlie would be meeting her at the clinic in Santa

Monica at ten to finish sorting and packing records and small equipment she planned to store near her home. How long would it take her to reach Rodeo Drive from Santa Monica? She retrieved her cell phone from the pocket of her shorts and punched in the address. She seldom had reason to visit L.A. and she'd never considered shopping on Rodeo Drive. On a few memorable occasions she'd visited the Los Angeles County Museum of Art to view traveling exhibits. It had to be only a short drive from the Museum to Rodeo Drive. Although it might have been fun seeing the famous designer stores, she certainly couldn't afford to shop there. As for appropriate clothes, she owned a few professional looking dresses and suits and some evening wear. But most of her wardrobe consisted of practical swimming suits, shorts, tee shirts, Levis and sweats. The small legacy her father left her had helped her finish college and graduate school, and the rest went to open her clinic. All money she'd earned after that she spent to support the clinic and maintain a modest living.

With rent, utilities, salaries and all those unexpected extra costs, money for clothes remained on the last page of her budget. Looking at fashions she liked in magazines and as worn by some of her clients was free. Some of them no doubt were as fashionably attired as the woman Carstairs had informed her she would impersonate, Silke von Chassen, a minor international celebrity. But she couldn't help remembering the old cliché her father used for a man or a woman who, in his words, "put on airs" by wearing expensive fashions. "Don't they know," he'd say, "you can't turn a pig's ear into a silk dress or purse." Or words to that effect. She loved beautiful clothes, although she hated to admit that her father might have been right many times. Monsieur Jacque seemed to think she was attractive. And she wanted to win. She hoped Carstairs would prove to be her fairy godmother.

Number Two Rodeo Drive must have skipped the drab month of February. Although the calendar said March was a week away, baskets of spring flowers hung from ornamental light poles lining the cobbled streets. Store windows glittered. and fashionably dressed pedestrians walking in and out of shops added an ever shifting rainbow of out-of-season color.

As directed, Angela waited, watching the scene from the corner of the famous street until Evelyn Carstairs, joined her. Only a few minutes after greeting Angela, the Charades game show producer led her down Rodeo Drive where she opened a massive gold filigreed door to one of the exclusive Rodeo Drive shops.

The two women stopped inside the door and waited while their eyes adjusted to the subdued light. Even after she'd begun to make out parts of the room, the reflections from the window behind her prevented Angela from seeing the woman before she rose from behind a replica of a Star Trek glass desk.

She wore black. Not simply a black dress, but a severely tailored black dress, sheer black hose, black nondescript heels and black rimmed glasses that seemed to magnify her piercing hazel eyes, now focused on Angela.

"May I help you?" she asked. At least those words came out of her mouth, but her eyes continued to assess

Angela's gray sweats in a way that suggested Goodwill was a few blocks north.

Carstairs stepped forward. "Our appointment is at one thirty."

The woman's gaze slid past Angela and her body tensed. Her closed-lipped smile and hesitant nod acknowledged the producer instantly, but could not hide the flush of embarrassment on her cheeks.

"Yes, of course, Ms. Carstairs," she said. "Madame is expecting you. If you will follow me."

Without waiting for a response the woman in black turned on her heel and with the long-legged stride of a former fashion model, she lead the way across a polished marble floor to an opaque glass door with the word Salon written on it. On the other side of the door, a petite, silver-haired woman in a sculpted gray suit stepped forward to greet them. She only glanced at Angela before extending a ring laden hand to Carstairs.

"We were delighted to receive the inquiry from your secretary, Ms. Carstairs. I am quite certain we can accommodate your needs once more. My associates and I have collected a few samples you may find attractive." She indicated the right side of the room where two clothing racks on wheels stood hung with colorful garments.

"Your selections will be modeled, of course. Please be seated," she added, indicating two plump occasional chairs upholstered in a creamy shantung silk.

"I've rung for tea, unless—?" She looked from Angela to Carstairs, "you'd prefer a glass of Prosecco while you view your selections."

"Thank you, tea will be welcome." Carstairs

answered without consulting Angela who was doing her best not to appear intimidated by both the luxurious surroundings and the famous silver-haired designer she'd only seen on television. When she'd signed to compete for the Grand Prize, she had understood the show would choose the celebrity she would imitate, the places she would go and it would also provide her with a suitable wardrobe for her masquerade. What hadn't been said was the kind of wardrobe. And once she'd been told where she was going and who she was supposed to be, she should have guessed why Carstairs wanted to meet her on Rodeo Drive.

For the next three hours the producer and the salon owner chose clothing they decided that the internationally known playgirl Silke von Chassen would wear on a ten day Caribbean cruise. Model after model paraded their selections. A discussion followed, with each of the women putting forward their case for the fashions they considered most appropriate. Not once did they turn to Angela for an opinion.

Three hours later, after a short visit to Jimmy Choo for shoes to match their final selections, Angela, laden with packages, followed the producer into Minnie's, a popular coffee shop where they both ordered coffee and croissants.

Neither of the women spoke after ordering until their selections were placed in front of them. Carstairs turned to Angela only after she added two scoops of sugar to her coffee, stirred, and sipped.

"Except for lingerie," she said, "and at least one swimming suit, I believe the clothes we have with us today and what will be delivered should be sufficient for the cruise. You do have a swimming suit, yes?"

"Of course. I probably have twenty, but not one Silke von Chassen might wear, even unseen in her own shower."

Carstairs sighed. "Lingerie?"

"Not anything Victoria's Secret would approve of, but as it won't be seen..." She reached for her coffee. "Mmm good."

Carstairs frowned, set her cup down. "A bikini, I think."

Distracted, Angela's gaze swept the room lingering on several of the fashionably attired women, most of whom sat alone with an extensive collection of shopping bags on the floor next to their feet.

"In that case, I'd prefer to choose my own suit, but not today. I'm exhausted. How do these shopaholics do it?"

Carstairs, who'd reached for her coffee, hesitated. She also surveyed the room. 3 "Many of them have nothing better to do," she said, "which reminds me—in her bio, you did note Silke does not swim."

"Then why would she require something to swim in?"

"Good point, I suppose, but when we spoke she mentioned several resorts she visits each year. Many of them are quite famous for their fabulous shops, some for their topless beaches. Perhaps she likes to sunbathe?"

Angela suppressed a smile, but couldn't resist asking, "With or without a suit?"

Carstairs reached for her croissant and broke off a piece. "Exactly. It's a masquerade. You'll need a suit."

Angela decided she liked Carstairs, and half an hour

later, after they'd compared notes on what they knew or thought they knew about well-known celebrities, they'd finished their coffee and were on their way to the door when they were stopped in the foyer by a beautiful, expensively dressed woman. She would be a perfect Rodeo Drive model for one of the designer salons specializing in so called "plus size" fashions, Angela thought. The woman acknowledged the hasty introduction to Angela, then turned to Carstairs. Obviously a business acquaintance involved in the Hollywood scene, the two women carried on a brief conversation about Monica Thorne.

Not quite gossip, but close, Angela, who tried not to listen, decided. But she couldn't help overhearing Carstairs say, "It's wishful thinking. Pryce isn't likely to marry her, or anyone soon, for that matter." The other woman agreed and after a minute or two longer she said goodbye and made her way into the restaurant.

~

Chapter Five

Angela spent over a month researching, the life and family history of the woman she would portray, minor celebrity and international play-girl Silke von Chassen. Much sooner than she felt she'd be ready, Angela opened the door to the V.I.P. lounge at Miami International Airport. A smiling hostess behind a tall lectern inside the door, glanced at the first class ticket Angela presented and then opened the heavily padded doors leading into the lounge.

A wall of glass overlooked the airport tarmac. A bar in the center of the room was surrounded by thickly cushioned bar stools. Small tables were scattered throughout the room. Men and women seated alone, in pairs and in small groups, filled the deeply upholstered occasional chairs and long couches. Business travelers, Angela decided.

Some talked quietly. Others thumbed through magazines or read pocketbooks. A few hunched over the low, chrome and glass drink tables, and gazed intensely at multicolored laptop computer screens and smartphones.

Angela fought back an impulse to stare. The entire scene left her with the impression of an Architectural Digest magazine spread of an upscale living room or a 007 movie set.

A harried looking cocktail waitress moved among the tables distributing drinks and taking orders.

"Just wait in the V.I.P lounge," Charades producer, Evelyn Carstairs, had said. "You'll be paged by a company chauffeur. He'll drive you to the harbor. You're a lucky girl, and you will sail away on Pryce Line's newest, most luxurious cruise ship, the Queen of Charades. Relax, have a drink. Remember you're on vacation.

Angela grimaced. "Some vacation."

Carstairs had grinned. "Well, sort of."

A vacation. Why not, Angela decided. This could be fun, she told herself. Relax, enjoy. Her gaze scanned the room in search of a table. After all, she hadn't had a vacation since she finished high school, and she'd never been on a cruise ship. For that matter, she'd never been in a V.I.P lounge before today.

She checked her watch. Even after the stop in Atlanta, her flight landed almost fifteen minutes ahead of schedule. If she could find an empty table, she would have time for one drink before she was paged. She wanted a drink, not because she was nervous or anything like that, she told herself.

After walking the length of the room without seeing an empty seat, she turned back toward the entrance to the lounge just in time to see a couple leaving a table.

Relieved, she slid into one of the empty chairs facing the lounge entrance doors. Then turning, she spotted the busy waitress who managed to avoid locking eyes with her by looking at something somewhere above her head. She couldn't help wondering if the real Lady von Chassen would have better luck placing an order?

Before Angela could signal her again, the waitress moved to the other side of the room. At that point, she decided to forgo the drink and began rummaging in her overnight case for a novel she'd wanted to read. Her hand closed over it as the lounge doors swung open. Startled, Angela looked up.

For a moment he stood framed in the doorway. It had been more than a month since she'd seen him in the wings of the Studio. He'd been dressed casually that morning in brown gabardine trousers and a camel-colored sports jacket. Mindy, one of the other two contestants on the game show Charades, assured her it was "cashmere."

Angela wasn't surprised. It looked expensive. He looked expensive.

And still looks expensive, she thought, only more so. Working in Santa Monica and dating Edward Fournier she'd become aware many men considered three thousand dollars plus for a suit from Barney's New York or a British-made bespoke suit from a London tailor an acceptable price. Today Jeremy wore a blue-gray suit. The fabric Angela identified as a silk blend, the design, Italian. Exquisitely tailored, it fit so well it might look effeminate on many men, but not on this man. If anything, it seemed to accent his muscular, broad-shouldered, slim-hipped body. A body, she realized, her fingers itched to touch.

A slightly bemused smile played at the corners of his mouth. He stood motionless, casually surveying the crowded room, until his gaze came to rest on her. She would have sworn his eyes were even bluer than those in the portrait she'd seen on the cover of Time. Her reaction to the easy self-confidence they projected was immediate, instinctive, primitive, an almost physical assault on her senses. And, he didn't try to hide the fact he was aware of her reaction. When he moved from the door to her table the smile his lips had only hinted at became even more amused, broadening and deepening the creases at the corners of his mouth.

Did he recognize her?

"Hello." His voice resonated warmly. "I see you have an unoccupied chair." His gaze once more swept the room. "There's a crowd today. Unless you are expecting someone, perhaps you'd be kind enough to share your table?"

Angela hesitated, clutched the book she'd retrieved from her bag. She could detect no hint of familiarity in his greeting.

When she'd first seen him looking at her, for an instant she thought he'd recognized her. But, now as he stood over her waiting politely for a response, she saw no glimmer of recognition in his eyes.

Snap out of it. Just because he wears self-assurance like some kind of Medal of Honor doesn't mean he recognized you. You were masked. Why shouldn't you share your table? It's not as if your paths will ever cross again. Forget it, he's gorgeous. Enjoy!

Angela acknowledged her inner voice and with a

tentative smile said, "Yes, of course, please." She indicated the remaining chair with a wave of her hand.

Almost immediately she wondered if she'd made a mistake. His smile, she realized, when he'd seated himself in the chair across from her, was a bit too self-satisfied, his introduction too unnerving.

"Jeremy," he said, offering her his hand across the tiny cocktail table. "I promised myself when I saw you from the doorway I wouldn't say anything as trite as, 'Hello, beautiful, it seems only hours since we last met.'"

Angela felt her stomach drop. "I...I'm sorry, I don't..." she began.

"On the flight," he said.

"The flight?" Surely she would have noticed him. He'd hardly been out of her mind for the past several weeks.

"Actually we might have met if there had been time. You were seated ahead of me in first class. I missed my first flight and took a hop from D.C. I boarded your plane when it landed in Atlanta. Angela's face flushed. "Oh," she said in a rush of comprehension. The relief she felt all too apparent in her face, her voice.

Jeremy looked at her quizzically, but before he had a chance to question her reaction, the cocktail waitress, who'd managed to avoid Angela's arrival, appeared at the table.

"What'll you have?" she directed her question to Jeremy. Once more ignoring Angela, "Ah, prompt service," he said, "My mother would have insisted on ladies first." He nodded at Angela. "So, what will it be? Milady?"

"Silke."

"Not exactly a common name?"

"No, my...my...grandmother's name," she lied.

"And my name's Maisie," the waitress interrupted.

Angela managed not to smile, "A Riesling, please, Maisie. A Franken wine, if you stock it."

The waitress shifted her full attention from a clearly intrigued Jeremy to Angela.

"Hey, I had some the other day. The wine supplier said it was from Germany. Something with a weird name, Inneren I think. Good stuff."

"Thank you Maisie, you seem to know your wines." The waitress beamed.

"If you have a bottle chilled..."

Angela paused and fixing Jeremy with a mischievous smile said, "And if the gentleman will join me...my treat of course." She was immediately rewarded with Jeremy's frown.

The waitress looked at Jeremy. He looked at Angela.

"I would be a bore not to accept such a gracious offer," he said

"Smart," Maisie said, and flounced off in her ridiculously short skirt.

Jeremy sat back. It had been a long time since a woman, other than Samantha, or his sister had challenged him. He was used to being in charge, expected to be in charge. And, he recalled, the last time a woman had bought him a drink, he'd been a college freshman. Two years later that one drink had caused him more pain than he ever wanted to experience again.

He leaned across the table. "Did I pass the test?"

In spite of herself, Angela smiled. "You passed."

"And if I had refused your offer?"

Angela's chin rose. She straightened in her chair. "As you invited yourself to my table, I would, in your words, consider you a 'bore' and expect you to find another table."

"I would not care to be classified as one. My mother, I'm certain, would not have liked that."

"A wise woman," Angela quipped.

Jeremy leaned back, amusement sparkled in his eyes. "I'll admit to a certain curiosity about your choice in wines," he said. "You've clearly taken advantage of one of my weak spots, untasted wines. Naturally, my mother would also have taught me not to accept gifts from strangers," he said gravely.

Angela didn't miss the past tense referral to his mother and felt a twinge of regret, but almost laughed when he added in a business like voice, "I must, however, make you a counter offer."

Angela's eyebrows rose.

"I promise I won't think of you as a temptress if you'll agree to have dinner with me," he added with a disarming smile.

The intensity of his gaze and the memory of the first time she'd seen him left her breathless and strangely annoyed. Why did she have to meet him here, why now, when there was no hope of getting to know him? "I'm afraid I..." she began.

"Naturally, we'll go Dutch." His smile broadened into a playful grin.

Angela couldn't suppress the laughter. Reaching across the table, she shook his outstretched hand.

"Deal!" she said.

Careful, the voice cautioned. Yet, she sincerely wished some day she could keep the promise.

Jeremy gazed at Angela thoughtfully. Short, curly blonde hair framed her small, oval, face. A face, Jeremy knew, an artist such as Botticelli would have painted had he not preferred dark haired angels. The tiny cocktail table couldn't cover her figure or a pair of legs a runway model would kill for. And, while Dolly Parton's breasts deserved adulation, hers though smaller, were downright spectacular. She owned, in his experienced opinion, an absolutely sensational body. He'd been attracted to another woman not long ago. She too had been blonde, a different shade of blonde, perhaps, but that woman's hair was quite long and tied up with a black velvet ribbon. And there was something about this woman's voice. He was certain he'd heard her voice before, could she be an actress?

Perhaps he'd remember later, but now, looking at her closely, he understood why, when he'd stepped through the padded lounge door and spotted her, he'd gone directly to her table. She'd looked up at him, drew him in —her large, wide, indigo eyes, fringed with long ebony lashes, questioning beneath winged brows. They mesmerized him, spoke to him of bottomless seas he knew and loved, of tropical islands and pirate treasures. What were they hiding? He could almost feel the question forming in her mind. 'Do I know you?' And he couldn't shake the impression he knew her. Did she also wonder where they had met, if they had met? They had, he was almost sure of it.

No wedding ring, he noted, surprised at how that observation pleased him.

"How was your flight?" Jeremy began.

"Pleasant. And yours?"

"Excuse me." Maisie held out a bottle for inspection. Angela looked at her blankly. "Your wine?" Maisie prodded.

"Yes. Thank you." Angela accepted a proffered glass, sipped, nodded her approval and after the wine had been poured, raised her glass.

"Ciao," she said, regaining her composure.

Jeremy raised his glass and sipped. "Salute, to you also, Milady."

Neither of them noticed the lounge hostess approaching until she stopped at their table.

"A chauffer from Pryce Cruise lines is outside asking for you Ms. von Chassen. He said you were expecting him."

"Yes, thank you." Angela smiled up at the hostess. "Please, ask him to wait."

"Going, so soon?"

When the hostess returned to her station, Angela faced Jeremy. There was no mistaking the chill in his question.

She reached for her glass and then without drinking from it, set it down again. Any explanation she made, she realized, would not change the fact she had agreed to go to dinner with him knowing she had no intention of doing so.

"It wasn't an out and out lie," she began. "I did say I would go out with you and I meant it. It's only that...I—I don't know exactly when."

"You had no particular date in mind?" he leaned toward her pinning her with his gaze.

"I...well," Once more she reached for the glass in front of her and put it down again. "To tell the truth, I don't know you. I'm simply not in the habit of going out with a man I just met. Women who do frequently end up dead."

"Then, I look like a serial killer?"

"Not exactly a...serial killer."

"Who then? Exactly?"

Angela lowered her gaze to the table. "You'll have to admit you came on fast, and even Ted Bundy was supposed to be extremely handsome and..."

Jeremy reached across the table and took the glass from Angela's hand.

"So you think I'm handsome enough to be a serial killer, then?"

"I didn't say that!"

"Which was it you didn't say? You don't see me as a Ted Bundy or you don't see me as handsome?"

Too unnerved to think clearly, Angela missed the amused tone in Jeremy's voice. She hadn't meant to insult him. How had he managed to twist her words?

"I meant what I said. You certainly must realize you are handsome!"

Jeremy fought back an impulse to laugh. "But, you don't think I'm a killer?" he asked gravely.

"Of course not!"

Noting the sparks beginning to gather in her eyes,

Jeremy picked up the glass he'd taken from her and offered it to her.

"Before you throw the remaining wine in your glass at me, let me remind you, you did agreed to dine with me."

A grin tugged at the corner of his mouth. "And, speaking of dinner, we really should be going." He pushed his chair back, walked around the table and pulled out hers.

Attraction fought with reason. There was no point in kidding herself. Whatever was going on between them, it might cause her to let her guard down. Was he suggesting he'd be on the cruise? If so, she couldn't afford to take the chance he might remember where he thought he'd seen her. Angela rose from her chair, retrieved her travel bag from the floor, and turned to face him again.

Lowering her voice to a whisper, she said, "Assuming we could be going in the same direction, which we obviously shouldn't be, whatever would make you think I'd offer you a ride anywhere, mister, mister... You are without a doubt the most arrogant..."

"The name is Jeremy. Remember?" he said. Cupping her elbow, he guided her through the lounge doors.

In the lobby a uniformed chauffeur stepped forward. "And the fact is, it appears we are going in the same direction Let me be the first to introduce you to the amiable Howard, chauffeur extraordinaire for the Pryce Cruise Line, which I happen to know has the only cruise ship docked in the harbor at this moment."

"Mr. Pryce," the chauffeur said, tipping his hat, "good to see you sir. Welcome to Fort Lauderdale Lady von Chassen. May I take your carry-on bag?"

Beside her, Angela felt, rather than saw Jeremy stiffen? Uh, oh, she thought turning toward him. Has he remembered something?

But, he only studied her for a long moment. Then with a bow he said, "I'm afraid I've been operating under a misconception. My apologies, your Ladyship. I should have recognized you from a photograph of you I saw last week in the London Times...a photograph which, by the way didn't do you justice."

Angela swallowed a sigh of relief, gave Jeremy her brightest smile, glanced at her watch and suggested, "Shouldn't we be going?"

The white Rolls Royce limousine glided gracefully out of Miami's international airport into Fort Lauderdale's rush hour traffic. After leaving the airport, Jeremy, much to Angela's dismay, had chosen to sit in the front seat with the driver. Now staring at the back of his neck, her confusion deepened when he closed the sliding glass partition between the front and backseat of the limousine.

Outside the car window the city streamed by, but she hardly noticed. In the airport lounge, he seemed to feel the same attraction she had for him when she'd first seen him at the studio. And, even when she'd tried ignoring the obvious signals, he continued to press her for a positive response. That is, it seemed until the chauffeur addressed her as Lady von Chassen. His attitude toward her changed instantly. Why? If there'd been some history between Jeremy and Silke, a failed romance, a feud of some sort, wouldn't Carstairs have mentioned it? The producer had certainly been free with details of Silke's many liaisons. On the other hand, why should she? What

Jeremy Pryce did and where he chose to travel was certainly not important to the show's producer. Was she simply a pawn? After all, a million dollars was a lot of money. Hadn't Monsieur Jacque warned her? Hadn't she first seen Jeremy on the stage of KCBT? Was it just a coincidence he'd walked into the V.I.P. lounge at the airport, that he would be on the cruise? Could he part of the Charade? If he knew who she really was, would he disqualify her? Come on Angela, just because of what happened with Edward, you can't start seeing all of life's coincidences as conspiracies. Jeremy Pryce is CEO of Pryce Cruises. Why wouldn't he be on one of their ships? But, she'd be lying to herself if she denied the chemistry. And she could lose everything if she didn't keep her attraction to him under control.

It was not until their driver guided the car into a sharp turn through a security fence onto a tarmac road marked "Harbor" that Angela realized they'd arrived. Almost before the car came to a halt Jeremy was out of the passenger door. With a perfunctory wave to her, he headed off toward a large, gray block building and disappeared inside its massive doors. A blue and white sign over those doors read Pryce Line Terminal.

In the back seat of the Rolls, Angela slid forward. Balancing on the edge of the burgundy leather seat, she stared up at the ship. Beyond the tinted glass the huge white liner rose out of the crystal blue water of the harbor. Its turreted forecastle caught the golden rays of the setting sun and shimmered enticingly, like a fairy-tale castle in a children's book.

What would be her options, she wondered, once

aboard that illusion? She was no fairy-tale princess. The ship was real. She wasn't. The very real Silke von Chassen, who might expect to be carried off by some Prince Charming, wouldn't be sailing tonight.

On the other hand, Angela Hamilton's encounter with Jeremy Pryce might be the closest she'd ever come to encountering a "real" Prince Charming. Every time he looked at her she melted. She had to be honest with herself, she didn't know what would happen if he got too close. If Jeremy Pryce was on the cruise somehow, she must avoid him. She couldn't allow the attraction she felt for him to distract her from her goal. Her commitment to her patients, to opening a new clinic, to the career she'd dedicated her life to was at stake. She had to win.

The chauffeur slid open the privacy window behind the front seat. "I'll see to your luggage now, Lady von Chassen. May I suggest you wait here? It will be crowded in the reception area, and you'll be more comfortable in the car."

The luggage, of course...Angela nodded in agreement. If the chauffeur hadn't taken the lead she realized she might have climbed out of the limousine and proceeded to carry her own luggage to the terminal. Silke Von Chassen would hardly carry her own luggage. No doubt she'd been on many cruises.

But, Silke wasn't going on her first cruise. Angela Hamilton could hardly wait to board. She watched until Howard's broad back disappeared into the darkened interior of the building. Then, like a disobedient child, she opened the passenger door and stepped out to be greeted by an almost overpowering chemical odor, the result of the Florida sun melting the surface of the asphalt coated pier.

Hot and humid, the moisture laden air coated her skin and soaked through the once crisp, white cotton suit she wore. In spite of the heat, Angela shivered with anticipation. Whatever else happened, she told herself, she would enjoy the cruise. As for her encounter at the airport, she would worry about Jeremy later. Why worry about something that hadn't happened?

When Angela joined the line to board the Queen of Charades, it seemed that half the population of Ft Lauderdale was also on the gangplank with her, and no one could wait to board. She pulled her flight bag closer to her body and moved forward slowly, a few steps at a time. Somehow she managed to avoid bumping into the people ahead of her or having anyone bump into her from behind. Until, some twenty minutes later, in sight of the lobby entrance, she was jostled from behind. Caught off balance, she avoided falling against the man moving forward ahead of her, straightening, she glanced over her shoulder. Behind her she met the eyes of a stout middle-aged woman in a colorful Mumu.

"Well! Can't you see it's your turn?" the woman demanded. "Are you boarding or not?

Embarrassed, Angela murmured, "Sorry," and stepped into the ships lobby. The smartly uniformed ship's purser stood behind a tall podium holding a computer.

"Passport?" he said without looking up.

Angela extended her passport. He opened it then raised his eyes to meet hers. Angela froze. What was wrong? She'd gone through customs with her real passport. The one the purser held was a copy of Silke von Chassen's passport.

The purser looked down again at the passport and the photograph. His brow furrowed, and he looked up again at Angela. He hesitated then said, "My apologies Lady von Chassen. I should have recognized you."

Why? Angela wondered. Had he met Silke on another cruise?

His arm outstretched with the document still in his grip, the purser extended Angela's passport. But, before Angela could reach for it, his gaze slid to the large lady behind her who now stood open-mouthed, staring at the back of Angela's head. He said, "And the rest of your party?"

"Party?" Momentarily confused, Angela hesitated then glanced behind her again and saw the woman in the oversized Mumu.

Lady von Chassen would certainly be traveling with someone, wouldn't she? Of course, a maid was one detail Carstairs hadn't mentioned, possibly hadn't intended to.

Turning back to the pursuer, she raised her chin, looked into his eyes and lied. "I'll be cruising alone this time. My maid is ill."

"I'm sorry to hear that, Lady von Chassen. If we can be of any service, any service at all, please inform our staff."

"Thank you. I'm certain I'll manage without her," she said, and dismissing him with what she hoped was a regal look, she took the passport from his outstretched hand and glanced at it surreptitiously. It certainly looked okay for a copy. She'd been careful to use her real passport in the terminal when she went through immigration. Then, she'd placed her genuine passport in a locked section of her carry-on bag.

Angela had been nervous about using the phony passport but Carstairs assured her as long as she carried her own there should be no problem. The cruise would only be sailing to American ports. She would go through customs with her authentic passport only to board, and she would not need it again until the ship returned to Florida. Even if one of the ship's officers questioned the passport she used when she boarded, the rules of the game specified no person related to the cruise line could win the game. Supposedly no one on board would know her true identity, with the exception of the captain of the cruise ship.

Maybe, Angela thought. But, if that was true, how could the game be played fairly so that the show's fans had a chance to win? There had to be someone on the ship other than the captain who knew her true identity.

～

Chapter Six

After she'd been escorted to her suite by her steward, Angela found her way back to the promenade deck. On the port side of the ship, passengers crowded the rail calling to friends and relatives on the dock. Most of them were young, probably on a honeymoon, several appeared to be middle-age couples, perhaps on a second honeymoon. She had expected to see children. But, with the exception of a sad-eyed young boy in a wheel chair being pushed about by a woman who appeared to be a nurse, she only noted two or three children chasing each other around the deck.

Angela found a place at the rail and stared unseeingly at the dock far below. An unexpected wave of regret swept over her. *If I'd married, would we taking this cruise together, or any cruise?* After several years of marriage would we go on a second honeymoon? Did Edward ever mention a cruise, the Caribbean—a first honeymoon? I *might be sailing alone, but I'm not sailing with a man who only wanted a brood mare for a wife.*

"Stop it!"

"Were you speaking to me?"

Startled, Angela turned to face the person who'd joined her at the rail. A woman of two or three years younger than herself, with flaming red hair, and wide-set eyes so round and blue they reminded her of a china doll she'd coveted at age seven when she saw it in the window of an antique store,

Angela shook her head. "No. Guilty...of talking to myself that is."

"Perfectly natural. Doesn't everyone talk to themselves when they travel?"

"Thanks. I suspect the story that only people over eighty talk to themselves is another one of those myths parents like to tease children with."

"It's not fair, is it? My name's Heather," the woman offered her small, beautifully manicured hand, a surprisingly strong hand, Angela noticed.

"I'm..." Angela hesitated. "I'm, Silke."

"Terrific name. It's German isn't it? I remember the name from a character in a children's book my grandmother read to me when I was six. She pronounced it "Silk-uh" just as you do."

"I like it," Angela said, relieved to note Heather hadn't asked for a surname or notice any hesitation.

"Have you sailed on the Q.C. before?"

"No," Angela admitted.

"Isn't it a gorgeous ship?"

"Absolutely!" Did her voice reflect her excitement?

Would Silke von Chassen be excited? Probably not. She'd have to be careful.

"Even though I've been on the Q.C. before, I'm dying to tour the whole ship again."

Heather's smile, warm and welcoming, and her excitement about touring the ship matched her own. It would be difficult not to like her, Angela decided.

"There hasn't been time to tour it yet. I didn't want to go inside and miss our departure."

Heather's eyes sparkled. "Me either, but I'm about to go up to the forward deck, for a drink and a better view. I like to be up there when we clear the harbor. It's so exciting to sail out of the channel into the ocean, don't you agree?"

"There is something awesome about all that water," Angela hedged. She certainly wasn't going to tell this stranger she'd never been on a cruise ship.

"I thought I'd go exploring, first," she said.

Heather nodded. "Open seating tonight—plenty of time to go exploring before dinner."

Both Carstairs and Mad Martin cautioned her about "hiding out on the trip." It would constitute automatic disqualification. And they'd never actually said so, but Angela believed it was more than likely someone on the ship would be watching to make sure she obeyed the rules of the game. Even if the charming red-head was a plant, what could go wrong?

"Am I correct, if you've never sailed from Fort Lauderdale you would enjoy seeing the channel on the way to the ocean?" Heather asked.

Angela's answer was easy and immediate. "Thank you, I'd love to."

"Let's go."

Angela followed Heather up several sets of stairs she'd heard her steward Rashid refer to as ladders when she followed him from the lobby to her suite.

The stairs weren't as steep as ladders, but looking down, she realized it was a long way up. At the end of the climb, they came out onto a broad deck Angela realized must be at the prow of the ship.

A tropically themed cocktail bar stood near the edge of a covered swimming pool surrounded by what appeared to be hundreds of small, unoccupied tables, brightly colored deck chairs and no passengers. Clearly, the majority of the *bon voyage* crowds remained behind enthusiastically hanging over the rails facing the wharf, waving farewell.

"Let's take a table near the pool. We'll have a good view from there," Heather directed.

According to Carstairs, Silke prefers the Mediterranean or the Adriatic for cruising. She told me Silke never cruised in the Caribbean, Angela thought. What she didn't say left too many possibilities. An international traveler, Silke might know this area well. She could have water skied, sailed, or swum here—no—she couldn't swim. After the way her parents died, apparently the media discovered Silke can't swim.

"Somehow I've missed the Caribbean," she replied

Not that Heather noticed her lack of a yes or no answer.

"Good," Heather said, "new places, nothing like

exploring—after we find a table, and order our drinks, I'll play travel guide."

Angela managed to say, "Thanks" before Heather added, "I love the trip out of this harbor. Both sides of the channel are lined with waterfront homes. I think you might enjoy seeing them. Some are quite attractive."

The houses on either side of the channel, so close to the water probably were attractive. Angela thought. She'd been lucky to meet Heather, someone who seemed to enjoy her company and asked her to remain with her on deck until they reached the ocean.

How long does that take? Angela wondered, Maybe I should excuse myself, say I'm tired. I shouldn't become too friendly—I'd like to stay...

Before she could reach a decision, a white-jacketed waiter materialized at their table the moment they sat down. He offered an extensive drinks menu, made a suggestion, and they both ordered Mimosas.

The ship's loudspeaker interrupted Heather animated description of the sights with a booming "All ashore who are going ashore," warning. And before Heather could finish her remarks, Angela felt a slight vibration rising from the deck beneath her feet. Sounds, not unlike the rumble of a threatening storm, signaled the ship had weighed anchor. They were underway. Distant voices of friends and relatives left behind on the pier faded. A clean, fresh salt water breeze washed over the pool deck. The oppressive mugginess, so uncomfortable before the ship began to move, vanished as a small tugboat prodded the great ship out of the safety of the harbor into the channel leading to the sea.

Effervescent Heather obviously loved to talk. Angela heard most of her recent history before their drinks arrived. She'd just completed an MBA at Harvard, and said she would be settling into a career in a few weeks. Angela listened, asked polite questions, and avoided a detailed recital of her own history by repeating what Carstairs had told her about Silke's education: A Liberal Arts degree from Wellesley, and some vague plans about what she might do with it, then she changed the subject.

"Am I correct, you've been cruising in the Caribbean recently?"

Heather laughed, a low musical laugh. "Oh, yes, recently, and long ago. My cruising initiation is one of my grandmother's very favorite stories. She loves to tell strangers I was still in diapers the first time I sailed in the Caribbean. She assures me she chased me all over the ship to keep me from falling overboard. I must have loved it then because I still do. There's nothing like it. You'll see. The water's bath-tub warm and so blue you'd swear it's been dyed."

"The photographs certainly appear too good to be true."

Heather leaned forward. Her eyes brightened even more. "Photographs don't begin to capture the beauty of the ocean, the charm of the ports. I've sailed there at least once a year since I was a child."

"Then, you must be familiar with the ports of call."

"I am. But they never seem familiar in a boring way. What I love best about them is they're never exactly the same. Discovering what's new, different, since the last time I was there, is part of what makes this cruise so much fun. Not that exploring the ports is everything."

Heather's blue eyes shimmered. "It still thrills me to be on board as a ship leaves the harbor. It's in my blood. It's genetic, my brother says. Our ancestors on both sides of the family were sailors, and ship builders."

In her blood. If so, it's catching. My heart's beating in overdrive. I can't believe I'm here, on a ship. It's moving. I'm going to the Caribbean!

The waterfront homes Heather promised they'd see began to slide by on both sides of the ship. The two women pointed out the ones they liked, and those they decided "lacked something."

Angela began to relax. She'd convinced herself following Heather had been a good idea when she became aware of a man approaching their table. She looked up and recognized the man who she'd noticed in the lobby during her encounter with the purser.

"Burt," Heather sat up abruptly in her chair, obviously more than a little pleased to see him.

"Off island hopping again, Heather?"

"Can you think of anything more fun? But, what are you doing on board? No, don't tell me old-nose-to-the-grindstone couldn't be taking a real vacation?"

"Why not? Would you believe me if I admitted work interferes with my tennis game?"

"Burt, you are impossible. I'd believe in unicorns before I'd believe you were on vacation. Why don't you join us?" She patted the seat of the chair next to her.

"And your friend is?"

"Oops! I am being rude. Before you sit down, let me introduce my delightful new acquaintance."

Heather smiled at Angela. "Silke, um, Silke, I'm afraid I..."

Burt's pale gray eyes focused on Angela.

Pinned beneath their unwavering gaze she felt him study her now as he had during her brief encounter with the purser. She wanted to look away, to squirm, and knew she could not. Determined to ignore the warning signals flashing in her brain, Angela pushed the sunglasses hiding her eyes up to the top of her head, returned his smile, and offered her hand. Whatever was on his mind she would not let him know how apprehensive he made her feel.

With practiced ease, Burt took her outstretched hand, and bending forward kissed it.

"A pleasure, Lady von Chassen."

So he had been listening in the lobby. It took every ounce of her self-control not to jerk it away. Never in her life had a man kissed her hand. But, if the intent of the kiss was to rattle her...he wasn't going to be successful.

"Silke, please," she said, widening her smile. "I prefer Silke."

Unaware of the tension, Heather stared at Burt, then at Angela. Her eyes lit up. "Lady Von Chassen?" She turned to Angela. "A title...you didn't tell me. I—didn't recognize you. I must have seen your photograph in the London Times. In February you sponsor the Orchid Ball."

The words spilled out of Heather's mouth like water from a fountain. "What fun, Silke," Her voice sang on, "You must, you simply must, promise me you'll come shopping with me when we dock in Nassau. I can hardly wait to spring your title on a vendeuse at Coles on Bay Street. I must have something stunning to wear to the Mardi Gras Ball in St. Thomas. You are going, of course. And I can't wait to introduce you to Mademoiselle Dubrie, she's just the snottiest clerk this side of Paris. She still treats me like I'm a school girl."

"Really?" Angela couldn't help smiling.

A mischievous grin turned up the corners of Heather's mouth. Her eyes danced with delight. "When I introduce you, she'll turn herself inside out to serve us. Naturally, I wouldn't dream of purchasing anything she'd suggest. We'll move on to Carticr's—I'm sure you love Cartier's"

Angela struggled to keep herself from laughing at Heather's infectious enthusiasm. She talked so fast. It's a wonder she finds time to breathe, she thought.

Heather tore on, "Actually, I might buy something there. I saw the sweetest little accessories tray in Cartier's catalogue. It had these elegant, stalking Cheetahs. But..." Heather paused mid-sentence and raising her hand to her mouth talked through her fingers. "Oh, I'm sorry Silke. I should have asked. Perhaps you have other plans for Nassau."

"Yes," Burt said, "Lady von Chassen may have other plans for Nassau?" He looked at Angela, waited.

There it is again. Angela thought. No, not my imagination. Whenever he looks at me, says anything to me or about me, it ends with a question.

"I wouldn't miss it." Angela smiled at Heather, and looked back at Burt in time to be rewarded with a scowl.

The ship had almost reached the entrance to the

harbor by the time the trio finished their drinks. Just beyond the end of the channel, she could see the Atlantic. Angela shivered. It was indeed awesome. Now, she thought, now the game begins in earnest.

Entranced with her first view of a new ocean, Angela didn't see the man coming up from the stairwell until he'd gained the deck, walked up behind Heather, stopped, winked at her, and tapped Heather gently on the top of her head.

"Ouch!" Heather yelled, and whirled on her attacker. "Jeremy! You beast!"

He grinned at Angela and seated himself in the last empty chair.

"When did you get back from D.C...?"

"Yes, I am the beast, your brother the beast," he said. Then, reaching across the low table, he shook Burt's hand. The two men feigned surprise at seeing one another.

"Vacationing Burt? When did you get back from Greece?"

Burt's smiled broadened. "Good to see you on board. Do we dare hope for your company on the courts of Saint Thomas, or is this a business cruise?"

Jeremy shrugged. "You know me Burt, a little of both. But, after D.C., I suppose I could call this a pleasure cruise."

"And so," Heather interrupted. "What about Greece? Burt? Was it heavenly?" She sighed. "I haven't been there in an age."

"It's still in the Mediterranean."

"Too cute, big brother, I didn't ask you, and I was

almost ready to say something kind and sisterly about you."

Jeremy turned to Burt. "Hey friend, sisterly love? Ever heard of it? What about brotherly love? I'll bet you know about that. Aren't there seven boys in your family?"

"Five, plus me."

"Girls?"

"Nada."

"Ah, that explains why you haven't turned into a serial killer. Something I may have been suspected of quite recently?" Again he winked at Angela.

Heather looked from Jeremy to Angela. "Brothers," she said, spewing out the word.

"If I had known he would be on board, Silke, I'd have been delighted to introduce you to a charming, intelligent man, my brother, unlike the gentleman who joined us who claims to be my brother." She glared at Jeremy, "I'm sorry to say this man clearly considers himself our family's favorite comedian, a personality quirk he assumes whenever he gets together with his straight man," Heather added, her gaze zeroing in on Burt who grinned.

Angela laughed. "Thanks Heather. However, I believe I've already enjoyed the unique experience of meeting your brother."

"Really, when did you become so lucky?"

"A few hours ago in the airport lounge."

Jeremy nodded. "You forgot to mention we also shared a ride to the harbor from the airport."

"Did I? It must have slipped my mind. I didn't realize you knew I was in the same car with you after you climbed into the front seat, and closed the glass partition in my face."

"That sounds like our Jeremy. Sorry Silke. As my grandmother regularly says, 'Boys will boys, and given any opportunity men will revert to boys.' You'll have to take my word for it that occasionally I've noticed my brother behaving like the gentlemen he was raised to be."

Watching them together, Angela thought it couldn't be clearer Heather adored her brother, and he adored her.

"Okay, okay," Jeremy said. "Game, set, match, little sister. If I admit I behaved boorishly, apologize to Lady von Chassen, and buy the next round of drinks, will all be forgiven?"

He smiled at Angela, and once more she felt her heart do a tap dance.

Angela glared at him. Damn you Jeremy Pryce, she thought, the last thing I need on this trip is a distraction like you. Heather's delightful and knowledgeable about this cruise...could keep me out of trouble. I don't have time for another heartache.

"How about it Silke?" Heather interrupted, "Shall we ransom him from purgatory?"

"Of course. A toast to brothers," she said as she raised her glass but didn't drink. Then setting it down, she pushed back her chair and rose. "Thanks Heather, it's been fun. Jeremy, if you're issuing rain checks for the drink offer, I might collect sometime. Gentlemen," she addressed both men, "it's been, um, pleasant."

"I hope the boys aren't chasing you away."

"No, not at all. I'm just going to freshen up before dinner."

"Are we on for the Nassau shopping trip?"

"Wouldn't miss it."

"Good. Then if I don't see you at dinner this evening, when we dock in the morning, I'll meet you in the lobby at nine."

Only if you're alone when I arrive, Angela decided.

Chapter Seven

First seating began at seven, second seating at nine. Angela guessed Jeremy was unlikely to dine early. Determined to avoid him, she arrived promptly at seven.

Because she could choose her table on the first night out, she knew exactly what kind of table to look for and the kind of table mates she wanted. The tables varied in size. Some would accommodate only two diners, others as many as eight. Once inside the oversized double doors she paused to scan the dining room. Windows running the length of the room offered an unobstructed view of the ocean. Angela caught her breath. Poised to plunge beneath the horizon, the sun hung low on the horizon setting fire to the sky and the tips of the restless waves fashioned by the moving ship.

Across the room she spotted a table for four next to a window. Three people, an older couple and a middle-aged woman, were already seated there. Angela knew exactly where she must sit. Less than a minute later she stood beside the table she'd chosen. An older, middle-aged man taking on the role of host confirmed the fourth seat was vacant and invited her to join them. After they'd introduced themselves, Angela knew she'd made a wise choice. Not only did she gain a spectacular view by the windows, when she introduced herself, no one recognized or commented on the name Silke. The couple at the table, Joan and Jack Crawford, said they were retired, Jack from the Marines and Joan from teaching. This cruise, they shared, would be their long awaited second honeymoon. Joan blushed when Jack said honeymoon. Angela suppressed a smile.

The middle–aged woman, who introduced herself as Irene Ackerman from Omaha, didn't become talkative for several minutes until the conversation at the table turned to the Islands when Joan Crawford said she hoped the weather would be pleasant. Irene volunteered she was a professor specializing in Caribbean history and its indigenous peoples. As for the weather, she summarized it succinctly with one word, "warm."

During Angela's limited preparations when she learned she'd be cruising in the Caribbean, she looked for books on the region and developed an interest in the history of the Islands.

"Yeah," Jack said. "Hey how come it's called the Caribbean, isn't it part of the Atlantic?"

"It certainly is," Irene agreed. "But the geography of the region has a lot to do with its name."

"Geography? A bunch of Islands? Not much geography there," Jack said.

"Yes, not like a continent but the islands make a major difference in the climate because the perimeter of the Caribbean Sea is mountainous," she explained, "with the volcanic chain of the Lesser Antilles rising on the East. The volcanoes of Central America on the West also form a wall isolating that part of the Atlantic Ocean, separating it from the Pacific for about 750 miles from east to west."

"And that affects the weather? How?" Jack asked. "What am I missing?"

"Think of the Caribbean as a huge bowl filled with water, protected by volcanic walls. Because it is so well protected, the cooling trade-winds mitigate what would be oppressive heat and also bring rain from the Atlantic creating a tropical paradise without comparison."

Their waiter arrived as Irene finished her explanation of the climate. They all ordered. By the time the food was served the conversation shifted to a discussion about the services and amusements on board the ship and on shore.

"I'm for the casino," Jack said. "Talked to someone in line at the tour desk. Claimed some guy on the last cruise picked up fifty thousand playing roulette."

"Great way to give away money," Joan said. "You can forget that Jack," and turning to Angela and Irene she ignored Jack's "Women don't know how to have fun" reply.

"Can't agree with that," Joan said. "I'm saving my money for the St. Thomas duty-free shops I read about."

"Good idea," Irene said, "You could spend a whole day and never see all of them. You'll bargains on china, crystal, perfume, art and designer clothes if you are willing to do some comparison shopping."

Joan's eyes sparkled. "Comparison shopper —that's me!"

"Forget the perfume," Jack chimed in. "Duty-free Scotch. Now that's a real bargain."

The waiter arrived to refill glasses, make suggestions for dessert, and take orders.

"I'll have this one," Jack said pointing at the Bacardi Rum Cake. "I heard Rum is special out here."

The waiter guaranteed it and moved on to the three women. He suggested many passengers liked the Mango or Guava Sorbet for desert.

Irene confirmed it was "delicious" and added Flan de Café con Leche, a local version of a custard, with coffee would also be a good choice.

Joan chose the sorbet and Angela decided to try the flan.

After the waiter returned with their desserts, Angela turned to Irene. "Didn't flan originate with Spanish explorers?"

"Probably," Irene said.

"Are there local foods that originated with the Arawak-Caribe Islanders?" Joan asked.

Irene nodded. She was 'in her element,' now. "Specific native foods include the staples, cassava and manioc, both roots. Cassava was dried and ground into a meal to make bread. We know Manioc as tapioca. Fish, prepared in many ways is, of course, popular."

"I vaguely recall reading somewhere that none of the native peoples survived after the Spanish explorers arrived. Supposedly, when they discovered how lovely the

Islands were, they weren't willing to share paradise with the natives," Joan said.

Irene shrugged. "Not true. Most historians consider that a myth. While it's true the Spaniards and other European settlers almost eradicated much of the original population, many survived."

She took a sip of her coffee. "Many also intermarried with the explorers, and later with Africans brought to the Islands for slave labor. The descendants of the explorers, natives and the slaves have a unique and thriving culture. I believe you will find them both welcoming and charming."

Jack put down his fork, "I'll bet the pirate Blackbeard was one of the greedy ones who wouldn't share the islands. Wasn't he supposed to live on one?"

"True, he was one of the earliest residents of St. Thomas."

"How about the descendants of Blackbeard...any around?"

They all turned to look at Jack.

"I'm serious," he insisted.

Everyone laughed except the professor. She nodded.

"It's possible, I suppose. But, many people confuse Blackbeard and Bluebeard. The Bluebeard story tells us Bluebeard murdered his brides. If that were true, one has to wonder how he'd have any descendants, or if he did, would they admit he'd fathered them?"

"Why did he kill them?"

"According to the myth, they were dishonest."

"Dishonest?"

"He told them they could open any door in the castle except one."

"Yeah, got it." Jack grinned. "Figures. Women. They opened it."

"Yes, they all did."

"What was behind the door?" Joan asked.

Irene smiled before answering, "The skeletons of his former brides."

"Whoee! Couldn't trust them? Man ought to be able to trust his wife to do what he asks," Jack said. "Sort of like entrapment though."

"Oh, it wasn't because they opened the door."

"No?" Jack asked. "Then what was it?"

"After he caught them, they all lied and said they hadn't opened the door."

"No kidding. Seems like a dumb reason to kill someone."

"Couldn't agree more," Irene replied. "Later Blackbeard was credited with the Bluebeard story, probably because he was a pirate. But the story goes Bluebeard killed his wives because he hated liars."

"If people killed each other for lying, the planet would be decimated." Joan said.

"And Jack, if you plan to see Blackbeard's castle," Irene said, "I'm afraid you'll be disappointed. His so-called castle is a tower. There are some unique things about it. You can climb its ninety-nine steps to the top or take a taxi to the crest of the hill where there are a couple of historic houses with pools, an open air veranda at the tower with a drinks bar and a terrific view of the harbor and cruise ships."

"It sounds charming," Angela said.

Jack turned to his wife. "Not to me. If there isn't a castle. I think we should tour the Islands. Like the Prof here says, it'll be warm, and I heard there are some great beaches. Private too."

Joan brightened. "We could take our suits, and a picnic."

"Hey, if the beaches are private, bring the picnic, forget the suits."

"Really, Jack." Joan blushed again.

"To each his own. I'll bet the natives didn't have suits."

Irene's expression said she was patient, not pleased. She turned to Angela. "There's another tower on the Island, or maybe I should say under the Island."

"Under?"

Yes, fifteen feet underwater and air conditioned. The Coral Underwater Observatory. It's the only observatory of its kind in the Islands with an unobstructed view of the fish common to the Caribbean. Quite entertaining."

"How far is it from the dock?" Angela asked.

"I'm not certain, but not far. Any taxi driver can take you there. You could visit both towers and still have time for some souvenir shopping before you are due back at the ship for sailing."

"Thanks, Irene. I think I'll visit both places."

"Well, hey," Jack interrupted after dessert was served. "Anyone ready for some nightlife? Joan and I are taking in the nightclub revue."

"Not me," Angela said. "It's been a long day. I overheard someone saying there's a talented pianist in one of the lounges. I think I'll find out."

Chapter Eight

He waited in the foyer of the main dining room until the double brass elevator doors closed on the four passengers from the table by the window. He watched the lights climb to the decks above noting where they stopped. Just curious, he told himself.

When the elevator returned to the foyer it brought down new diners. He remained where he was near a huge artificial palm and scanned the women—until, the last woman emerged from the elevator and entered the frosted double doors of the dining room.

His first choice, he decided was the best choice. The first night on board wouldn't be a good time to institute his plan. He'd have to be patient. San Juan was four days away. He had time to be patient. In the meantime, it pleased him that none of the diners exiting the elevator appeared to be aware of him standing there. They certainly didn't indicate they saw him...not that he expected them too. Passengers looked right at a uniform and didn't necessarily see the person wearing it.

Then too, he considered himself an average looking man, an average looking man who'd grown from an average looking boy. A boy who'd sat unnoticed in the back of the classroom, and years later, a hopeful young man, on a bench with other substitutes holding his breath while the coach scanned the waiting players for a replacement on the field. How many times had they looked at him and not seen him? Only every day of his life.

An old scene played before his eyes. The memory was still fresh. "That's him, over there, at the back of the room. He would be an ideal candidate for student leadership," the teacher said, indicating his place near the tall windows.

He sat up very straight in his chair. And the principal looked past him to the next boy. The one he'd heard his father say once, when he was sober, "...came from the wealthiest family in town."

Later, when he'd grown older, into "an average looking college student" attending parties, he faded into the wallpaper of his fraternity, and watched, not nearly as hopefully anymore, while the prettiest girls scanned the sidelines looking for dance partners and picked the men on either side of him.

They didn't see him then. He no longer expected them to recognize him now. Hadn't he proved it in Italy, Greece, Spain?

A half smile played at the corners of his mouth. How things had changed! Now when he approached them, they would not walk away as they once had, at least not more than once.

～

Three decks above the dining room, Angela followed several people when they exited the elevator at the mezzanine level and went directly to the Calypso lounge. The walls inside were covered with colorful paintings of mythological sea nymphs and ancient Greek ships rowed by sturdy looking sailors that testified to the source of its name. After a brief survey of the room, Angela found a table situated well away from the crowd surrounding the piano.

With a sigh, she sank into a deeply cushioned chair and admitted to herself she was tired. Tonight she'd like nothing better than to stroll the deck breathing in salt air, far away from the crowds. Up to now she'd realized she'd been lucky. The Crawford's were so interested in professor Ackerman's stories that they hardly noticed her. According to the rules of the game, she had to be seen to be identified. Hiding out would disqualify her. Being too notable might expose her as a fraud. That is exactly why meeting Jeremy at the airport and again on board with Heather had originally worried her. But being with people who were sure of who she was proved to be lucky. It kept her visible.

Silke von Chassen, she knew, wasn't one to miss a shopping trip or a party. She should stick with Heather, and when she wasn't with her, be where she'd be seen. No dark decks or early bedtimes for her.

Angela censored the mental view she had of the king-sized bed with the satin comforter she'd only glimpsed a few hours ago in her suite. So inviting and so not the woman she was impersonating. Forget it, the voice in the back of her mind ordered. Listen to the music.

She heard the first notes of a song she should recognize, but couldn't quite place. In the front of the room several people crowded around the piano. She guessed some were singles. If so, one or more of the men might take notice of a woman alone. Couples sitting around the room caught up in each other wouldn't be aware of her. It wasn't even ten o'clock—too early for party-girl Silke to wander around on deck, alone. Was someone watching? If so, she'd be seen enjoying the music in the Calypso Lounge. The music was good as promised and the next song one of her favorites, "The Best is Yet to Come."

Was it? She wondered. Maybe she'd already experienced the best life offered, Although her mother hadn't survived childbirth, her father, a swimming coach, loved her and took her with him wherever he traveled.

He taught her to swim before she could walk, and she had a shelf full of swimming trophies she'd joyfully earned while still an adolescent. After her father died, she finished college and not too long after that she'd been able to open her own physical therapy clinic. What she hadn't had in life was a so-called "normal" childhood, living in one house, attending neighborhood schools, making friends, and later, when she was old enough, hanging out with girlfriends, studying boys, and talking love.

The song the pianist began with, like most popular songs was all about love, the kind that, when it came, lasted. Love? It didn't happen for her. Although she'd thought it had once. If she'd had that neighborhood house, the school, the girlfriends, maybe she would know what love looked like. Instead she fell for the first man who came along. It took almost a year before she painfully discovered how naïve she was. When it was over, she still didn't know what love looked like, but she knew what it didn't look like. With her former fiancée, Dr. Edward Fournier, it would never have been love. All he'd demanded was her soul. Did all lyrics lie about love? If love, the real kind, came her way, would she recognize it? How? She'd been so wrong the first time.

The song ended and another began. When the waiter appeared, she glanced at her watch and ordered a glass of Chardonnay. Ten-thirty. She'd stay put until midnight, she decided. Leaning her head back in the chair, she let her mind drift.

Only nine more days, win or lose, I'll be on a plane home.

Two hours later Jeremy felt guilty when he found her in the back of the lounge. He hadn't intended to catch her unaware. Yet it seemed to him each time they met, he had. The way her eyes widened, and her body tensed when he'd approached her at the airport. Then, before the ship sailed he'd found her on the Lido deck with, of all people, his sister. Again he'd noted the closed-lipped smile during Heather's introductions and the way her hands tightened their grip on the arms of the chair. In fact, from the moment they'd met, she'd made it abundantly clear she didn't know him and didn't want to. At the airport he'd decided her cautious reaction was what any woman traveling alone might exhibit when approached by a man she didn't know.

Later, when she seemed to accept him as safe, he'd entertained the idea that perhaps his unexpected arrival might have startled her. Somehow, he couldn't shake the conviction she knew who he was not only at the airport but again when they'd been formally introduced. A gentleman, he told himself, would stay away from her. Looking down at her now, finding her asleep like this, made him feel like a voyeur. Leave, he ordered himself, but he stayed. He could not leave her there alone, so vulnerable while she slept.

Lady Silke von Chassen was an enigma...a question mark in his normally orderly, predictable existence. Ignore five-foot-seven-inches of toned, long-legged temptation with hair of spun gold, the face of a goddess, a living breathing sexual fantasy? Not a chance. She was everything most men would lust for in a woman. No question about it, he shouldn't be anywhere near her, not when he had a job to do. With her on board, he knew what would happen. He was in trouble.

"Sleeping Beauty, I presume."

Angela sat up straight. Only half awake in the dimly lit lounge, it took her a moment to make out his face: square jaw, bronzed skin, an arrogant smile and those eyes, brilliant blue, so intense they drew her in once more, dared her to turn away.

"Jeremy!"

"The last time I checked. Sorry didn't mean to wake you. Past your bedtime is it?"

"I wasn't asleep." Her eyes flashed, "I was—concentrating on the music."

"That music?" He glanced to the low stage at the front of the room.

Angela looked past him. The piano bench stood empty, the crowd gone. She felt the heat rise in her face.

"Just resting your eyes?"

Angela started to agree and then, unable to suppress her amusement any longer, she laughed.

"Well, I was."

"Perhaps a stroll in the night air is in order," he suggested, and offered his hand to help her rise.

At the prow of the ship, they paused to watch the luminous fluorescent trail the ship left behind in its wake. A soft breeze caressed their faces, while behind them the sound of laughter spilled out into the night when a hatch opened somewhere. Jeremy slid his arm around Angela's waist and held her tightly against him. The light of the full moon cascaded over her shoulders draping them in a silver shawl. He looked down and her eyes met his. The laughter behind them drifted away and for a few moments they stood wordless, only distantly aware of the pulsating engines carrying them deeper into the Caribbean night.

Angela trembled while his fingers traced a line up her throat to her chin and across her cheekbone. He combed a strand of her short windblown hair from her cheek, and smiled when the wind caught it again, and it danced out of his fingers. In the moonlight his eyes, brilliant blue in sunlight, were dark, bottomless and still. His grip tightened pulling her closer. Mesmerized by his unreadable gaze, her heart seemed to falter. Then, almost as if he suddenly realized what it was he wanted, he tilted up her chin, and lowered his mouth to hers. Their lips met. The kiss began tentatively then deepened until every fiber in her body seemed to vibrate to some unheard note singing in her blood. Tightening his arms around her waist, he drew her even closer, and she could feel the urgency of his heart beating against hers.

Then abruptly, without warning, his hands dropped to his sides. His eyes hardened, questioning.

Confused, she stepped back. Her throat tightened.

"I'm sorry. It's late," Jeremy said, "Rude of me to impose on your evening."

Angela shook her head. What had happened?

"It's late," Jeremy repeated. "I'll see you to your suite."

Angela clenched her fists at her side, "Thanks but, don't bother."

"It's no bother..." Jeremy began.

"It's early," Angela said, "and as it appears you have something better to do, I'll see myself to my suite when I'm ready."

~

Chapter Nine

When the ship docked in Nassau at eight a.m., Angela was determined to enjoy the rare treat of breakfast in bed. She sat propped up against satin pillows with the ship's daily paper spread out on the bed beside her. After several minutes reading the programs of the day, she paused to spread a second freshly baked muffin with "lemon curd," an English jam her cabin steward, Rashid, strongly recommended.

"Delicious," she murmured to no one, licking the jam from her fingers.

She had not forgotten her promise to go shopping in Nassau with Heather, and now she wished she hadn't agreed. Suppose Jeremy was with her? Annoyed, she pushed the papers aside. I don't have to go. The words rose in her mind. Plenty to do on board and still be seen. There's an aerobics class. I could jog around the deck, get a massage. I'll telephone tell her... she glanced down at the paper again, read that "a scuba diving trip is scheduled to leave the ship at nine a.m." She loved to scuba dive. It must be heavenly in the Caribbean, she thought. Out of the question of course. Impatiently, again she brushed the paper aside. Anyone that reads the celebrity stories in Enquirer knowns Silke can't scuba dive and probably knows why she can't swim either, she thought.

She sighed and threw the paper on the floor. Just as well, she decided, remembering last evening. She'd been surprised to hear Jeremy say he didn't know how to scuba dive. For him to admit he didn't know how to do anything was unexpected. She'd have to take a chance he wouldn't be with his sister. On second thought, she would go shopping with his sister. Realistically, Jeremy wasn't likely to go shopping with his sister, and she liked Heather.

When Angela arrived at the lobby an hour later, at least half the passengers on the Q.C. appeared to be milling about while waiting their turn to disembark. She scanned the crowd. A part of her hoped she wouldn't find Heather among them. She wanted to visit Nassau, wanted to shop, but not where Heather wanted to shop. The three thousand dollars she'd received from the sponsors of the game show, money Carstairs jokingly referred to as "walking about money," wouldn't go far in a Cartier's or a Coles. She'd heard the Straw Market was the place to go for souvenirs. If Heather spent the day shopping at the up-scale stops, she'd miss the opportunity to tour Nassau, a place she might never visit it again.

Somehow, she promised herself, she'd manage to slip away from Heather to at least visit the Straw Market where she'd been assured they carried the kind of mementos she wanted: straw hats, baskets, maybe string purses.

If Heather did appear, how difficult could it be to convince her she didn't need another pair of diamond earrings or the latest Gucci gown? Silke could be expected to already own every jewel, every toy, every couture gown a wealthy socialite believed she had to have. If I play my part right, she thought, I can convince her there isn't a trinket or a dress on the Island that Silke von Chassen would covet. At least I hope so.

Only a moment later she sighed when she spotted Heather on the opposite side of the lobby standing next to Burt. Her shoulders tightened and her back stiffened. What was it about him that made her nervous? They haven't seen you, she thought. You can leave before they do. But, before she could turn away, Burt's sharp-eyed gaze zeroed in on her, and with Heather following him, he began forging a path toward her through the crowd.

Angela forced a smile. Get over it, she told herself. If she was right about Burt, if he was a plant from the show, or even a game show fan wondering if she was the mystery celebrity, becoming tense or defensive around him could only increase any suspicion he might have as to her true identity.

She needn't have worried about Burt. After an abrupt "Good morning, Silke," and a reminder to Heather not to forget they'd be meeting for dinner, he left them in what seemed to Angela too much of a hurry for good manners. She was surprised her new friend didn't appear to notice how quickly Burt disappeared.

Instead, Heather linked her arm through Angela's and

said, "You look rested. I'm so happy you decided to come along." She led Angela through the lobby where they followed the crowd to the bottom of the gangplank onto St George's Pier.

Chapter Ten

After leaving the two women in the ship's lobby, Burt went directly to Jeremy's suite. A temporary residence for the Line's executives, much larger than the ship's average balconied suite, it consisted of an office, a spacious living room, a bedroom and bath.

"Have a seat, Burt." Jeremy indicated a large leather chair directly across from him. "Care for some coffee?" He pointed to the silver carafe in the middle of the conference table.

"Maybe later," Burt said, dropping the folder he carried onto the table. "I had a cup about thirty minutes ago with MacDonald. He's still reviewing the reports from the Lyre that Pete Cuzak believed pertinent."

Jeremy's jaw tightened. "Any luck?"

"Nada. Not that we could expect much this early in the game."

"Of course, you'd be the best judge of that. I don't

have to tell you how critical knowing who murdered Margret Kopinski is to the Line."

Burt nodded. "While I can't promise it will answer more questions than it raises, there is one thing..."

"Yes?"

Burt pulled out a small notebook from his jacket pocket. "I don't think I mentioned that when I landed in Athens, the superintendent of police, Giorgis Papadakis, met my plane. An angry man. He's the one who advised me the victim's suite had been cleaned at least an hour before the Lyre notified his office of her death. By the time his crime scene team reached the ship any chance of finding a significant lead had been wiped out."

Jeremy's face darkened, his eyes narrowed, "Yes, headquarters notified me in New York before I left for Fort Lauderdale. Who ordered it? Why?"

Stone-faced, Burt looked at Jeremy. "Exactly. Why? Before we go on—" He reached for the folder he'd brought with him, opened it and slid it across the table. "I'd like you to review what I knew when I wrote the report. Page five," he added.

Jeremy flipped through the pages of the report. "According to this, Harry Carter, the cleaning supervisor, received a message to sano out suite B112 on the Lido deck ASAP. You interviewed him, and he confirmed this?"

Burt grimaced, shook his head. "Neither. Not possible. Not in this life, anyway."

Jeremy leaned forward. "Dead?"

"Very. I spoke with Pete Cuzak formerly our head of security on the Lyre. He said after the crime scene people in Athens left the ship he interviewed every member of the crew who knew Harry.

"As the report states, Carter couldn't be found when the authorities boarded in Athens, no one seemed to know where he was. And—" Burt paused, frowned, "He didn't turn up while I was in Athens. After the ship sailed from Greece, Pete reported the cleaning crew gathered on the aft deck to discuss what they thought they knew. They'd been questioned by the Greek police, and they decided putting together what each one had said, they might figure out what had happened to Harry, and what the Greek police might need to know. After they'd shared information, they told Pete that the last time they saw Harry, suddenly he'd burst out onto the crew deck. Without seeming to notice them there, he raced past them, climbed over a rail about half way down the deck and feet first, plunged into the harbor."

Jeremy interrupted, "How many witnesses?"

"Five. They didn't add much to what they'd each independently told the crime team detectives when they were interviewed. It was later, after I left the Lyre, when the story of Harry's apparent suicide spread, and a different crew member who works in the laundry contacted Pete. He described seeing Harry a few minutes before he jumped, apparently *before* his crew saw him on deck.

"He said Harry was crouched down in a corridor near the laundry, batting at something with both hands as if fighting off a swarm of insects. When he learned later what had happened, he told Pete he'd looked closely, but he couldn't see any sign of whatever it was Harry seemed to be fighting off."

"Sounds like he might have been hallucinating."

"Likely he was. At least that's what the crew told Pete."

"Jumped in the harbor?" Jeremy repeated.

"Right."

"Anyone pull him out?"

"The Greek port authority police retrieved a body after the ship sailed. They didn't find any identification on it. They didn't know if he was ours. The superintendent ordered an autopsy, but he'd suspected it was more than likely Harry Carter. If the autopsy confirms that belief, Papadakis will forward a full report of the findings to our authorities. In the meantime, I believe you knew I ordered Personnel to transfer Pete Cuzak and the men involved with the clean-up crew to the Q.C. I wanted to be sure I could question them again if any new information comes in. As for the Lyre, her new security officer will continue to be on the lookout in case someone on board is peddling hallucinogenics. Until the autopsy is completed we haven't proven drugs had anything to do with Harry jumping. If there is someone on board pushing, they'll find him."

"Anything else...?" Jeremy indicated the report in front of him. "Anything at all you want to add before I read this?"

"Yes. It's in there, but for what it's worth, it was over twenty four hours before I reached Athens and boarded the Lyre. With so much time elapsed, I'm not sure how much credence I can give to what the clean-up crew told me then. But they claimed, even before being questioned by the port authority, they'd all decided something bad had gone down in that suite."

"Meaning what?" Jeremy asked.

Burt nodded. "They said the bedding lay twisted half on, half off the bed as if it had been violently kicked there. One of the four down pillows usually provided for the suite beds was on the floor, with what seemed to be a dusty white footprint in its center. They also noted what might have been a message printed in bright red lipstick on the bathroom mirror. They couldn't make it out. Apparently whoever wrote it, or found it, didn't want it read. They also mentioned they found several paper tissues with lipstick on them under the sink, possibly used to erase the lipstick on the mirror."

Jeremy sat back, his eyes boring a hole in the opposite wall as he focused. "The report I read indicated you've concluded the clean-up of the suite appeared to be done to buy time before the body was found?"

"It fits," Burt said. "When the crew vacuumed the closet floor they found no clothing, not even a suitcase in the closet, no toiletries in the bathroom, no sign of a former resident. As I pointed out in that report, neither the crew nor Cuzak knew there'd been a murder in that suite. The purser said a woman, a famous model...you'll find her name in the report, had reserved that suite. Pete could find no computer records of her boarding or leaving the ship. The purser, a guy name of Boyle—I had him transferred to the Q.C. along with the clean-up crew— said she didn't appear on his passenger list. But the stewards responsible for that suite remembered her. And immigration recorded her passport before the ship sailed for Greece. She had to have boarded."

Jeremy leaned forward. "If that's how it went down, the perp managed to have the body moved to the morgue and under some pretense got Harry to order the clean-up," he said.

Burt agreed. "The crew, to a man, clearly didn't believe Harry Carter had anything to do with either the death of the passenger or the order to clean the suite. And one of them—it's on page seven—claimed he'd been close to Harry Carter."

Jeremy found the page and read the crew member's statement: "I don't get it. Never saw Harry with no drugs. Didn't put up with any of the guys using. The kind a guy he was, don't see him jumping off no deck. Always bragging about his wife and kid in Tampa, and how he couldn't wait to get back to see 'em."

"He was plenty angry about the Greeks suggesting the perp must have been Harry," Burt said.

Jeremy opened his mouth as if to speak, then closed it. He sat for a moment staring into space, then shook his head. "If I'm reading you right, Burt, my next question has to be whether you believe the murder and apparent suicide are related."

"We can't prove they aren't."

"You have no reason to believe any member of the clean-up crew could be involved in either the murder or in moving the body from the suite. Right?"

"No reason that makes sense."

"Right." Jeremy looked thoughtful. He steepled his fingers in front of him on the table, looked down a moment, then nodded. "Transferring Cuzak and the crew to the Q.C. may, as you say, allow you to review what they said they knew. Are you suggesting it could be one of them?"

"Yes. Except with a yes, I'm admitting to a hunch. We can't prove Harry ordered the cleanup or someone posing as Harry. If it wasn't one of the clean-up crew, it had to be a superior, someone with enough rank that Harry wouldn't question an order to have a suite cleaned at three a.m. I suspect Harry found out about the body in the morgue. If I'm right, he realized he'd been duped into being an accessory."

"You believe it came down that way?" asked Jeremy.

Burt turned his hands palms up. "For what it's worth, I'd say I do. Nothing in Harry's service record points to him as stupid. I also can't help believing Cuzak or one of the crew heard or saw something they didn't consider significant at the time, but after a while they might recall it and tell someone. And if a passenger on the Lyre was our perp, chances are we will never know who killed Kopinski and indirectly maybe Harry Carter."

Burt shook his head. "Official interrogation is stressful." He added, "By letting the details of the experience simmer a few days, I agree there is a chance the memory of someone or some incident leading to a viable suspect will surface."

"Okay, I want you to go with that and see where it leads." Jeremy rose, and Burt followed. They shook hands. At the door Jeremy hesitated. "In the meantime," he said, "I believe I overheard you were meeting Heather at Graystairs for dinner. Is that still on?"

"As far as I know."

"Anyone else going to be there?"

Burt grinned. "It's a possibility. Care to join the party?"

"The food's the best."

"The view should be terrific, also."

Jeremy opened the door. "See you there then."

Chapter Eleven

In Nassau, at the end of the pier, Heather asked, "Which will it be—Bay Street—we can walk, it's only a block." Then, without waiting for an answer, she added, "We'll stop by Cartier's first. I saw the loveliest sapphire earrings, perfect match for your eyes. You simply must try them on."

"Sapphire's? No doubt they're lovely, it's just that..."

Heather stopped abruptly and covered her mouth with her hand "Oh, I'm so sorry Silke. Of course you have lovely sapphires...your mother's favorite stone."

They were? Angela caught herself before voicing the question. Silke's mother. Of course, Heather meant Silke's mother.

"Yes, well..."

"Rude of me to remind you of your loss."

"Not at all," Angela said. "She's been gone a long time. It's just that I didn't realize her taste in stones was so widely known." True, she thought, she didn't know.

They had stopped at a corner when Heather suggested sapphires and now looking around her Angela recognized the name on the sign, Bay Street. Coles? If they were close to Coles, the Straw Market must be nearby, she realized.

"What about Cole's?" Angela suggested. "I believe you wanted to find a dress for Mardi Gras."

While she might be taking a chance that she'd be recognized by the snotty sales woman Heather wanted to impress, Angela seriously doubted it. Carstairs and Mad Martin insisted she was "practically" Silke's double. If the vendeuse was a snob, as Heather's description of her suggested, would she dare challenge Heather's introduction. After all, Heather was no longer a teenager, but a potential heir of Pryce Shipping and Cruise Line.

"Actually, that's a good idea. Then later, since you've never been there, we'll tour the Straw Market? It's quaint."

"Sounds like fun." Angela agreed, anything but Cartier's she thought.

"Perfect. We should have just enough time if we go directly to Coles now. I promised Burt we'd meet him at Graystairs for dinner."

"Graystairs?"

"It's *the* restaurant in the Bahamas. Been in business for over two hundred years, sooo romantic," Heather added.

"Oh. I wouldn't want to intrude."

"Not a chance. Burt insisted I invite you to join us, and if you like stone crabs—yum, yum, the very, very best. I know you'll love Graystairs."

"Three's a crowd."

"Not to worry. Jeremy's coming too. Four's a party."

Trapped! Angela thought.

The two women hadn't walked far when Angela saw the large white and pink banner. "Coles of Nassau, A Ladies Boutique Established in 1956 by an Old Bahamian Family" the sign bragged. Hung suspended over a red brick walk leading to the shop, the sign couldn't be missed. A surprisingly small building surrounded by tropical palms, painted pink with a startling white trim. After her visit to Rodeo Drive with Carstairs, Angela realized Coles wasn't at all what she expected an exclusive boutique to look like. Instead, she noted with pleasure, it reminded her of her own six-year-old idea of the perfect doll house. But six-year-old storybook houses sometimes held witches. Too late to turn back now.

"Here we are," Heather said, and held the door open for Angela. "I can hardly wait to introduce you to that snotty vendeuse I told you about," she whispered. "She won't dare treat me like an annoying adolescent this time, not after I introduce you. She'll gush all over herself trying to please Lady von Chassen and her friend."

Given the clerk's passion for the rich and famous, Angela wasn't so sure of that.

The inside of the shop lived up to Angela's concept of a fashionista's treasure chest. Although she was anything but a compulsive shopper, beautiful displays of brightly colored resort wear beckoned.

But instead of taking the time to look around, Heather asked for the clerk she wanted to impress; instead, she got the store manager.

"I'm so sorry," the manager said a few minutes later. "I'm afraid Lana's not in today, you know, one of those colds that drag on. She's been out for several days." She flashed her expensive white capped smile, and said, "Let me send for someone to help you," and without waiting for consent, the manager left the two of them standing in the middle of the store.

While Angela breathed a sigh of relief, thinking maybe they could just look around after all, Heather fumed. "Personalized service not available from the person I personally wanted to help me right now," Heather said. "You see Silke, the woman's a sadist who'd do almost anything not to wait on me. How does anyone get the flu on a tropical island anyway?"

Angela swallowed a laugh. "If she's that rude, the flu probably arrived with a New York tourist who deliberately breathed on her because she was rude," Angela suggested.

Heather's anger collapsed. She shook her head at Angela, and covered her mouth with both hands. "Bad, Silke, really bad!" she mumbled between her fingers.

And they might have succeeded in suppressing the laughter, if one of the clerks hadn't approached them at that exact moment and said, "May I be of service?"

Both women turned, looked at her, and doubled over in the middle of the store, laughing until they had tears in their eyes. The clerk, obviously mystified, stood staring at them.

Ten minutes after they'd arrived at Coles they left and headed for the Straw Market down Bay Street toward Christ Church Cathedral. Talking when they left the store, neither of them noticed the man who fell in step several feet behind them

"Too bad about the dress, Heather."

"Not a problem. I'll have time to buy one in St. Thomas. The shops there are fabuloso. Besides, someone's bound to tell Ms. Arrogance I arrived at the shop with the one and only Lady von Chassen." Heather shrugged. "That's almost as good as being there in person. She'll absolutely hate that she missed meeting you. Now we have plenty of time to poke around the Straw Market. You wanted to see it, and it's advertised as the best in the Bahamas."

"Isn't it very old?"

"It is, or was. Of course, the fire in 2001 did a lot of damage. Being rebuilt, I don't suppose it will ever be quite the same. But, you might like it Silke, especially if you like handmade stuff."

At the Straw Market, Angela, fascinated with the seemingly endless variety of colorful straw goods, wood-carvings, scarves, and costume jewelry, stopped every few feet to look and ask questions. Once she stood mesmerized in front of one of the stalls for fifteen minutes while watching a woman sew brilliant straw flowers onto a huge basket. She didn't buy much, a small string purse for her best friend from her swimming competition days, a wide brimmed hat for Charlie, her intern, and a scarf for his fiancée. Delighted with the market, she happily might have spent the day there if Heather hadn't held up her wrist and tapped her watch. "If we leave now," she said, "we'll have time to see more of the Island and visit the

Queen's staircase. It's a short cut to Graystairs, and it's historic."

"I think I read about it, too, built by slaves during Victoria's reign?"

"It was. Sixty-five steps carved out of limestone with only sharp axes. Originally intended to make it safer for British troops to reach Fort Fincastle. I don't know how safe it is now." Heather grimaced. "I wouldn't want to slip on those stairs."

The man in dark glasses stepped from between two of the stalls and followed them to the Queen's Staircase. Her attention fixed on the rugged steps, Angela didn't note the dark haired man elbowing other tourists out of his way several steps up behind her.

It wasn't until he reached for her shoulder that Heather saw him and yelled, "Watch out!"

Instinctively, Angela grabbed the railing and fell hard on one knee.

Only Heather's warning, the metal rail beside the steps, and her own trained reflexes kept her from tumbling down the rugged stairs to almost certain death. Above and below her, people were shouting at the would-be attacker who shoved them aside in his race back up the stairs where he disappeared into the crowd gathered at the top.

Shocked, Angela pulled herself up with Heather's help. A shudder went through her.

"God!" Heather wrapped an arm around Angela's waist and kept it there until they'd reached the bottom of the stairs where they paused.

"Are you okay?"

"I'll admit I've been better." Angela glanced back at

the stairs. "Wouldn't you know, the first time I've worn them." She bent down and brushed dirt from the knee of her new white slacks.

When she stood again, Heather, her voice awed, said, "He wanted to hurt you. He could have killed you. He almost pushed you down the stairs. He did it deliberately."

"Deliberately? Why would he do that?"

"I don't know. But I saw it on his face. That look, wild, it was...determined! It wasn't an accident. He knew exactly what he was doing."

Angela stared at Heather and shook her head. "Wouldn't it seem more likely he was just in a hurry, and I happened to be in the way?"

Heather held Angela's gaze for a moment. Then slowly nodded. "Maybe," she said.

Time to change the subject Angela thought. "Shouldn't we be going?" She held up her watch for Heather to see.

"Six, already? Oh. I promised Burt we'd be there by six-thirty. How's your knee? Is it hurting? We can flag down a taxi."

Angela looked behind her at the staircase with the lush tropical plants flourishing at its base. Her face grew pensive. Then she turned back to Heather, and shook her head. "No, it's fine. I can walk, thanks to you. If you hadn't yelled, I might have had more than a sore knee and..." She laughed, adding, "I most definitely would miss dinner."

Heather's eyes brightened. "We couldn't have that. I told you when visiting Nassau, no one should miss having dinner at Graystairs. Let's go. Those two men must be starved."

"True," she said. "We can't have that." The incident on the stairs would be just the catalyst needed to bring out the protective instincts of a man like Jeremy, Angela guessed. "Before we go, there is one thing..."

Heather waited.

"About what happened... I wasn't hurt and we really don't know..."

"That's it, we don't know," Heather said emphatically, a note of anger barely concealed in her voice. "We don't know why a man I feel certain I've seen before, attempted to push you down those stairs. Burt is responsible for the safety of every passenger on the Line. I have to tell him. Not to mention Jeremy. And I for one don't want to hear what my brother would say if he found out about it another way."

The tension in the back of Angele's neck tightened. "I understand your position, Heather. I suppose it would be best—but," she suggested, her voice hopeful, "can't it wait until morning or at least until we're back on board. Why ruin what promises to be a lovely evening?"

Heather looked thoughtful. "Sure, I don't see why not. It isn't as if I could point out the man tonight."

In April, the average temperature in the Bahamas hovers in the eighties during the day, cooling early in the evening. With Angela stepping carefully on the uneven path, the women reached Graystairs shortly after six thirty and well before sunset.

When they'd passed through the massive gates and began the ascent up the stairs leading to the entryway,

Angela couldn't shake a mixture of nerves and anticipation. At the top of the stairs, the huge doors to the entryway of the 250 year old hotel stood open. Although it was still daylight, the carriage lights on either side of the doors were lit. The massive chandelier inside the entrance glowed, suggesting a welcome Angela questioned.

Heather had assured her the five star restaurant offered fine food, great service and by implication a romantic setting no visitor to Nassau should miss. But Angela wasn't an ordinary tourist and Heather's description only triggered Angela's memory of the last dinner she'd shared with her fiancé in another romantic, not-to-be-missed restaurant. She'd been in love, or at least she'd been fool enough to believe she was. He wasn't. A fact she didn't know at the time. Only later, much too painfully, she discovered what he wanted from her. It wasn't love but something she would only give to a man who loved her, children, but Edward Fournier wasn't that man.

Inside Angela and Heather joined Jeremy and Burt seated in a room called The Parlor, a room any wealthy Victorian would appreciate, complete with velvet draperies and a grand piano. After pre-dinner champagne sours, and the usual courteous inquiries about their shopping trip, the two men ushered the women into a private dining room overlooking lavish tropical gardens.

On the table, flickering hurricane lanterns illuminated the intricate pattern of the crocheted table cloth, light danced in crystal stemware, and cast rosy shadows on the room's walls. Captivated by the beauty of her surroundings, Angela read the menu suggestions with unseeing eyes. Not that it mattered, she realized with relief. When the waiter appeared, Jeremy ordered for all of them. The Bahamian dinner was served on the famous restaurant's signature, navy blue-banded china. It began with a silky lobster bisque followed by an entrée of seafood en papillote accompanied by sugar peas and a plate of papayas so fresh Angela concluded they'd been picked moments before being served.

Each course was also served with a serious wine from what Burt said was the restaurant's impressive 27,000 bottle cellar of vintage wines. Dessert was optional, and Angela passed.

Across the small table, so close she could smell his cologne, a scent rich and masculine like the man who wore it threatened to undo Angela's attempt to portray a cool reserve. Determined to ignore the question so clearly written in his eyes whenever his gaze met hers across the table, she turned to Heather.

"Your description of the food couldn't have been more accurate. I'd never tasted Bahamian style food before. It's delicious. I suspect you've come here often."

"Since I was fifteen, or only as often as I could talk big brother here into paying the bill." She winked at Jeremy. "Our grandmother doesn't believe in spoiling kids. She always expected us to work holidays and summers while we were in school—for minimum wages, of course. Minimum wage doesn't buy an olive in a restaurant like Graystairs."

"And speaking of credit, you now owe me how many dinners?" Jeremy faked a scowl, but couldn't hide the playful humor in his voice.

Bright-eyed, Heather poked her brother in the ribs.

"Nary a one, until you pay me for all the buttons I sewed on your shirts when you were still in school. However, as I'll be working in the Los Angeles office starting in June, I might consider inviting you to dinner at Spago's. Everyone raves about Wolfgang Puck's duck with plum wine sauce, and I know your weakness for his chocolate cake with vanilla Bourbon sauce."

"One dinner there ought to take a healthy bite out of your first significant paycheck, kid." Jeremy laughed easily, then shook Heather's outstretched hand to seal the agreement. "It's a date. It will be my pleasure to see you don't have a nickel left."

Angela shifted in her chair. How was she supposed to ignore him? Jeremy Pryce didn't fit the template in her mind of who a wealthy CEO with his privileged background should be. For that matter, his sister for all her sophistication charmed everyone around her with an easygoing attitude and obvious willingness to share her life while understanding that of others. Even Burt, with his questioning attitude, seemed to relax, at least when he wasn't looking at Heather. For the first time, it dawned on Angela that Burt was probably in love with Heather, and it was mutual.

The gracious atmosphere, delicious food and lively conversation all worked to lull Angela into an unguarded state. The enchanting setting and the people in it all seemed contrived, an evening too perfect, too story-like to be believable. She wasn't ready for the jolt she experienced when Jeremy's eyes met hers again with a challenge, a dare, a look that said not if, but when? Unimpeded, his gaze traveled down to her mouth and lingered there while distant music pulsed, and the room grew much too warm.

There was no point in lying to herself. She wasn't free to let her attraction lead to any kind of emotional involvement. Even if the attraction was as mutual as it seemed to be. Sooner or later he would discover she wasn't who she said she was and...? She refused to think about it.

Breaking eye contact, Angela looked down at the table. She picked up her unused dessert spoon and slid it back and forth across the crocheted table cloth. She shouldn't be here. She shouldn't be with these people. They seemed friendly, seemed to like her, accept her, but she knew better. When she broke her engagement to Edward Fournier, he and his mother let her know she was a fool. They made her lack of marriageable assets exquisitely clear. No lowly physical therapist possessed the social credentials, not to mention money, required to marry him. His mother told her she was "grateful" that she broke the engagement.

Angela glanced at Jeremy, wealthy, sophisticated, out of reach. Her vision blurred, her chest ached. She looked down at the silver spoon in her hand, gripped it more tightly. And what about the clinic? The voice taunted. She took a deep breath. How could she let a silly infatuation keep her from her goal? She had to win...had to build a new clinic. Suddenly she felt cold.

"Silke?" Startled, Angela looked up from the table. "It must have been an unpleasant thought." Heather said. "Your face, you looked so grim."

"I—no, not really. I was thinking about how much patience it must take to learn to crochet."

Heather shrugged. "I don't think I ever consider it. Maybe it's relaxing for some people, like weaving hats from straw. The people at the market seemed to like what they were doing."

"The things that can be done with straw—amazing." Burt said, and directed his question to Angela. "I suppose you spent most of the day there?"

Why did Burt's questions always sound like interrogations?

Angela looked at Heather. Heather looked away. "Not as much time as we should have."

"Speaking of time," Jeremy signaled the waiter hovering in the doorway. "It's not much of a walk to the dock, but I think it's time we started back. I still haven't heard the piano player in the Calypso lounge. Someone did suggest he's so smooth he can lull you to sleep." His grin widened and he winked at Angela. She felt her face flame.

"Perfect. We can stop there for a nightcap." Heather said.

It was almost ten when they reached the ship.

He stood in the shadow of a parked taxi. He waited and watched them approach the gangplank—Pryce, his bratty sister and the cop, Chaney. Good, she was with them. They thought they were so smart. They hadn't found out who she was, and he'd recognized her almost immediately. Weren't they going to be surprised when they found out? Too bad she'd already be dead.

Chapter Twelve

Angela awoke early. Beyond the glass doors leading to the balconies, the world waited for morning. She hadn't slept well, probably, she told herself, because that one drink after dinner dragged on and the conversation that followed continued until almost midnight.

After several moments of staring out into the darkness, Angela decided she might as well make her way to the small cafeteria near the forward pool where she'd been assured she'd find coffee any time of the day or night.

Hot and fresh the coffee tasted good, "...better than what I brew at home," Angela told the sleepy steward on duty, which earned a smile and an oversized cup of coffee to take with her. Before moving on, she checked the location of the deck she wanted. Posted on bulkheads throughout the ship, colorful maps served as road signs for the passengers.

After checking her course, she headed for the bow

where, the steward had assured her, she could watch the sunrise.

To her surprise, the big pool on the deck sat empty. "A ship never sleeps," Heather had said. Maybe, Angela thought, but if the passengers partied all night apparently they must stay inside mornings to avoid sleepwalking overboard. My good luck, she thought looking out to sea.

Beyond the rail, the horizon reflected a pastel dawn. Gradually, it spread out until it became a ribbon of color unfurling in a measured advance, laying a path to Angela's feet across the undulating ocean.

Overwhelmed by the beauty of the rising sun's promise for the day, she longed to stay close to the rail where she could watch the restless waves endlessly shifting on the face of the sea. But she chose a chair against the bulkhead, one slightly shadowed by the overhanging promenade deck, a place where she could be seen, without necessarily being noticed. Satisfied with her selection, she sat down, wrapped herself in a terry cloth pool-robe, adjusted the straw hat she'd carried, placed her book on the seat beside her, and leaned back in the chair.

Soothed by the rocking motion of the ship and the rhythmic throb from the great engines at its heart, she slept.

The sun continued to rise. Passengers wandered out onto the pool deck, admired the ocean and went back inside to breakfast. None of them coming or going seemed to notice the woman wrapped in a robe, asleep in the deck chair, her hat shadowing her face.

It was a couple of hours after Angela fell asleep that Jeremy, in swimming trunks, a towel wrapped around his waist, came out on deck. He looked at the pool and then back across the deck where he saw the person he'd been looking for. Skirting the pool he squatted on his heels in front of a boy in a wheelchair.

"How about a game of water polo?"

"You want to play with me?" the boy asked. "Really?" he questioned, his eyes wide.

"Sure. It's not much fun tossing a ball around by myself. You do like to play water polo ball, don't you?"

"Oh, yes. Please sir." He breathed out the words on a sigh. He hesitated, looked back over his shoulder, "I must ask Ms. Kettering."

"Is that Ms. Kettering over there?" Jeremy nodded in the direction of a slim young woman talking to one of the ship's officers.

"Yes."

"Well, suppose I ask her?"

"Oh, yes, please sir."

"Happy to, if you'll just hold onto our ball for a moment." Jeremy dropped the red ball into the boy's lap, and the child immediately wrapped his small arms around it as if it might disappear.

When the officer beside Ms. Kettering introduced her, it was more than apparent from her face she would have given Jeremy almost anything he asked for.

Only a few minutes later, Angela awoke to the sound of a child's laughter. Surprised she had fallen asleep in the deck chair, she sat up abruptly. With the glare off the ocean blinding her, she could barely make out the people on deck. She dug her sunglasses out of the pocket of her robe, straightened the broad-brimmed hat that had slid to the back of her head and replaced her glasses.

On the other side of the ship's rail, the sun stood off to the East, not quite high enough to be noon. Given its loca tion she decided it couldn't be later than ten. It took a few seconds for her eyes to adjust to the glare off the ocean before she identified the source of the sound that had awakened her. Then she spotted them.

Two figures at the far end of the pool engaged in a game of water polo. She recognized Jeremy immediately and then the boy with him. When she'd boarded the Q.C. he'd arrived on the promenade deck shortly after she had. Sad faced, apparently handicapped, he'd stared vacant-eyed at the harbor while a woman who appeared to be a nurse of some sort pushed his wheelchair in circles around the promenade deck.

Angela recognized the look on the child's face. She'd seen it often enough on the faces of new patients arriving at her clinic for their first therapy sessions. It wasn't so much a look of hopelessness as it was of endurance. Anger rose like bile in her throat. No child should wear that mask, that adult mask, stoic, frozen in pain. No, she wouldn't allow her patients to settle for *that*. If she could gain their confidence, convince them to come with her into the water, within a few weeks of gentle therapy the despair she'd first seen on their faces would vanish, to be replaced first by cautious smiles, then surprise or excite-ment. The realization they were gaining on their disability followed, weeks later, by determination and yes, finally, hope.

Puzzled, she watched the man and the boy. It almost

seemed Jeremy knew what he was doing. She suppressed a cheer when he repeatedly forced the child to fight for points. The boy was neither a competent nor a strong swimmer. On land, his pale legs would leave him at a disadvantage in the world of the walking, but in the smooth waters of the pool he darted for the ball like an oversized guppy, quick and agile. His arms, strong from lifting himself in and out of a wheelchair, allowed him to send the ball high over the net. Several times it flew beyond a long-armed reach, and the boy laughed to see Jeremy chase after it. Handicapped children, she knew, more than children without disabilities, were quite sensitive to being treated as if they couldn't compete. The boy would have lost interest immediately if he could not challenge the man, or if Jeremy allowed him to win. Where was the sophisticated, cynical playboy she had presumed him to be?

In her deck chair across the deck, Angela enjoyed the game immensely. In fact, before it was over she forgot she was trying to stay out of sight and without thinking she tilted her broad-brimmed straw hat back to better view the game. About thirty minutes after Jeremy's arrival, the young officer left and the nurse came to the edge of the pool to call a halt to the fun.

Jeremy scooped up the boy and headed for the ladder. He placed the child in his wheelchair, removed a silver chain with a Dolphin medal attached to it from around his own neck and draped it around the boy's neck. The two shook hands before the nurse wheeled the chair away. Not until Jeremy reentered the pool did Angela remember where she was. Sliding back down in her beach chair she tipped her hat forward, picked up her book from the chair beside her and pretended to read.

Sunlight gilded, the waves danced to the rhythm of Jeremy's passage back and forth across pool. The muscles of his back rippled and gleamed. A strong, graceful swimmer he cut through the water effortlessly. Angela shifted, uncomfortable in the deck chair. Unwillingly, she recalled the way his arms felt that night on the deck. Watching him now, she could almost feel them close around her again, pulling her against his hard, lean body. Foolishly she'd clung to him the way the water did now. She could taste his arrogant mouth on hers—the flavor, salted now with soft Caribbean days, nights. A fine veil of perspiration coated her skin. Nights. The word settled in her limbs leaving her weak. When he paused and began to climb out of the pool, she slid down further in her chair.

"Hormones," Angela muttered, "damn hormones."

"Up early Milady?" Jeremy reached for one of the pool towels stacked on the table beside Angela's deck chair flinging drops of pool-water onto her open book.

"Oops!"

Her eyes narrowed.

"If it's a whodunit, I hope you weren't at the point where the brilliant detective revealed the name of the killer. That would be tragic."

Angel suppressed a groan and regarded him critically. "Tragic? Ridiculous. And stop calling me Milady. For you, the name is Silke."

Jeremy settled in the chair next to her. "I'd say it's a matter of opinion, mine in this case. With eyes that send up fireworks like yours when you're annoyed, I doubt there's a princess on the globe that can match them. However, today your wish is my command, fair lady. Since I'd like you to join me for lunch."

Angela glanced down at the wet pages of her book, then up to his wet swimming trunks.

"When?" she said sweetly.

His gaze followed hers..."now, after I change into something more suitable."

Angela seemed about to smile then bent over laughing.

Jeremy's face reddened. "I didn't think it was that funny," he said, eliciting more laughter.

"No, oh no," she said, pressing her fingers to her mouth. "It's just that," she said between her fingers—"just that the page you soaked is about how the police finally caught up with Bundy."

Jeremy scowled, looked bland for only a moment. Then his eyes crinkled, and he laughed with her. "Right," he said, "the airport. Which reminds me, I seem to recall after you decided I didn't look handsome enough to be another Bundy, you promised to have dinner with me."

"I never said you weren't as handsome as Bundy. And it's my impression that the dinner obligation was taken care of at Graystairs last night."

"Dinner with my sister doesn't count."

"No?"

"No. Suppose we start over. "Have lunch with me, and I promise never again to address you as Milady."

Hormones? Careful Angela.

The word ignited her memory. She was back in Bel Air. Excited about the dinner party Edward's parents were giving to announce their son's engagement. She arrived early. The soft footed houseman ushered her into the study and left her there while he went to inform Edward. He'd no sooner closed the door than she heard voices. It took less than a moment to identify their source coming from beyond the French doors leading to the pool. Through the doors lightly curtained windows she saw Edward and his mother seated on the pool deck. I'll surprise him, she thought recalling how often he'd told her he hated it when she was delayed by one of her patients. But before she could tiptoe across his mother's prized, antique Kazak carpet to the doors, Edward's deep bass stopped her.

"With both a husband and a son who are doctors, you of all people, Mother, should know about chemistry, how misleading it can be. Not that I believe you are wrong about Angela. She's not, as you put it, our kind. However, I have no intention of being trapped in a marriage based on a random hormonal response to the opposite sex."

"Then explain why, Edward—Is there a shortage of attractive, socially eligible young women in the greater Los Angeles area? Were there none at Berkley?"

"Of course, Mother. If I took the time, I might find one more attractive than Angela, but few would have her characteristics I'm looking for in a wife, more importantly, the mother of my children. If there's anything that's clear about recent genetic research, it's the importance of genetic heredity in producing healthy, attractive offspring. Angela comes from a long line of healthy intelligent men and women. Over a century ago, Alexander Hamilton being only one of the first. Her father was a world famous

Olympic swimming coach, her mother a concert pianist. When her mother died from childbirth complications, her father coached Angela from childhood to be a swimming star."

"Hamilton, yes, and I can take your word on her genetic history, but I don't see what a winning medals in swimming competitions has to do with..."

"Not much, possibly, except it proves she's strong, healthy and can be trained."

Edward leaned his head closer to his mother's, and lowered his voice. "Exposure to our life style, the money I can provide to see she dresses well, introduction to the right young women in our social set, a mother-in-law who is the perfect example of what I'd expect from a wife. You see Mother, Angela Hamilton will be the perfect mother to my children, your grandchildren."

Angela froze. Later, she couldn't remember how she got out of the study door and into the hallway where she almost collided with the startled houseman. She brushed past him without responding to his "Is anything wrong, Miss?"

Had it really been eight months since that night? What was she thinking? Was she so lonely now that she had to know she mattered to someone? Hadn't she learned? No, never again would she allow herself to be that naïve. She would not allow herself to be that damaged by another man, one who could buy anything and anyone he chose to.

Angela lifted her head and forcing a smile, faced Jeremy. "Oh, I am sorry, another time perhaps. I have a spa appointment in..." she glanced at her watch, "twenty minutes." She lied.

Jeremy studied her face, then nodded. "I can take another rain check. It would be a shame to miss the Q.C.'s spa. It's been written up in almost every travel article about cruising as being the best."

"Yes," Angela said, and without meeting his eyes she looked away, pretended to search for her book before she spotted it where it had fallen from her lap. Jeremy leaned over the arm of the chair, retrieved it and glanced at the title before offering it to her. "Physical Therapy for the Autistic Child," he read aloud before handing her the book. "A little light reading. Interesting," he added, the unstated questions implied were not lost on her. "Who would have believed Bundy was autistic," he said, handing her the book.

"Thanks." She choked out the word, gathered her things and fled through the nearest bulkhead doorway.

Back in her suite, intent on changing out of her swim wear to something casual for a gourmet cooking class at the noon the ship's head chef was holding Angela almost missed seeing the small manila envelope propped up next to the telephone. Jeremy? So soon? Why couldn't he leave her alone? She picked it up, found it surprisingly heavy for such a small envelope. Based on its weight and the fine cotton texture of the paper, she guessed it was probably some kind of invitation, the kind a woman like Silke would receive. Reluctant to open an envelope addressed to someone else, she stared at it for several seconds then turned it over. The back was not sealed, no return name or address. Necessity won out, she lifted the flap, and wasn't too surprised to find a dinner invitation inside for the following evening, the night before the ship reached St. Thomas. What did surprise her was its source, the ship's captain.

She'd been lucky until now, she told herself. Meeting Heather when she'd first boarded allowed her to appear to be mingling with the other passengers, but kept her from meeting many of them. On her second night in the dining room, one of the passengers at her table had pointed out the Captain's guests—a sports star, actress, politician and a celebrated journalist. Dining at his table would be like sitting beneath a microscope.

Angela dropped the invitation on the bed. In the bathroom she showered and after changing into cotton slacks and a light blouse she considered practical for a cooking class, she returned to her bedroom. The cream colored envelope, small and accusing, remained where she'd dropped it on the bed. She considered claiming illness, but someone might ask Rashid, her steward, or Anastasia, her butler, if she needed a doctor. She couldn't expect them to lie for her. Besides, if someone on the ship was keeping track of her, making certain the rules were followed, she'd have to accept the invitation.

Chapter Thirteen

The gourmet cooking class proved to be fun. She also attended a lecture on the flora and fauna of the Caribbean late that afternoon. She'd expected Dr. Ackerman, the historian, to be the lecturer and was surprised when it was a man. After dinner in the main dining room, she attended a comedy show that lasted until midnight. Then, careful to avoid the Calypso room, she had a glass of wine on deck under the stars at one of the ship's open-air bars and went to bed at two a.m. The following morning, the fourth day of the cruise, she awoke and checked the electronic clock on the nightstand. It was seven a.m. She'd overslept. The ship would dock at nine. She climbed out of bed and reached for her robe. In the living room of her suite the sun backlit the two sets of double doors leading to her two balconies. Yawning, she stepped out onto the balcony on the right.

Why two balconies? When she asked Rashid, he'd explained that her suite sat at the prow of the ship, below the ship's bridge and above the exclusive deck for the passengers of the most expensive suites. The point of having balconies port side and starboard was so that the occupants could choose one or the other. If you were close to shore, you might see land from the port-side balcony. If you stood on the other balcony you faced starboard and most likely would see only water. All she could see now was the endless blue Caribbean and a few drifting white clouds that seemed to be parading along the ship's route. She'd hoped to see some Islands, or even St. Thomas. She went back into the living room and stepped out onto balcony on the port side of her living room and sighed. Where were the islands? The first night, Professor Ackerman had said there were several in the Antilles chain. No luck. She would have to wait until the ship reached St. Thomas. After learning some of the history of the Islands the first night out, she could hardly wait.

Two hours later, Angela showered and dressed, stood on the weather deck watching the shore while the Queen of Charades glided into the harbor at Charlotte Amalie, the capitol city of St. Thomas, and weighed anchor.

Above the sugar sand beaches, steep emerald hills garlanded with strings of tiny white houses each crowned with a geranium red roof. A gentle breeze emanated from the shore, caressed Angela's face and filled her senses with the island's exotic perfume: tropical flowers, rich, dark soil, salt air and, strangely, an odor Angela could only identify as cooking spices.

At the base of the hills, local taxis lined the single road bordering the harbor. Their drivers sat slumped in their vehicles, silently watching, until the ship secured its mooring and the thump, thump of its great motors shuddered and stilled. Then the drivers seemed to rise as one, leaving their taxi doors ajar.

They stepped out onto the narrow street and stood waiting, taut with expectancy as the bright sun created their silent, slender, black shadows. They didn't have long to wait. In less than an hour, all the taxis were filled with excited passengers, most of whom went directly to the dozens of duty free shops lining Veterans Drive.

Angela had read about the duty free shops in the cruise brochures, but she was unprepared for the seemingly endless display counters crammed with priceless gold and jewels or the magnificent displays of couturier clothing and museum quality *objects d'arte*. Not even Beverly Hills famous Rodeo Drive offered so much manmade bounty in such small spaces. Intrigued, she paused before a glass topped counter to admire an exceptionally attractive display. "Lovely," Angela murmured, and before she could object, the clerk behind the counter unlocked the cabinet and laid the tiny, jeweled butterfly mask on a blue velvet pad in front of her.

She didn't notice Jeremy step up beside her until he said, "You have a good eye. Unless I'm mistaken, it's a vintage piece designed by Mario Buccellati sometime in the late twenties, early thirties."

The mask, studded with diamonds, rubies, and emeralds, merely lovely beneath the glass, proved stunning laying before her and much too much like the one she wore on the game show the first time he had seen her. She inhaled slowly, smiled at the clerk and turned to face Jeremy.

"Possibly," she said, "a bit gaudy, perhaps," she added. Surprised she hadn't choked on the lie.

"Not a description I would have chosen. I see it as a rare work of art, incredibly lovely, unique and somehow right for you. Are you certain you don't like it?"

"Surely you'll agree," she said, in what she hoped was an arrogant Silke voice, "one can have too much jewelry? And now, if you'll excuse me, I'd like to see the Coral World Marine Park before it becomes, like this place, too crowded."

"Right," Jeremy agreed, ignoring the implied slight. "Better yet, for a real Caribbean experience you'd see much more and avoid the crowds if you took me up on my offer to take you sailing. There are dozens of secluded coves on the island where you can view the marine life from the comfort of a boat."

Angela glared at him. "And I'll bet you know every one of them. You just can't take no for an answer, can you Jeremy Pryce? Now if you'll excuse me," she headed for the door.

Outside Angela signaled the first passing taxi. "Coral World," she instructed the driver. But, when he put the car into gear and began to pull away she saw Jeremy in the rearview mirror step into the dusty street and stand there watching the retreating car. Just when she believed she'd conquered her infatuation, he turned up again, tempting her.

Damn him! Must he look so lonely?

"Stop," she leaned forward and ordered the driver. "I forgot something. Well, someone," she said settling back into the worn seat.

Puzzled, Jeremy watched the taxi stop and do a U turn. After she refused to meet him for lunch, dinner, or "only a drink," and feeling a bit like a stalker, he'd located her in one of the jewelry shops on Veterans Drive. Once there, he had convinced himself that with dozens of tourists between them, when she saw him he could pretend to shop and she could pretend she didn't know he'd followed her. From the moment they met at the airport in Fort Lauderdale, his gut told him the attraction he felt was mutual. He also knew that somewhere, locked in the dim halls of his memory, he'd seen that defiant lift of her chin before, watched her lose the struggle to suppress a smile, a smile he knew now she only succumbed to when accepting she'd been caught in some denial. Self-confidence and persistence he had plenty of, and he was determined to break through the façade she hid behind of a jaded, too-rich playgirl. Certain she knew the attraction worked both ways, he still found it difficult to hide his surprise when she came back to where he stood in the street, leaned out the taxi window and said she would accept his invitation to go sailing if he wanted to wait until after her visit to Coral World.

Jeremy agreed, and they arranged a time and place to meet. Pleased, but puzzled, he watch the taxi pull away and wondered why she agreed to spend a day alone on a sailboat with him? Surely she knew what could happen. When he had suggested sailing after reaching St. Thomas the night they dined at Graystairs, she seemed less than pleased with the idea. Of course, he reasoned, inviting her for a sail could prove to be nothing less than an extraordinary inspiration on his part.

Not that he believed it. He was, he admitted, occasionally arrogant but not that arrogant. When he'd approached her at the airport, watched her tilt her chin, and raise it in a regal if not subtle signal that for whatever reason she recognized him but would not acknowledge she knew him, he didn't accept the warning. He didn't believe her then and refused to now.

He couldn't deny the chemistry between them, and she had to know it was mutual. He'd seen the desire to laugh linger, teasing the corners of her mouth until it overcame those reluctant lips, and lit her face. The same smile she attempted to hide, but couldn't the day he met her in the airport lounge; the one she failed to deny now when she realized he'd seen her arrive at the Marina.

Angela called his name from where she stood at the locked gate on the other side of the fence guarding the moored boats. Before the sound of her voice died, Jeremy climbed up over the stern of the Sun Dancer. He reached the chain link fence in only a few long-legged strides. How did she manage it, he wondered? She looked even lovelier with that ridiculous, oversized sun hat perched on the back of her head. Even more enchanting than she had the night he found her asleep in the Calypso room. He'd been afraid she'd back out. And again he felt certain that all he needed to do was to have her to himself, away from the crowds, for his memory to return.

"Any trouble finding the right dock?" he asked, unlocking the heavy metal gate between them, and swinging it open.

She shook her head, stepped past him and stood beside him on the dock. "None at all. The taxi drivers in

St. Thomas must know every marina on the island. Mine not only recognized the name of the marina, he knew the name of the boat and who owned it."

"Not surprising. Pryce Line ships bring a lot of business to the local economy. The Sun Dancer's right over there." He indicated a sleek, white sailboat moored a few feet away, and was pleased to see her smile widen. "Oh, it is lovely," she said.

"Unless you've enjoyed your quota of submerged Island residents at Coral World, I know a quiet cove with a beautiful beach where you're certain to see many more of them. If we leave now we'll have time to explore it."

Jeremy reached for the small backpack she was carrying, and slung it over his shoulder. "Sensible wearing that hat. The sun is brutal on the water. Usually there's some sun screen below, but I couldn't find any."

"I always carry sun screen. Will two small tubes do?"

He laughed. "Not if we go aground on a deserted island. A situation one can always hope for, of course." He grinned at her. "And clearly the lady is fully prepared."

Her eyes narrowed. She didn't return the smile. "And miss the ship?"

"If you're worried, don't be." He looked at her thoughtfully. "The truth is I'm playing hooky. I'm due back by five. Plenty of time to secure the Sun Dancer before the Q.C. sails." He pointed up at the boat's ensign flying in the breeze. "With this breeze, we should be able to see quite a bit of the Island without relying on the engine."

"Really? I meant to ask someone on the ship how large the island is and how many people live here."

"It's about twenty-four square miles, roughly the size of Manhattan, big enough for the current population of about fifty-five thousand, most of them happier residents than Manhattan's three million, I suspect."

"My enthusiastic taxi driver would agree. He claimed he drove a taxi in New Jersey for a year, couldn't wait to get back to Charlotte Amalie."

Jeremy took her arm to help her aboard. "You'd find few residents who'd disagree with him."

Angela looked down at his hand, brown from the past two days at sea. It felt strong, good, too good. She looked at his profile. If an artist set out to create a perfect "male" face he wouldn't look further than Jeremy Pryce. His keen blue eyes, broad forehead and strong jaw, shouted male, not to mention the sculpted athletic build he owed as much to genetics as time in a gym. No, she didn't want to be attracted to him. If she wanted to remain incognito, she couldn't trust anyone right now, especially herself with this man. He didn't just hold her arm, potentially he held her future. Jeremy was anything but stupid. What if he remembered where he'd seen her before? Panic swept over her. What am I doing here? She stopped.

"Did I hurt your arm?"

Angela shook her head. It wasn't a good idea to let him see she was nervous He might ask questions, questions I can't answer, she thought. "It's only that," she looked away, seemed to be examining something behind him and lowering her voice to almost a whisper added, "I haven't been sailing on a small boat for ah...for several years."

Jeremy removed his hand from her arm, studied her. A last minute excuse? No. She appeared poised, ready to run. Afraid? Maybe she hadn't been kidding about Bundy. Jeremy held her gaze. No, he thought, not afraid, sad. And then he remembered Heather's words when he'd suggested inviting Silke for a sail.

Silke's parents died while boating when a yacht captained by its drunken owner rammed their small sloop. Of course she'd be sad.

"Sorry, stupid of me. It didn't occur to me you hadn't been on a small boat since the accident."

"Sorry?" Her mind raced. Her stomach fluttered, tightened. Even if he'd realized she wasn't who she claimed to be, he couldn't possibly know how her father died, could he? Speechless, she stared at him.

"I should have asked if you *liked* to sail or if being on a sailboat might bring back unhappy childhood memories."

A child's memories. A giddy sense of relief welled up. Of course. Now his apology made sense. When Carstairs, the game show's producer, briefed her for the masquerade, she explained how Silke lost her parents in a tragic sailing accident. "She was only three. Chances are good," she'd added, "Silke does not consciously remember the accident. Subsequent news stories noted she was wearing a life preserver. The impact threw her clear of the sinking boat and a sailor on board another vessel saw her and went in after her."

Angela felt the tension seep from her. "You have no reason to apologize. What happened, happened a long time ago. I have no memory of that accident, and I love to sail."

Jeremy looked relieved. "There's a fine breeze. If we get underway now, we should be able to reach my favorite beach in about forty-five minutes." He gestured to the short flight of teak stairs leading below deck. "If you brought a swimming suit, you can change below while I cast off."

Angela reached for her back pack. "It's in here," she said.

"Good. You'll find a life vest below. Put it on."

"Aye, aye captain." Angela smiled, gave a mock salute, and turning, went below deck.

It hadn't occur to Jeremy telling her to 'put it on,' sounded more like a command than a suggestion until she saluted. He liked her sense of humor.

When his grandfather decided it was time for him to sail the family sloop without adult interference or direction, he'd been twelve going on thirteen. He would be, John Pryce told his grandson, fully responsible for sailing to any cove on St Thomas he designated, and for getting them both safely there. Once they arrived, he'd be expected to choose the best anchorage without beaching the boat, and close enough to the shore so they could swim to the beach.

Jeremy knew he would never forget that first trip at the helm of a sailboat. He'd sailed as his grandfather's "first mate" since he was eight. Until that day he'd never felt the responsibility for the safety of another person. Nor would he forget agonizing over the choice of when to switch from sail to motor to enter the designated cove under power. Most of all, he would remember his grandfather's pride in him when they'd arrived at the cove and he'd correctly judged a safe depth to anchor the boat, one that only required a short swim to reach the shore. Much later he realized that first trip was only the beginning of his grandfather's plan to groom him for a future position with Pryce Cruise Line. It was also the beginning of his love affair with sailboats.

Once while in college he invited a woman he'd been dating to sail with him—only once, a mistake. He glanced over his shoulder to the steps leading below deck. Today could also be a mistake, but somehow, with this woman, he didn't think so.

~

Chapter Fourteen

In the cabin below deck, Angela stripped off the shorts and cotton shirt she'd worn and changed into her new swimming suit. Silke would approve of the suit, she thought. It wasn't at all like the conservative one-piece suits she wore at the clinic. Hot pink, the bikini bra barely covered her nipples, while the scrap of cloth secured low on her hips with four thin, silk, cords could barely pass for a handkerchief. An impulsive choice purchased for the cruise. It fit like her own skin. So? So what! There was nothing wrong with her skin. And anyway, she reasoned, men were used to seeing women in bikinis, weren't they?

Occupied in maneuvering the Sun Dancer out of the crowded harbor, Angela realized Jeremy didn't notice her when she returned to the deck. Unwilling to interrupt his concentration, she stood behind him while he expertly maneuvered the sleek sailboat out of the marina to sea. A good sailor herself, she couldn't help but admire his skill. And, in spite of her determination not to allow him to become too important, being with him felt comfortable, safe and natural. Now, as she watched his bronzed, strong, competent hands on the wheel turning the Sun Dancer into the wind, she caught herself remembering the first time she'd seen him in the wings of the set before the game began. Tall, broad shouldered, strong jawed and smiling across the set. Too far across the stage to see the color of his eyes, she could still feel them on her—curious, questioning. What would it take for him to remember where he'd seen her and recognize she'd known all along who he was and that from the first, every exchange between them had been built on a lie? The breeze skipping over the waves and across the bow of the boat brought with it the scent of something masculine and seductive that mingled with salt water and reminded her of the night he'd kissed her on the deck and the mindless way she'd responded to his need with her own. Until her reason won out despite his handsomeness and wealth. And since when have wealthy men been anything but a disaster in your life, Angela Hamilton? They're arrogant, self-centered and only after what they think they're entitled to. If she had an ounce of sense, she reminded herself, she wouldn't be here. No doubt *shouldn't* be here.

Several minutes passed before Jeremy killed the auxiliary motor, raised and secured the mainsail then turned to Angela. His gaze began at her eyes, and traveled to her bare feet before gradually moving back up slowly to her eyes where it stopped. He seemed to be assessing what he'd seen. Angela fought back an almost overpowering urge to turn away. Little Red Riding Hood probably saw the same look on the face of the wolf.

"Nice suit," he said, then, with what seemed a deliberate dismissal, he turned away, gripped the wheel, and began to spin stories of the Caribbean, its islands, beaches, coves and the history of the men who sailed there.

Confused, Angela sat down and leaned back on the large, blue leather, U-shaped settee behind Jeremy. Lulled by the melodious tap, tap of the waves she ignored the sound of his voice and her mind drifted back.

She'd been truthful when she said she loved sailing, she thought, or at least she had before that night at Catalina. She hadn't sailed since then, surprised that sailing today did not trigger the guilty feeling it might have nine years ago.

It happened on her eighteenth birthday when her father decided she needed a break from training. The next swimming meet would be held in Nebraska in less than a month. A national meet, the winners would be competing to represent the U.S.A at the summer Olympics in Japan. Frank Hamilton seldom relented enough to let her have time off from training, and she was thrilled when he rented a boat in Long Beach and they set out for a long weekend of sunshine and fishing.

After her father's death, she'd fought back the guilt, finished her education and begun her career. But, she hadn't been able to swim since that day. Two quotes she'd read a few months later comforted her. They echoed in her mind now.

Let the past remain in the past.

And

The only honest way to live today is to
honor the past and live in the present.

She did honor her past, maybe someday, she told
herself, she might be able to live in the present.

With a sigh, Angela turned her attention back to that
present at the moment Jeremy ended a story she'd only
half heard about the indigenous Caribe's, the original residents of the Caribbean. What little she'd heard reminded
her of the famous historical writer she'd met that first
night on board. Maybe she'd see the professor again before
the end of the cruise, she thought, just as Jeremy pointed
out a flying fish off the bow.

"Look at those 'wings,'" Jeremy said. "Those
pectoral fins allow them to soar above the ocean. An
ichthyologist I met once while visiting Barbados told me
they could reach speeds of about thirty-six miles an
hour, in flight."

Angela stood up and joined him at the helm.

"Are there many of them in the Caribbean?" she
asked, shading her eyes for a better look.

"There probably are. According to that expert, flying
fish prefer warm water with a temperature above 20
Celsius. There are more than sixty species, twenty species
found in the eastern Pacific Ocean, about sixteen species
in the Atlantic Ocean, but most of them are found in the
Caribbean off the coast of Barbados."

"They are spectacular." Each day in the Caribbean
she encountered something more to enjoy and meant it.
Jeremy knew so much about the area. Maybe taking a
chance to spend the day with him wasn't as reckless as she

first thought. "If we're lucky maybe we'll see more," she said, before returning to her seat.

They'd been underway about forty-five minutes without seeing anymore flying fish when Jeremy lowered the sails; switched on the boat's engine and began to maneuver the Sun Dancer to the place he intended to anchor. With the sails down, the boat glided into a small secluded cove of clear water that reflected the boat's passage like a shadowed future in a glittering crystal ball. He'd visited most of the ten beaches National Geographic touted as the most beautiful in the world, he'd told Angela. He didn't tell her secluded Paradiso beach remained his favorite. A place to swim, snorkel or a perfect place for him to lie on a perfect beach and let the sun warm his soul and shut off the clamor of his mind orchestrating his daily life.

While Jeremy worked, Angela's gaze swept the lush tropical forest on gentle hills, banded at their base by a thin ribbon of white beach that hugged the turquoise sea. Before the engine completely died, she left her seat and hurried to the bow.

They'd anchored in water about twelve feet deep, approximately one hundred and thirty feet from the beach, an easy swim to shore, she noted, even for an average swimmer,

Leaning over the bow she looked down into water so clear she could see the sandy bottom and she immediately became enchanted with an impossibly fat orange-stripped fish swimming lazily past the boat to the opposite side of the cove.

"Healthy looking, isn't he?"

Startled, she turned to face Jeremy who'd come up behind her.

"He certainly is. If he's planning to reach shore, I doubt he'll arrive before sundown," she added.

"What would be the point? He's a perfect example of life in the Caribbean. None of its creatures, including humans, hurry. Food's available and nutritious, the weather smiles on the islands most of the year, adequate shelter, even rudimentary shelter is generally sufficient. It takes the threat of a typhoon to encourage the locals to increase their pace beyond a definition of what we land-lubbers would consider leisurely."

"No doubt," she said, recalling the glowing descriptions of the islands given by her taxi driver and in the Pryce Line brochures she'd read before flying to Fort Lauderdale. "But that's what attracts the tourists, especially newlyweds, isn't it?"

"True, Pryce Line does its best to give tourists a taste of paradise by transporting and entertaining anyone who wants to escape reality, from newlyweds to overworked men and women. Personally, I find the job rewarding."

"It seems to me Pryce Line caters more to the wealthy than to overworked tourists."

Jeremy shrugged, "Also true. They pay the most. Our cruises are designed to offer people like you and me any luxury money can purchase aboard a floating hotel."

You anyway, Angela thought. "Exactly," she said.

"I doubt you've considered the wealthier passengers choose the more expensive suites and cruises that embark during the most desirable times of year," Jeremy said, "because they do. The Line finds it economically feasible to offer special prices to people who want to splurge on a few days living a life style they'd never be able to afford on shore."

"You realize, of course, that sounds suspiciously like a sales pitch."

He frowned. "Sales pay the bills. They also keep many tourist related businesses in the world happy and prosperous."

Her eyes scanned his face. She hadn't intended her comments to sound belligerent. He was sincere, she realized. Clearly, she'd hit a nerve. Pryce Cruise line had a great reputation. She'd owned a business and knew what she'd said was unfair. Then too, he had to know a woman like Silke would be too self-centered to consider the interests of cost-conscious tourists.

"Just curious."

Angela ignored the questioning look on his face; she shrugged, stepped away from him, and gestured toward the beach. "Are we going ashore?"

"We can," Jeremy said, "Unless you'd prefer diving first. The Sun Dancer comes equipped for diving. I don't know how, never took the time to learn. But my friends tell me I do well topside backing them up."

"I don't swim."

"No." He didn't sound surprised at her abrupt answer. She looked away, studied the shore. Perhaps given Silke's history he didn't expect her to be a swimmer. He could believe she still carried the emotional scars of her parents' deaths. Of course he would know nothing of her own scars. None of his business, she concluded.

"Okay with wading?" he asked

"How deep?"

"Deep enough to snorkel. Ever tried it?"

Once, it seemed so long ago now, Angela would not have considered anything as tame as snorkeling. She would've taken Jeremy up on his offer to loan her the scuba gear and been over the side almost before the engines stilled. The first time in, she would dive all the way to the bottom of that warm translucent water into an enchanted world she could only envy now from above. At first, she knew she'd be awed by the multitude of its colorful residents. Then, her previous diving experience told her, they'd accept her, and she would swim with them, playing tag until she ran out of air.

When she surfaced, she'd drop her gear on board and reenter the water. She wouldn't hurry, but would swim a lazy side-stroke, stopping occasionally to tread water, admire the scenery and congratulate herself on how happy she felt. Someday, someday, she promised herself, she would be able to swim again. And, she would return to Paradiso, not alone. She studied Jeremy while the voice at the back of her mind nagged. Once he knows who you are, Jeremy Pryce will not be part of that someday. Enjoy today.

Certain Silke wouldn't be likely to stick her head underwater for any reason, Jeremy said, "Have you ever tried snorkeling?"

"No," she lied, "never tried it."

"Nothing ventured, nothing gained," Jeremy said, "Live dangerously. This is a great place to learn. Okay?"

"I suppose."

It would be a good idea to go along with his suggestion. She'd wade out a little way then pretend she didn't like wading in waist deep water. He'd fail to teach her and give up. Jeremy didn't strike her as a man who would be patient with a wimp. Maybe then he'd pursue another woman, when they returned to the ship.

"We'll take the masks along. There's bound to be some bread in the picnic basket I brought. We'll have lunch first. Then feed the fish."

"Feed the fish?"

"Right."

"You're kidding?"

"No. A local fisherman showed me how when I was still a boy. You enter the water slowly, stand very still, the fish become used to you and your mask and some of them will eat out of your hand."

Angela smiled. It was a playful side of Jeremy she hadn't seen. The boy behind the face of a powerful, widely recognized CEO. And for a moment she wondered what would happen if her mask should fall. Would he see the woman beneath the mask, be willing to eat out of her hand, or would he swim away?

Across the water, the deserted beach beckoned.

Jeremy untied the ropes securing the dingy to the side of the boat and lowered it into the water.

"Ready?" he indicated the ladder leading down to the boat and helped her over the side to board.

When they reached the beach Angela stepped out of the dingy. The powder-white sand slid like silk beneath her bare feet. The palm trees beyond the narrow ribbon of beach swayed seductively. Her blue eyes gleamed. She turned and smiled at Jeremy. "A movie set," she said, "too beautiful to be real."

"I'm glad you like it."

"Like it? I love it."

Jeremy congratulated himself. It hadn't been a mistake to bring her here.

"Do you come here, ah, often?" Alone? The word, unspoken, trembled on her tongue. Who Jeremy Pryce brought to Paradiso and what they did here was none of her business. The only reason she was there was to convince him she wasn't his type, she told herself.

"At least once a year." He picked up the snorkel masks from the bottom of the dingy and tossed them onto the beach. Then he lifted out the large willow picnic basket, he brought with him to the boat, a portable ship-to-shore radio, and set them down in the sand next to the masks. After turning the dingy upside down to dry, he picked up both the basket and the radio.

"May I carry something?" Angela offered.

"Thanks. I've got it. There's a great spot for a picnic right under that clump of trees," he said, indicating the direction with nod of his head.

"Looks inviting. Just enough cover, but with a great view of the cove."

"Lead on, I'll follow," he said and fell in behind her to enjoy the sight of her hips swaying in a scrap of cloth as she plowed through the sand.

Jeremy took the picnic basket and the ship-to-shore radio he'd brought from the boat and set them down in the sand, under the trees. "Why don't you make yourself comfortable while I see what's for lunch," he said.

Angela remained standing, "Need some help?"

"Thanks but the chef gave me strict orders on how to present a gourmet picnic." Jeremy grinned. "I'm to follow directions and report back to him."

"I take it that basket doesn't contain the typical checked table cloth, paper napkins, plastic forks, potato salad and hot dogs?"

"Horrors, No! Julia Child would turn over in her grave." Jeremy said, "And our illustrious head chef would bar me from the ship's dining room. Make yourself comfortable. This should only take a minute."

Intrigued, Angela sat down to watch. She'd attended plenty of picnics, but this was the first time she'd ever been with a man who took charge, and she decided she might like it.

~

Chapter Fifteen

After removing a white linen table cloth from the oversized willow picnic basket, Jeremy spread it out on the sand. He tugged at the corners until he appeared to be satisfied with its placement. Then he reached back into the basket and produced two matching linen napkins, two china plates, silver service for two and two crystal wine glasses, glasses, Angela guessed, that cost more than a month's rent on her tiny apartment.

Noting how deftly Jeremy prepared the improvised table, Angela guessed it wasn't the first time he'd entertained someone with a picnic. "Lovely," she said, "I believe you can tell the chef your table is flawless."

"It does look festive. But, I'm hungry. It will look even better with food on it. How's your appetite."

"After all that fresh air, I'm starving. What's on the menu?"

"It just so happens I can answer that question," he

said and reaching into the basket once more, he pulled out a menu with a flourish of the wrist.

"Let's see, there's smoked turkey breast, with sun-dried tomato aioli, avocado, bacon, spinach and fresh sliced tomatoes on Andre's special bread. For dessert his own chocolate macadamia cookies, or should Madam prefer, cupcakes, with caramel filing, or for a lighter dessert, grapes, an assortment of cheeses, and what is a picnic without wine to wash it down," he added, removing a bottle of chilled Veuve Cliquot from a special refrigerated container inside the oversized basket.

Angela's comments about checked table clothes and hot dogs, plus her wide-eyed surprise as he laid out the linen, sterling, crystal and gourmet picnic made him curious. If he didn't know better he would have said that being treated to a unique meal in an exotic location was a new experience for Silke. During the next thirty minutes, her obvious pleasure in the food and the setting pleased Jeremy. Until the last cupcake and the last grape disappeared, they ate and talked and were both surprised to discover they shared an appreciation of the history of the Antilles and its peoples.

Jeremy lifted his glass and proposed a toast. "To the incomparable Andre and his culinary talent."

"I'll drink to that," Angela said, and added it was a fabulous picnic. "I believe with your faultless presentation, you both deserve a toast, except, uh, oh, I would but," she looked into the glass. "It appears to be empty."

Jeremy reached across the cloth table and took her glass.

Angela laughed, "It seems I can't keep a glass in my

hand around you," she added, referring to the struggle for hers in the V.I. P. lounge at Fort Lauderdale International.

Jeremy smiled, poured the wine. "Boy Scout training, ever helpful." He lifted his hand, palm facing her with three fingers together, in the Scout salute.

"You help little old ladies cross streets."

"I haven't had the privilege since I was a boy scout." He smiled that wolfish smile again. "...of helping ladies cross streets. Although, since then you could say I've help a few younger ladies travel from point A to point B. The idea is to get close, travel together, enjoy the trip, and arrive safe and happy on the other side, for mutual plea-sure, that is."

Angela felt the color rising in her cheeks. What did she expect? She'd been certain all he wanted was sex, and she'd believed if she made it clear she wasn't dishing it out, he'd give up, and they'd simply have a pleasant day. With his looks and position, he had his pick of women. And she'd come willingly, well almost. The way he'd been looking at her since they sat down for the picnic, she suspected her plan wasn't working out the way she wanted it to. She should have known better. Just looking at him raised her temperature and sent her hormones spinning. She lowered her gaze and sipped her wine.

Jeremy lifted the bottle. "More wine?"

"No," she shook her head, looked away.

"I like your bikini," he said. His gaze roamed once more from her eyes all the way to her bare feet. "What there is of it," he added. "On you, it's very becoming."

The intensity of his words weren't lost on Angela She shifted, looked away, again.

Jeremy's eyes narrowed. Embarrassed, she was embarrassed? Once more, she surprised him. She appeared to be a thoughtful, intelligent woman, and the kind of a person who took the time to amuse a lonely boy in a wheel chair. Considering that fact, he hoped she didn't agree to go sailing with him because she felt sorry for him as well. Yet when she looked at him, he couldn't shake the conviction that she was attracted to him. Time to find out, he decided.

Without warning, Jeremy rose to his feet and stepped over the remains of the picnic on the makeshift table. Angela's eyes widened, she straightened. Leaning down, he removed the glass from her hand and placed it in the open basket.

"Ready?"

"Ready for the beach?"

"Or whatever."

Angela's shook her head. "I'm not sure I want..."

Jeremy smiled. "Let's find out." He reached down, helped her to her feet, wrapped his arms around her and lifted her up onto her toes.

She tensed and tried to break away from him, but his arms only tightened.

Angela took a deep breath, and he felt her relax. He smiled, placed his fingers under her chin, tilted it up and said, "Look at me."

Her blue eyes widened, dilated. She looked into his eyes then closed her own. Arms around each other, they sank down onto the sand. She smelled of chocolate and wine and he kissed her again, deepening the kiss. Their tongues met, explored. Her mouth was soft, moist, welcoming, and he knew he'd been right. His hand slid up her back. Stroked it, fingered the thin bikini cord. But before he could untie it, Angela grabbed his wrist, pushed his hand away. Jeremy leaned back. "No," she said and scrambled away.

He'd gone too far, been in too much of a hurry, Jeremy thought. He reached for her hand. But, still on her knees she backed further away.

"Silke, I," he began, "I thought you wanted. . ."

"No, you don't understand," she said, "I...can't."

Silent, they stared at each other.

The sound of Burt's voice shattered the silence.

"Q.C. to the Sun Dancer. Come in please. Over."

Jeremy scrambled to his feet and retrieved the radio from where he'd placed it under one of the Palm trees.

"Sun Dancer to the Q.C. Over"

"Suggest you return to the ship, immediately. Situation with a passenger—female. Over."

Frozen in place, she watched Jeremy's face darken. "How serious?" he asked.

"Fatal," came the clipped reply.

Angela got to her feet. Fatal? A heart attack she thought, an older woman, maybe, but the shock on Jeremy's faced signified something more tragic, perhaps the death of someone young? She thought about the boy in the wheelchair. She hoped he was okay.

"Not more than an hour," Jeremy said, the words brisk, cold.

Angela didn't wait for the call to end. There are doctors and nurses on all cruise ships aren't there, someone to certify a death, however unexpected, she thought as she returned the remains of the picnic to the basket and closed the lid. But why would the death of a passenger require the CEO's presence?

Back on board the Sun Dancer, Angela went below deck and changed out of her bikini into the slacks a blouse she'd worn to the boat. Jeremy intent on maneuvering the Sun Dancer through the waves seemed to have forgotten her, Angela realized. The return trip took less than an hour.

At the marina, a taxi stood waiting for them near the gate when Jeremy maneuvered the Sun Dancer into its slip at the dock. Within minutes, they were speeding back to the harbor at Charlotte Amalie.

Burt met them in the ship's lobby.

"Sorry to spoil your day," he said to Angela.

"Are they here?" Jeremy asked.

"Yeah. They arrived about twenty-some minutes after I notified you."

"Let's go," Jeremy said with barely a backward glance for Angela, who stood staring after him.

"I'll telephone you later," he said over his shoulder.

"How long has she been dead?" Jeremy asked.

With her rich brown coffee and cream skin, six foot something detective April Jones, a bigger than life local crime scene investigator, seemed to fill the tiny cabin that contained Burt's office.

"Hasn't been confirmed yet," Burt said. "We'll have to wait for the coroner's report."

"Too early for much speculation," C.S.I. inspector Jones added.

"Any chance this one is related to the Lyre murder?" Jeremy asked.

"For my money—obvious, manual," she said. "From what I read in that report, there are similarities. Could be. There's the bath powder on the body. Too much like the signature of a serial killer to ignore."

"Anything we can use to determine if the perp could be a crew member?"

"Sorry, gentlemen. That would be too easy. The tech couldn't lift any identifiable prints."

"We should be so lucky." Burt shrugged.

Jeremy said, "The Captain would appreciate speaking with you before you leave, detective."

"Of course," Jones agreed. "At this point I doubt we'll find anything further to delay the ship leaving on schedule. Our team will fly to San Juan tomorrow and meet with our local officers there. If you hear anything or think of anything we should know, we can discuss it then."

Jones rose from the chair in front of Burt's desk. She offered her hand to Jeremy who had stood quietly near the door during most of the meeting listening, while she and Burt shared information.

"Pleasure meeting you, Mr. Pryce." Detective Jones shook his hand. "Sorry about the circumstances."

Burt also stood and came around his desk. "Good to see you, Jones. You're a long way from Quantico."

"You too, friend. We miss your ugly face out there. Stop in the next time you dock here, and we'll share a story or two."

"Will do, April, Thanks."

Efficiently, detective Jones and her team completed their preliminary study of the crime scene, secured the scene and arranged for the body to be moved off the ship.

Detective Jones, an FBI crime scene investigator, under maritime law could have ordered the ship to remain. Burt, Jeremy and the Captain were all grateful she had not. A delay would have been difficult to explain to passengers.

After a short report to the ship's captain. Jones sent the Q.C. on its way to Puerto Rico. The crime scene secured, she and her team would finish what they started when the ship reached San Juan.

Six o'clock came and went, no message, no Jeremy. Angela realized she'd believed he meant it when he said he'd telephone. Whatever happened while they were sailing was obviously more important than calling her. What did you expect? The less you see of Jeremy Pryce, the better. You want to win, don't you?

Do I, she thought, recalling the final few moments on the beach at Paradiso. Do I really?

What if Burt hadn't called? You can avoid him if you really try, she told herself.

And suppose I don't try? What would be his reaction if he did find out who I really am?

When he finds out who you are—that's it. Not an option.

At seven fifteen Angela stepped out of the shower.

She put on a light robe when there was a knock on the suite door. For one crazy moment she hoped it was Jeremy. But when she opened the door she saw Anastasia, the female butler who'd been assigned to her suite, standing in the corridor.

Angela frowned. Had she forgotten to tell the young woman she wouldn't need her tonight? "Yes," Angela said.

"I must apologize, Milady. The purser advised me you would be expecting me at seven? I'm afraid I'm a bit late."

"Late?" The purser, Angela thought, does he know everyone's itinerary? Why?

"The purser sent you? Did he say why?"

"Yes. He said you would require my assistance before the Captain's dinner. I'm quite sure I can help you with your dress.

Not until she'd boarded the Q.C. did Angela realize Silke traveled with a lady's maid. Nor would she have known about the maid if the purser hadn't questioned her absence. For reasons she couldn't pinpoint, it annoyed her that someone kept track of her personal life. Only a misogynist would imagine Silke or any other woman under the age of ninety-five couldn't dress herself for dinner with a ship's captain. Ridiculous—in fact laughable.

Stepping back she waved Anastasia inside. But, she wasn't about to take her annoyance out on the butler. "You may tell the purser that somehow we managed."

The blue silk dinner dress selected for her cruise wardrobe by Carstairs and her fashion consultant on Rodeo Drive was the work of Sophie Theallet, a French designer. It slipped over Angela's head like warm rain and draped her body in all the right places. A dress Carstairs assured Angela was "tight enough to show you're a woman, but one you can stand and sit in gracefully."

"I can sit and stand in a swimming suit more comfortably, and I'd have a lot more use for a swimming suit than a designer dress I'll wear once," Angela had said.

Carstairs only smiled at the snide remark. "Ask and ye shall receive," she replied. In the next shop they visited, a polka dot bikini was the result.

A worthwhile purchase, she decided, recalling the look on Jeremy's face when he saw her on the deck of the Sun Dancer wearing the colorful bikini.

Would Jeremy be at the dinner? She wondered. If so, what kind of reaction would tonight's dress, with its apparently modest, but impossibly suggestive neckline, elicit from him? She had not forgotten his reputation as an international playboy. A man who escorted the likes of actress Monica Thorne and so many wealthy young beauties on four continents. Designer dress or not, if anyone could recognize her as a phony he could.

Once dressed, she started to shoo the hovering butler out of her suite, when she remembered the missing bath powder.

Anastasia assured her she hadn't seen it recently.

"Maybe one of the stewards moved it. I can ask them," she suggested.

"Thanks," Angela said, "I'll ask."

The elevator stopped at every deck, loading and unloading passengers. And when Angela stepped out of the elevator, she found herself alone in the small foyer facing the two embossed, frosted glass doors that led to the main dining room, and realized she was late.

For only a second, she paused to tuck stray strands of the short bob she wasn't used to wearing behind her ears. Then taking a deep breath, she straightened her shoulders and pulled open one of the double doors.

"Ah, Lady von Chassen." The Italian maître d' greeted her warmly, and loudly enough to elicit the attention of several nearby diners who turned and stared.

"The Captain is asking for you," he added. "You will be pleased to follow me."

If he wanted attention, he certainly got it, she thought, following the stout little man down a short flight of deeply carpeted stairs. Angela looked neither right not left as they paraded the full length of the dining room. She felt, rather than saw, glasses and forks rise only to pause somewhere above the plates before reaching the lips of the diners. A low buzz of speculation followed them. She shuddered slightly. Although she'd been on board four days, this was the first time she'd become aware that her presence was on display, or rather Silke's presence. How many years had it taken Jeremy and his sister Heather to learn how to cope with such personal invasion? Of course, they'd probably grown up with copious attention; perhaps that made it easier. Not that she believed anyone could ever appreciate being the subject of the curious, unspoken questions she could feel hiding behind the eyes of strangers.

How long did it take any celebrity to become accustomed to poorly veiled curiosity without wanting to hide, she wondered. For the first time in her life, she felt empathy for the world's celebrities.

How long, she wondered, would it take for one of these diners to see past the right dress and label her a phony? Tonight she'd been noticed. Not good.

And she had not forgotten Jeremy's reputation. Hadn't he escorted almost every wealthy young beauty on four continents? If anyone should recognize her as a phony it would be Jeremy. Could that be why he hadn't called?

All the men stood when the Maître stopped at the Captain's table, all the men, except one who didn't notice their arrival until the stunning brunette at his side looked up and smiled. Once more, a feeling not unlike a sudden jolt of electricity shot through her when he rose and Jeremy's eyes met hers, and he smiled.

Before she could move, the captain, a handsome graying man of sixty some, waved the men into their seats and, taking Angela's arm, led her to an ornate Louis the Sixteenth style chair at his right. When she was seated, the captain, who obviously knew the difference between a lowly princess and princess of a ruling royal family, introduced her as "Lady Silke von Chassen."

Relieved he hadn't made the mistake of calling her a "royal highness," Angela acknowledged each introduction that followed with what she hoped was a gracious nod and a smile.

A smile less than believable, she knew. With each introduction, it felt even more frozen like a pose an actor is caught in during an improvisation game when the director yells "freeze!"

Most of the captain's guest were older, wealthy middle-aged business types traveling with their wives, husbands or possibly lovers. The women made it clear they enjoyed being at the same table with a celebrated "lady" something or other. Peppered with questions throughout dinner, about mutual friends, acquaintances, and the present disposition of her "great uncle's" endless attempts to regain the throne her great grandfather lost during the Second World War, Angela skirted a deluge of questions because she'd memorized Silke's biography. Like so many Americans, the women at the table didn't really care about Europe or European dynasties, it was enough that a "real live princess," royal or otherwise, was at their table.

The dinner, when it arrived, was delicious, the wine exquisite. The men talked sports, stock markets and then more sports throughout the meal, occasionally pretending to include the women at the table.

Angela listened, feigning interest, when asked, until the discussion turned to the national swimming matches in Omaha that would determine next year's Olympic contenders. A former competitor, she no longer swam competitions after her father died, but during her college years she had coached; and she recognized the name of a former student, one of the young woman competing for a position. When she caught Jeremy staring at her, her stomach tensed, and she looked down and away from the two men discussing the potential team selections. Did he remember her unwillingness to swim at Paradiso Beach?

Chapter Sixteen

He'd made it a point to avoid friendships, not that he couldn't have made several when he'd first gone to work for Pryce Cruise Line almost four years ago. Since reaching adulthood, he'd recognized many considered him good looking and intelligent. He'd worked hard at ensuring other men saw him as a man's man, but one of the so-called strong, quiet kind. He'd also built a reputation as a reliable worker, and he knew that with his duties over for the day, no one below decks would notice his absence that night. He stood in the foyer near the palm tree and watched while the Captain's guests left the dining room more than an hour after they arrived. It endlessly amused him that few people ever saw the person wearing a uniform.

He saw the von Chassen woman leave, followed sometime later by Jeremy Pryce and another one of the captain's guests. After they boarded the elevator, he returned to his berth below decks where he would wait until after one before visiting the suite of his chosen party guest.

Tomorrow the ship would reach San Juan Harbor minus a second celebrity passenger. Scuttlebutt in the staff dining room predicted Pryce would also be leaving the cruise to fly back to the States. Neither he nor that smart-ass cop Chaney, were any closer to figuring out who killed the women they knew about, much less the ones they didn't.

A sneer curled his lips. After tonight, they'd know for sure they were up against a better man. No doubt Jeremy Pryce, CEO boy wonder, would be the one to personally report back to Samantha that another of their guests met their end tragically. The national news would be full of the story. Game Show Contestant Unmasked in Death. Winner Remains Anonymous. Too bad he couldn't leave her a personal message, remind her of the good old times back home.

When the bitch heard what happened, she wouldn't be happy with her darling grandson, would she? Too bad he couldn't be there to see the boy crawl. A tight smile spread across his face but did not reach his eyes. Not that after tonight it would make a difference, even if she fired her grandson. The unsolvable death of another woman passenger, one even more famous than the last, would take care of Samantha Pryce and company. There would no longer be a cruise line for them to manage.

His teeth bared in a satisfied grin when he recalled the little chat he'd had with that reporter back in St. Thomas. Soon no woman would dare board a Pryce line cruise ship. As for that cop Chaney, he'd be taken care of.

He felt the muscles in his shoulders tense, his hands clenched. Why, that old deal breaker in Malibu might even feel bad when the police suggested Chaney slipped and fell overboard. He smiled at the thought. In the meantime he'd heard Pryce would be meeting Chaney in his office tonight. Good. A perfect time to pay a little visit to Lady von Chassen's suite. He'd return the bath powder he'd borrowed in preparation for his next visit, sometime after two. The dedicated gamblers would still be in the casino and the drunks would either be in one of the half dozen bars or passed out in a corridor somewhere.

When Angela left the dining room after the Captain's dinner, she tried to ignore the churning sensation in her stomach while she waited in the foyer with several other passengers and watched the colored lights above the elevator door make their slow descent. Intent on avoiding further conversation with the remaining diners from the Captain's dinner, she had no idea where she was going, only a vague longing to be somewhere where there were people, people she didn't know, who didn't know who she was supposed to be, people who would not notice her or ask probing questions, demand a reaction from her.

After she boarded the elevator, she still hadn't decided where to go, only where she wasn't going: back to her empty suite. Someone pushed the up button, and the gleaming brass doors closed. When they slid open again, she allowed herself to be swept out onto the mezzanine deck with several other passengers and found herself once more within a few feet of the Calypso Lounge. From where she stood, she could hear music. There would be a combo playing tonight, and someone at dinner mentioned a special singer, but she couldn't remember the name. Her first night on board she'd gone there for a drink, fallen asleep and been awakened by Jeremy. She hadn't been there again until that night in Nassau after dinner at Graystairs, when they all stopped for a drink and Jeremy suggested she go sailing with him when they reached St. Thomas.

Would she ever learn, she wondered.

On the beach at Paradiso she'd almost let her body take over her mind for one night between the sheets with a man she'd never see again when the cruise ended.

She hesitated near the door, but the music drew her. Perhaps music would help, she thought.

Not that it was important she told herself, but shortly before the end of dinner she'd overheard gossip about Jeremy being engaged to Monica Thorne. About the same time, she began to feel a little nauseated. Jealous? The word, unanticipated, surprised her. Jealous?

Ridiculous, she told the impertinent voice in her mind. Too much rich food. The chef's famous chocolate dessert alone was a guarantee of an upset stomach. Jeremy's relationship with Monica was certainly none of her business.

Keep it that way, the voice cautioned. Once the cruise ends there would be no more Jeremy. Monica would be a flickering image on a television screen. Yes, she told herself, music is all she needed—something soothing.

Inside the dimly lit Calypso Lounge, the wooden

handkerchief masquerading as a dance floor disappeared beneath the feet of a dozen couples swaying to the pulsating rhythms. Dance music played by the small combo calculated to insure maximum body contact. She paused just inside the door, allowing her eyes to adjust to the shadowy interior before finding a table. As before, the room wasn't over crowded. Many of the ships passengers would be attending the musical scheduled for the evening. Some would be offering bribes to the universe at roulette or counting on luck with every throw of the dice, while others wore out the hours shoving coins into machines that seldom if ever paid them back. Never in her life had Angela considered herself a gambler, at least not until she'd entered the game show. Yet, here she was on a ship in the Caribbean, gambling that she would not be recognized, that she would win a million dollars with a small, she told herself, a very small investment of her time. She hadn't counted on meeting Jeremy. The music of the song ended and a new one began again immediately.

A few couples and one or two foursomes sat talking and laughing near the dance floor seemingly unaware of the dancers or the music. Angela remained standing inside the door to the lounge. Gradually her breathing slowed to match the steady beat of the music, and she allowed it to carry her away from the turmoil threatening to pull her under. Someone had died on board. She didn't know who, only that an unanticipated tragedy may have kept her from following her heart, a tragedy that was sabotaging her goals.

The song ended and another began. Moving gingerly in the dimly lit lounge, she found an empty table near enough to the combo to appreciate the music, but far enough away from the other occupants to avoid being noticed. She sank into the deeply cushioned chair and admitted to herself she was exhausted.

When Carstairs first told Angela about the cruise she'd be taking, she'd been excited. Although she'd always lived near the shore and sailed with her father during summers for several years, she'd never been on board one of the beautiful cruise ships that traveled daily up and down the coast of California. For weeks after the news, she'd daydreamed about the coming trip. She'd imagined nights strolling the decks breathing in heady salt air, then finding her way to the stern of the ship to watching luminescent waves trailing in the wake of the ship. Like a heroine without a lover in a romance novel, she'd walk the deck until sated with the night, return to her cabin, settle into a cloud soft bed and fall asleep to the gentle rhythm of the ship's powerful engines, secure in the belief that if she waited patiently, someday she'd know true love.

The dream evaporated when she'd boarded the Q.C. in Fort Lauderdale. The cozy cabin she'd imagined proved to be a suite larger than her entire efficiency apartment. Not that she could complain. It did have a "cloud soft bed." Then, instead of walking the decks dreaming of a lover, the first afternoon after she'd boarded she met Heather and since that first meeting, she had been too busy to walk the decks or even to see much of the ship. Instead, she carefully considered everything she did while the nagging voice in the back of her mind kept reciting the rules.

And how could she argue with the facts? Silke von

Chassen would be unlikely to hang around alone on a cruise ship deck. Silke, the irrepressible party girl, would be somewhere where the action was, somewhere where the men were, and not alone either, never alone. Someone might be watching.

But, she was alone now.

Angela surveyed the lounge. The couples not on the dance floor were too involved in themselves to be aware of her, and if there were singles, they were seated in one of the groups. It wasn't likely she'd be noticed by any of them.

Like the first night she'd fallen asleep, a white jacketed waiter arrived promptly at her table. She had definitely decided to stay for a while and ordered Chardonnay. This time she promised herself she would stay awake. And, should she be approached by a man, she could use the same excuse that someone 'would be joining' her, soon. Not Jeremy. She wasn't likely to encounter him again tonight. At least she didn't think she would. No doubt he'd be with the gorgeous brunette she'd seen him with at the Captain's dinner. She settled back in her chair. If she understood what the gossips at dinner said about Jeremy and Monica Thorne, the wedding might be within a month or so. Jeremy and Monica Thorne were definitely engaged.

Men simply didn't get it, did they? They fought each other to be with women like Monica. The women observing all this cheerfully agreed certain women would marry anyone provided sufficient money and prestige came with the package. And they would know. They were steadfast in their collective opinion that Monica was one of them—as transparent as any cliché about water in a glass.

Tonight, with four and a half of the ten days behind her, Angela told herself, it didn't matter who got married, she should be celebrating. No one, not even Jeremy, seemed to have any inkling of who she really was. Although some of tonight's gossip proved to her it shouldn't be too difficult to be unmasked by anyone who watched the show and paid attention to the weekly clues. Even someone who didn't watch the show, because people talked, and if not in person, there was no lack of computer access on the Q.C.—everyone had a Facebook or a Twitter account, or both. Three of the women at dinner mentioned being fans of the game show, yet no one even looked her way. Why?

"Will there be anything else, Madam?"

Startled, Angela looked up to see the waiter hovering.

"No, thank you," she said.

He placed the wine on the small table beside her. She signed the check, added a handsome tip to the bill, and when he'd moved away, lifted the wine to her lips and sipped. Delicious.

There were advantages to being Silke, and fine wine was one of them. Glass in hand, she leaned back in the plush chair. Daydreaming, she pictured a new clinic, furnished with the latest and best equipment. Staffed with skilled therapists like Charlie, and enough patients to allow her free time to treat the disabled who needed physical therapy, and could not afford it. But, first she had to win.

Tomorrow, when the ship reached Puerto Rico, she

would disappear in plain sight. She'd be up at dawn and explore that part of the ship she should have explored at the beginning of the cruise. It would be interesting to see what kind of exercise equipment was available to passengers, and if there were accommodations for disabled passengers young or old. The ship's brochure claimed its "famous" gym and spa offered appointments twenty-four seven. Angela decided if she booked her appointments back to back she could exercise first, soak in the spa, enjoy a massage, a facial, have her hair done, and ask questions about the program while using up the entire day surrounded by people too occupied with their own exercise and beauty regimens to take note of her.

She'd been invited to join Heather for dinner at the Marmalade, a famous San Juan restaurant. From there they would go on to the Radisson Hotel around ten to attend a Mardi Gras ball. If available, Jeremy and Burt would join them, Heather had said. Angela felt bad about implying she would join them. Silke, however, would not be available. After she'd spent most of the day in the gym, she'd join the crowds who would disembark in late afternoon to visit the city and watch the Mardi Gras parades. She'd leave a message with her butler, Anastasia, and the suites steward Rashid, with apologies explaining she'd left the ship to meet a friend who lived in Puerto Rico, someone who contacted her when the ship docked. What was one more lie? She hoped Heather would believe it.

If all went as planned, Heather wouldn't consider it strange. For now, she'd simply enjoy the rest of her evening.

The music—good as promised...the song *Encore un*

Soir for romantic love, made famous by Celine Dion, said that if it came, true love, real love, lasted a lifetime, and a lifetime wasn't enough. Love, a lifetime kind of love hadn't happened for her and might never happen. While she enjoyed the music all the songs were about romantic love, and tonight, Angela felt certain, the lyrics lied, at least for her.

Before the song ended and another began, the waiter reappeared at her table to remove her empty wineglass. She checked her watch. Not yet eleven. She decided to order a second glass of Chardonnay. She'd stay put until after midnight. Sitting back in her chair she let her mind drift again. In only five more days, win or lose, the ship will dock in Fort Lauderdale, she thought, and she'd be on a plane home. If she could manage to keep up the masquerade for only a few more days...

Chapter Seventeen

"Silke."

"Jeremy! I was...concentrating on the music."

"It seems to me your bed might be more comfortable." His grin spread into a smile that turned up the corners of his mouth.

"I'm not tired."

"You're not!" He nodded toward the dance floor. "I've been informed the music is perfect for dancing."

He reached for her hand, took it in his. "And I promised you a dance." And before she could object, he cupped her elbow in his hand and guided to the dance floor.

They danced across the floor to the intimate rhythms of *You Belong to Me*.

For Angela, the gentle symphony of water parting and flowing beneath the ship, the shadowed lounge, the music, the other dancers seemed unreal, an old movie slightly out of focus.

Jeremey steered her back to the table. After they were seated, he said, "Heather told me you were partial to Armand de Brignac, or would you care for something else?"

Heather, Angela thought, busy little matchmaker. As for the wine, according to her biography, Silke did prefer it. Only the best for our girl Silke, Angela thought. "Doesn't everyone love champagne?" she said, mimicking what she considered a playful tone of voice, one Silke might have used.

Jeremy hesitated, shrugged. "Perhaps not everyone," he said, and turned away signaling a passing waiter to place his order.

In a flash of insight, Angela recognized that her thoughtless response disappointed Jeremy. Why? Given Silke's reputation, what had he expected? The waiter returned with the wine, two flutes and a wine bucket, before she could sort through the possibilities his behavior suggested. She'd been so certain she knew him. Angela watched while the waiter gingerly lifted the golden bottle and reverently wrapped it, covering its signature Ace of Spades pewter label in a white towel. With an experienced thumb, he expertly popped the cork, poured out a sample for Jeremy, then stood watching him while he sipped and nodded his head in approval.

The waiter then filled both flutes with the liquid gold, placed the bottle in the ice bucket he'd brought with him, and retreated.

His seductive smile back in place, Jeremy reached across the tiny table and handed Angela the second flute, then raised his glass. "For the lady with impeccable taste. I admit this wine is a favorite of mine, racy..." and looking at Angela's mouth, he added, "as smooth and silky as a lover's kiss."

At the price of one hundred or more dollars a bottle, which, according to her former fiancée Angela recalled, would almost guarantee the purchaser a night that ended in someone's bed, she took the glass.

Not tonight, not in my bed Jeremy, she thought, "Prost," she said, and lifting her glass, she sipped.

A little ginger, lemon, some spiciness on the tongue and, if a honeysuckle bloom could be labeled a flavor, she'd just tasted one. No wonder Silke liked it: A wine to be drunk slowly, one of the delicious encounters in a lifetime, a pleasure not to be rushed.

Angela looked up to find Jeremy watching her. Overwhelmed by the intensity of his gaze, the physical rush that swamped her senses each time he studied her, capturing her eyes. With an effort she looked down, stared into her glass. He's not who you think he is. The thought startled her. She could resist the man she believed him to be. Was she really so wrong? Angela sighed and set down the glass, carefully, gently.

Exactly what do you think you're doing? The voice demanded. He's not for you.

She closed her eyes. What do you know? All you do is caution, caution, caution. You've never known love.

"Is something wrong with the wine?" Jeremy asked.

She opened her eyes. For one embarrassing second she imagined she may have spoken aloud. "No, no, of course not. It's even better than advertised." Again, she lifted the glass to her lips, sipped.

Jeremy frowned, "Good," he said, but the frown remained. Had she said something wrong?

On the other side of the dance floor, the musicians finished the song they'd been playing, and she saw the pianist rise to his feet.

"Ladies and gentlemen, please welcome Ms. Geraldine Roclure, back with us after a successful season in Vegas." A dark-haired woman in a stunning red evening gown crossed the room and joined him at the microphone.

The combo played the first few bars of *I Need You Now*. Jeremy rose and extended his hand. "Another dance?"

Angela stepped into his arms. When she raised her head, he leaned down and kissed her, and she felt she would never draw a breath again without his lips on hers. They moved as one across the floor, as one while the music flowed. The singer seamlessly began another song. She caressed the words, *If You Really Love Me*, the lyrics narrating for Angela the words she could not speak. With her face against the finely woven wool of his tuxedo jacket and the dark scent of some masculine perfume emanating from his skin, the irony of the lyrics weren't lost on her.

"I try not to care when you stray
I know you'll return
into my heart, you know the way..."

Angela leaned into the reassuring arms that pulled her even closer.

"And I know for sure, someday you'll stay,

because you always say,
'I really love you.'"

Several songs later when the singer left the dais and
the combo took a break, Jeremy led Angela back to their
table. Lost in each other, neither of them noted the lone
figure at the back of the lounge who stepped out of the
shadows and slipped out the door.

Once seated, Jeremy said, "She has a compelling
voice, one of those singers who become one with the
emotion of the lyrics."

"You dance well," Angela said, changing the subject.

She couldn't trust herself to discuss the songs to let
him know how the lyrics hurt, especially when she'd
heard them with his arms around her

"Thanks. I like to dance. Or, I do now," Jeremy
corrected himself. He leaned back, seemed to relax, his
eyes alight, colored with humor. "Not that I thought I ever
would when I was eight and my grandmother enrolled me
in a cotillion class."

Ah yes, she thought, she'd treated children with minor
accidents accompanied by mothers of means who sat in
her waiting room and discussed with each other their
recalcitrant sons and, occasionally, daughters. Those
daring young souls, especially the boys who rebelled
when sent to classes to learn to dance.

Angela suppressed an amused grin while her mind
painted pictures of an eight year old Jeremy struggling to
lead other giggling eight year olds in Mary Janes across a
dance floor.

"Embarrassing?"

"Sure. Not the classes so much. My grandfather was an excellent dancer. There was this kid in my third grade class who saw me going into the dance studio one day after school. He and some buddies decided to make an issue of it on the playground the next day.

"When I got home from school that afternoon Sam didn't mention the principal called to tell her the other guy and I would be missing recess for a couple of days. All she said was that my grandfather once told her Joe Lewis moved like Fred Astaire in the ring and that the champs preferred their steak ice cold and raw for black eyes."

"Sam?" Angela repeated.

Jeremy frowned. "My grandmother."

Angela lowered her gaze.

"Family nickname?" Jeremy said, the question in his voice remaining.

Sam—Samantha Pryce—of course? Why hadn't she connected the dots? How many times had Heather spoken of her grandmother? And Carstairs? Surely Carstairs, producer extraordinaire, would assume Angela knew the name, the reputation of one of the wealthiest women in the country, the dowager queen of Pryce Cruise Line, Pryce merchant fleet. Why not just paint idiot on your forehead?

Angela forced herself to meet Jeremy's eyes. "If your grandmother is half as intimidating in person as she seems to be in the articles I've read about her, I can't imagine anyone calling her Sam to her face. She seems so—so..." she hesitated, remembering the woman, the diamond, the limousine, "so regal."

"I agree. Many people who meet her for the first time

198

are intimidated," he said. "An amazing woman. She seems to excel at everything she attempts, an excellent dancer, of course, at least as good as I am," he added with a straight face.

Angela couldn't help laughing, as much at herself as with Jeremy.

Jeremy refilled their glasses and the subject changed to sailing and their aborted trip to the cove at Paradisio beach. They both recalled admiring the aerobatics of the flying fish, the lazy passage of the fat orange fish across the cove, the delicious gourmet picnic.

Until Angela brought up the subject of the urgent call from the ship, and Jeremy changed the subject again, passing it off as something unavoidable and not important. His body language told another story, one he wasn't willing to share with her. Before she could think of a tactful way to find out who died and how, the combo returned to the podium. Jeremy reached for her hand.

After a couple of numbers, he tightened his hold on her waist and whispered in her ear, "It's almost two. With just a few more songs the combo will be closing down the place How about a night cap?"

"Here?"

"Too many people," he suggested, and with a grin he added, "to quote the cliché, my place or yours?"

Several decks below Jeremy's suite, a security officer monitoring dozens of cameras mounted in the ship's corridors turned away from the screen to answer a knock on the door. Behind him, the camera continued to record what appeared to be a red-haired man with a limp approaching the door of one of the executive suites. The Q.C. would be halfway to the port of San Juan, Puerto Rico, before that section of the recording would be seen and brought to Burt Chaney's attention.

Chapter Eighteen

"Welcome to my home." Jeremy acknowledged Angela's surprise when he ushered her through the door to his suite. She'd forgotten he told her it was on the port side of the ship two decks below hers. If she'd thought about it at all, she would have assumed it would be similar to hers. The last thing she expected to see when she stepped through the door was an office. A teak-topped conference table surrounded by several leather chairs, two computers, a printer and one file cabinet.

"Not the coziest place, I'll admit," Jeremy said. "But I believe we can sort out a night cap or two next door." He indicated another door in the wall beyond the conference table.

Inside the room Angela looked around and froze. "Attractive," she said, taking in muted geometrical designs of the carpet, drapes. Two chocolate brown leather couches and an oversized television screen dominated, and branded the room one hundred percent male.

Her mind issued a warning: Have one drink and leave.

Jeremy removed his jacket, and tossed it on one of the couches then headed across the room to a cocktail bar mounted on the opposite wall.

Angela stood just inside the door and watched fascinated by the way the fabric of his shirt tightened, outlining Jeremy's muscled back when he bent to open a small refrigerator door under the counter.

"Those couches aren't just big, they're comfortable," Jeremy suggested when he looked over his shoulder and saw her still standing by the door.

"I'm sure," she said, and dropping her purse on the nearest couch, she seated herself on the edge of it while Jeremy turned back to the bar and started removing bottles from the refrigerator.

Angela's stomach felt rock hard. So much for being in control, the voice at the back of her mind taunted.

Unsure of her legs, she stood, reached for her purse.

"Let's see, Kalua, Amaretto, Bailey's Cream," Jeremy recited.

When Angela didn't respond Jeremy turned to see her standing once more.

"Too late for a nightcap?" he asked. He set the bottle of liqueur on the counter and closed the distance between them in two strides. Without a word, he took the purse from her hand, dropped it on the couch behind her.

She was silenced by the stunning recognition of desire

in his eyes, as he took both her hands in his, and leaning down, kissed her slowly, deeply.

A hunger she'd denied from the first moment she'd seen him won out. She hesitated. When he released her hands, she wrapped her arms around his waist and pulled his shirt from the waistband of his trousers. Surprised, but pleased to recognize he wasn't wearing a tee shirt, she lifted the starched cotton and spread her hands across his broad back.

When the next kiss ended, Jeremy placed a finger under her chin, tilted it up and looked into her eyes. "Better than a nightcap?"

"Much better," she said.

With a husky sigh he stepped away from her, his hands clenched at his sides.

"I told myself I would not go near you tonight. Would you really like to leave?"

"Not a chance," she said.

In his office off the ship's lobby, Burt Chaney laid down the passenger list he'd been studying and ran his fingers through his short dark hair. He was tired and frustrated. A message from Venice to Pryce Cruise Lines main office in L.A. forwarded to him, advised the line the body of a woman found strangled in one of their narrow, poorly lit streets in early January was a British journalist, a missing passenger from one of Pryce Cruise Line's smallest, most popular ships.

The Romance sailed the Adriatic biweekly making a

round trip between Venice and Athens, and stopping along the way for their passengers to tour Ephesus, Dubrovnik, Cyprus, and Mykonos. The information from the Venetian authorities only added to Burt's growing conviction that all the attacks on the Line's single female passengers were the work of one twisted perpetrator. If he was right, the killer, male or possibly female, seemed quite picky in his choice of victims—not only single women, but each a celebrity. Could it be sheer coincidence? So unlikely it seemed too bizarre to be true. A killer with a grudge against the Line, possibly, a former, or god forbid, a current employee of Pryce Cruise Line out to destroy the company.

He checked his watch, two a.m. He needed more pieces of the puzzle. There had to be more information out there, although it wasn't likely to come in tonight. Sleep. He needed sleep for his mind to clear. When the ship reached Puerto Rico he'd contact the local authorities and Jones and her crew. They would be in San Juan by now. With luck she may also have found something for him. He laid the computer printout on his desk and reached for a file folder. Before he could pick it up there was a knock on his office door. Pete Cuzak, formerly of the Lyre and one of his most experienced security officers, stood at the door, a video camera disc in his hand.

Ten minutes later Burt turned from the computer screen. "You didn't recognize the man, if it was a man, not someone we've previously picked out in the corridors anywhere on the ship?"

"No sir. At first I thought maybe it was some guy

dressed for a masquerade party, Mardi Gras and all. I checked the ship's calendar for private parties. Nada."

"And you're sure he used a card key to go into Lady von Chassen's suite?"

Cuzak pointed at the computer screen. "Rerun it. Focus on his right hand. You'll catch a glimpse of the key card entering the slot in the door before it opens."

Burt paused the film, his face reddened. "Why didn't we seen this recording earlier?"

"Johnson just brought it to my attention when his shift ended. He had checked the recording and noted a time lapse. He recalled someone knocked on the door with a message from the Chief Pursuer so he reran the tape that covered the time lapse."

"Tell Johnson good work. I believe you said the guy in the wig hasn't been spotted again tonight."

"No sign of him. I've notified everyone on duty to report to me immediately if he's seen or if anyone they can't identify shows up in corridors," Cuzak said.

"Good, Not much more we can do until we reach San Juan. I'm going to turn in. But don't hesitate to wake me if he's seen again."

In his suite, Jeremy took Angela's hand and led her through the door on the other side of the living room. She'd made up her mind to have this night, this one night with him to remember, but inside his bedroom the sight of the king size bed unnerved her. She hesitated. His eyes roamed over her body in a slow, breathtaking look that awed her. She stilled. Without losing the grip on her hand he closed the door behind them and pulled her to him, took a deep breath, lifted her arms and wound them around his neck, buried her face in his shoulder. He tightened his grip and she spread her fingers, ran them through the clipped hair at the back of his neck and into the thick blond waves at the back of his head. He leaned down and his mouth closed over hers. A slow tide rose from her toes and rose up her body in an overpowering rush. Heat danced in her veins. The kiss seemed to last forever, and forever felt good, right. Her hands moved down his muscled back and tugged to free the remaining fabric tucked into his trousers.

He released his grip on her. She stepped back and with fumbling fingers unbuttoned the tiny white buttons of his shirt one at a time. He stood back from her and skillfully removed the gold cuff links at his wrists dropped them on the dresser next to the door, peeled off his shirt and left it on the floor where it fell.

When he reached for her again, she melted against him, hands open against his back again she wondered at the way his muscles moved—tightened then released like coils of steel. He was, she realized much stronger than she had imagined but gentle with her. His broad hands glided down her back leaving ripples of excitement in their wake. His hands lifted her hips, tilted them against him. She felt him harden against her. Her hands searched, slid inside the waistband of his trousers then moved beneath the slick leather belt at his waist. She unbuckled the belt. Her hands roamed down and he moaned. He removed her hands from below his waist, and with one motion, he scooped her up off the floor. She wrapped her legs around his waist, buried her face in the hollow of his neck and clung to him.

She would be sorry tomorrow. So be it. She would have tonight.

He carried her across the room and deposited her on the bed. He paused beside the bed. Looked down at her. Lust clouded his eyes. "Your dress," he said, as if it had only that moment dawned on him she was wearing a dress. "You probably should take it off."

Angela sat up. "My dress?"

He looked so confused, she almost laughed.

"Does it unzip somewhere?"

"In the back," she said and turned over on her side. She felt the mattress give beneath her when he sat down on the bed, felt his hands on her back and heard the zipper slide down. She sat up again, and he picked her up off the bed and set her on her feet in front of him.

He said, "No, let me," when she reached down to lift the hem of her dress. He lifted the skirt and pulled the heavily beaded dress up over her head then dropped it next to his shirt.

For a moment they stood beside the bed his hands on her hips his eyes on hers. "Like what you see?" she asked surprising him. He smiled, "Stunning," he said and pulling her to him with a low growl, he lifted her and laid her on the bed and followed her there.

She leaned into him and as her gaze searched his face her lips met his. Her fingers traced an outline across the broad cheekbones, the almost straight nose. Their tongues met and as the kiss deepened, she felt as if she'd never been kissed before. The kiss ended and she nuzzled his neck while his hands outlined her thighs, her waist, her breasts. His head came down and the tip of his tongue circled the nipples of one breast. She began to tremble and he lifted his head.

"I've wanted you like this from the first moment I saw you in the airport," he whispered, his voice husky with lust. "When I found out who you were, and Heather said you'd be meeting someone after the cruise. I knew being near you would be temporary at best. It made me a little crazy."

Tears formed in Angela's eyes, but she blinked them back. How could she tell him what those words meant to her and why they were true? He would never see her again. Her hand moved, and she stroked his shoulder and his chest, playing with the brown tips of his nipples, watching as they stiffened. His eyes opened wide and his hand tightened on her hips. She scooted closer him, and he rolled her to him, on top of him. Reaching behind her back he released the hooks on the flimsy lace covering her breasts. He tugged at the bikini pants she still wore and with his hand caressing her hips slid them down.

When he had them in his hand she saw him crush them in his fist and toss them off the bed. When he took her nipple in his mouth, the sensation surprised and startled her with an intensity she had never experienced, and she cried out.

He lifted his head and looked down. "I didn't hurt you?" His voice tense, anxious, questioning.

Angela laughed and rolled her head from side to side "No, no." She pulled his head down to her breast once more and moaned when he nuzzled there, her pulse racing. Some part of her brain startled almost in disbelief. And in that thought half formed, she recognized she'd never experienced what was happening to her now. She opened her eyes and stared up at him in wonder.

He smiled down at her, lifted himself on top of her and with one leg against the inside of her thigh, opened her legs. Supporting himself on one arm he began to explore her ear, her throat, with his tongue, pausing only to whisper words of pleasure that she couldn't comprehend as the waves of passion that danced in her body, rose and fell to heights and depths she'd never imagined.

She reached for the throbbing erection against her hip. Her fingers enclosed him, explored, and she felt him grow again at her touch.

His hand moved down her body. His experienced fingers caressed her hips her thighs, her belly and as her hips rose, her body clenched.

He smiled into her eyes, he hand slid further down her body, he began to explore the inside of her thigh with his fingers, warm they probed and then his tongue followed.

"No" she said, but he ignored her. She shuddered and with no control left she went with her body while it climbed. Helpless in shock while explosion after explosion ripped through her, the sensations lit up her brain, until at last she collapsed beneath him. Whispering words of pleasure, he moved up and over her again.

Stunned, she felt him slide inside her, fill her, and unbelievably she felt the tide of sensation begin to grow again, and again she rode with him on waves so high and so fast all thoughts of later drowned in the now, in the oneness.

And when he called out his release, she marveled at their simultaneous climax and wept.

Spent, on top of him, she kissed his throat, his jaw, his mouth. His arms tightened on her, and she felt him harden again.

He moved her off of him and onto her back. Leaning on one elbow over her, his eyes caressed her body. "This time," he said, "we take it slowly, I waited so long for this, sometimes I wasn't sure you would ever come to me." He smiled down at her.

"I had to, I had no choice." And as she spoke, she knew the words were true. She had to be with him once, this once that she would cherish long after she'd left him.

He said, "Don't make me wait so long next time."

She only smiled.

Several minutes later, sated, Angela lay back in Jeremy's arms and listened to him breathe slowly deep in sleep. She stared up at the light and shadow moving across the ceiling, reflections from the moon above on the sea below, dancing with her as she fell over the edge of sleep.

Chapter Nineteen

When the telephone rang at six the following morning, Jeremy eased Angela's hand off his chest and reached for the receiver. He eased out of the bed and crossed the room to the adjoining bathroom.

"Yes," he said when he'd closed the door behind him.

"She's here."

"Cuzak, what?" Jeremy eyebrows rose. He opened the door a crack. She lay curled up where he had left her, apparently still asleep.

Closing the door again, he listened to the voice on the other end of the line then repeated. "They checked her suite? Okay, right. You say Johnson's good at it. When he finishes the sketch...someone on one of the other ships... No, she's asleep. I'll make sure she stays here until I hear from you again. That should allow enough time to email it to every ship in the Line. I agree—he probably used the same get-up on the Lyre. Right, they'll check on all the transfers. No kidding, the Romance, too? That's a good idea. Headquarters can do a search. Right, I'll meet you in the lobby at seven."

~

Henry was tired. And he was angry. Where had the bitch been? He had hung around her suite until almost three. The ship was due in port by nine and he had to be at his desk to welcome the new passengers boarding in San Juan for the return trip to Fort Lauderdale. Where in the hell had she been?

"Rough night?" Betty the waitress in the crew's dining room questioned.

You would not like to know, Henry thought, but he pasted on the smile he knew she expected and grinned. From his first day he'd come on board, Betty made it known she was available. But then, most of the women he encountered in his life did the same.

He didn't question his attraction, good-looking men ran in the family. In his day his grandfather regularly reminded his grandson, he'd been the local stud of their county. But, as his grandfather told him, looks only go so far. They didn't mean women would put out for a man. If they did it was because they wanted something, wanted what men could do for them. With women, his grandfather taught him, smart men took what they wanted. Yeah, Henry thought, the old man learned that lesson. He never got over being dumped. Like they say, revenge is sweet. Too bad he isn't alive to see what his grandson is doing to make them pay. Sure, when the Pryce Cruise Line went under, he'd be out of a job. Not that the job mattered, except for the access he'd had to his choice of women. Yeah, but now with his routine down pat, it would work almost as well at a resort.

When he'd finished with that phony Lady von Chassen, maybe he'd just stay behind in San Juan, find a place at one of their upscale resorts. Plenty of single women available in resorts, plenty of resorts in the Caribbean. Lately he found himself getting impatient. The wait between his parties seemed too long. Maybe he needed more choices, more often. For now he cautioned himself, he must be patient. He had to be careful. He knew what the old man would have said about real men. "Real men are self-disciplined."

Jeremy chose a corner table on the executive deck. The ship would be in the harbor in a few minutes. No doubt the press would know something by now. They must know he is on board. After his testimony in D.C. before the congressional committee on passenger safety, the press would be circling, ready to move in when they thought they identified fresh game.

Although he could be reasonably sure they didn't believe he was on board the Q.C. because of the Lyre murder, even the press must know his position as CEO didn't qualify him to investigate murder. That didn't mean they wouldn't do their best to question him. And, he certainly couldn't ignore the serious pall the news of this latest death made on the Line. Until there were some answers, booking a cruise on a Pryce Line Cruise ship might be a questionable choice for a single woman. He had to be ready to answer their questions. But, he would avoid them until he had more facts, if at all possible. As for the rest of the coming day, the message he received early this morning guaranteed he and Burt would be with the local authorities for hours.

There would be no time to see Silke until they met for dinner at the Marmalade restaurant, hardly the place for him to discuss future arrangements to see her again and not much time tomorrow either. If the local authorities expected him to remain in San Juan he'd be stuck there. He hoped his stay would be brief. Once he'd seen Monica and done as much damage control as he could by accepting the blame for ending their relationship, he would only stay if his presence helped with the investigation.

The Q.C. ship would sail for home tomorrow and no matter what happened in the investigation, he must fly back to Los Angeles, no later than the next morning.

In the meantime, breakfast with Silke on the executive deck for breakfast was probably the only chance he'd have to ask the questions he should have been asking. What were her plans? Where would she go after the ship reached the States? He didn't have her address, much less a telephone number. Too many questions.

Didn't Heather suggest Silke was an expatriate, lived in Spain, or did she say France? Not that it mattered. From the moment he'd stepped through the door of the V.I.P. lounge and seen her sitting at that table, he'd understood he could not walk away from her without knowing when they would meet again. Whatever her plans after the cruise, he was determined to be part of them.

Maybe he was crazy. He'd only known her for a few days. Who was she, really? He felt he knew who she wasn't— an international, too rich, too famous, party-girl beauty. According to his sister, Heather, Silke was regularly chronicled in the pages of Vanity Fair and other fashion magazines. But the woman he'd met in an airport lounge, enjoyed dinner with in Nassau, sailed with to Paradiso, danced with in the Calypso Lounge, and who had spent last night in his arms, was not that party girl. He needed more time with her. Or maybe a lifetime—the thought startled him.

Now you've done it, the voice accused.

Fool!

When Jeremy had awakened her with coffee and orange juice, at first she'd been shocked. At least part of her was, she admitted now. But, she wasn't sorry about last night. On the contrary, if she could describe how she felt when she awoke in Jeremy's bed, her answer would be: thrilled.

More than an hour later, back in her own suite, Angela stepped out of the shower and reached for the heavy robe next to the shower door. She wrapped it around her, newly aware of her bare skin beneath the terry cloth.

Definitely not frigid, Dr. Edward Fournier. He had

been the first, the only man she'd slept with before Jeremy.

Sex with Edward? A "clinical experience" might be the better description she decided, now that she knew the difference. That less than the rapturous event promised by her friends and the romance novels she'd read since her teen years, had left her deeply disappointed and almost convinced she was frigid. That is until the night in Beverly Hills. After she'd overheard his conversation with his mother about his reasons for marrying her, she'd broken their engagement. Several weeks later, he'd cornered her at her clinic and suggested they should reconsider marriage, but she'd refused to discuss the subject. Angry, he'd struck back with a description of her sexuality as "non-female, frigid."

"Normal," she announced joyfully to herself. "I'm normal."

After last night, this was a day for celebration, a day for bath powder, perfumed body lotion, all the little luxuries the ship provided for suite occupants. Today she would celebrate. She wouldn't think of tomorrow. She looked for the powder where she'd seen it last night on the marble counter top. Gone? She opened the door to the cabinet on the right of the sink, extra towels, no powder. Rashid, the steward who cleaned her suite, was meticulous about returning all lotions, powders and cosmetics to the place on the counter they had occupied since the cruise began. But before she could search further, a gentle knock on the door to the suite startled her. Without closing the cabinet, she went to answer it. Anastasia, her face flushed as if she'd been running, stood in the corridor with an armload of creamy white roses and a smile wide enough to display her less than even teeth.

Jeremy. Angela hoped color hadn't risen in her own face. Wordless she stepped back, held the door wider and followed the butler in.

With the roses still in her arms, she handed Angela the card that came with the flowers and stood looking around. "I doubt there's a vase here, Lady von Chassen."

"Probably not, at least I don't recall seeing one." Angela opened the card.

"For Silke, a lady far lovelier than these flowers."

These are really for Silke, not me, she thought. She crushed the card in her hand and shoved it in her pocket.

"You can put them anywhere," she answered the butler.

Anastasia studied the bouquet, hesitated, scanned the room, turned back to Angela. "It would be a shame if they wilted."

"They are lovely," Angela admitted, and looking away she brushed back a tear.

What's in a name, a rose by any other name...? Shakespeare knew how it felt. They are beautiful, they are mine. "We'll fill the bathroom sink with water," she told Anastasia. "They'll keep until you can find a vase."

In the master bath Angela frowned. The cabinet doors stood open, the way she'd left them. "Anastasia, do you recall seeing a box of bath powder on the bathroom counter?"

After several minutes of searching both women failed to find the powder. "The steward may have moved it," Anastasia suggested.

Back in the bedroom the telephone rang.

"Good morning Lady von Chassen, what time may I pick you up for breakfast?" the low, resonate voice at the other end of the line demanded.

Speechless, Angela's hand froze on the receiver. "Oh," she said, and sat down on the bed. Naively, she simply hadn't thought beyond their night together. She bit her lower lip, forced a smile into her voice and agreed to meet him for breakfast on the executive deck at nine.

Angela dressed slowly, thinking. On the telephone he'd asked her what her plans were after the cruise ended. Would she be in The States, in Europe? Based on his questions, she gathered Heather believed Silke was an American expatriate with a home she'd inherited in Spain, or did she tell him Germany? If so, he wanted to know, would she be returning to Europe?

After the call she paced her suite for several minutes. What could she tell him except another lie?

Finally, torn between meeting Jeremy for breakfast and finding an excuse to avoid him, in the end she couldn't bear to pass up the opportunity to be with him, even briefly, knowing it would be the last time.

Although she'd avoided answering his questions earlier, she hoped they would not be asked again.

All the tables were filled when she arrived on the executive deck. Hardly ideal for an interrogation. When she located Jeremy at a table near the bulkhead that offered some privacy, she decided maybe it would still be okay. The smile he offered her when she approached his table lit his face. When he rose to seat her, she wondered how she could ever convince him to forget her.

He didn't look at all tired. She couldn't remember how late they'd fallen asleep only that she'd slept deeply and felt totally refreshed for the first time in months.

And even before he'd pulled out her chair, she'd seen the answer in his eyes. Unable to meet the message in his eyes without betraying her decision, Angela lowered her gaze knowing anything she told him now would be a lie. She inhaled deeply, she couldn't break down in front of him.

"Sorry about the early call," he began. "I hope you didn't feel I was rushing you out the door this morning."

"Rushing? Oh, no. Heather explained this is a business trip for you and I, we—thanks for the coffee and orange juice—great. I need coffee in the morning, an addict, I guess..."

The words trailed off. She hesitated, studied the napkin in her lap, lifted her gaze, studied the other diners, looked everywhere except into Jeremy's eyes.

But her mind was racing. Why is it so difficult? We are adults. Why can't I just say you were wonderful last night? I never knew sex could be like that. Thanks, thanks, perhaps we'll meet again someday, somewhere.

Instead she said, "I need to get back to my suite before..."

Jeremy reached across the table, laid his hand on hers. She stared at their linked hands, swallowed the lump in her throat, looked up, and met his gaze.

"Before the entire ship sees us together and knows

you didn't spend the night in your own bed?" he suggested.

Angela colored. Jeremy raised one eyebrow and smiled, his words almost a whisper, he asked. "Where are you going from here, Silke?"

Angela stiffened, stared at Jeremy. "Where am I going?" she repeated.

"After the cruise," he clarified.

Angela's chest tightened. "Um," she hesitated, caught her lower lip in her teeth.

Jeremy watched her closely, then said, "I believe Heather mentioned you might be spending the summer with friends in Spain."

"Spain," she repeated. You are beginning to sound like an illiterate parrot, Angela. Tell him you're meeting a friend after the cruise, preferably let him believe a male friend.

Angela shrugged. Then keeping her voice light, "A friend in Vermont suggested we meet sometime this summer," she lied.

"Then, you won't be traveling to Europe immediately?"

Angela shook her head.

"No set plans set you can't change?"

Angela felt her stomach drop. If only she had not agreed to meet him. She hated the lies. She was so much in love with him.

Holding her gaze with his, he said, "I don't think you need to be told, I'd like to spend more time with you." When she didn't look away, he continued. "I believe you feel the same way."

Angela understood it was not a question. They both knew the answer.

He paused, his hand tightened on hers. "Something has come up, and I'll be leaving the ship before it sails tomorrow. I expect to fly back to the West coast sometime this week. After I settle a few things, I can take some time off, meet you when the Q.C. docks in Fort Lauderdale."

Speechless, her heart drummed in her chest.

His eyes glowing, his hand tightened on hers, "I don't know if you've been to California, or if you'd like it, but I'm hoping you'll fly back to L.A. with me. I know my way around the city, plenty to see or do, the usual, theaters, museums. If that's what you'd like. Perhaps you've visited California, but if you've never taken a drive along the coast, you might think about that. We could see the local coast or go south to San Diego or north, up the coast, visit Carmel. It's gorgeous anytime of the year. Or, we could tour inland, the Napa and Sonoma vineyards are worth seeing, wonderful wine country. Of course, if you'd prefer we could tour San Francisco, ride the cable cars, see the Golden Gate Bridge, whatever you think you'd like to do?"

Would she like to see Los Angeles with him, California with him? The irony wasn't lost on her.

The places he named were familiar to her, even the ones she had never personally visited. But his questions were for the woman he thought she was. His questions were for Silke not for Angela. The incongruity of the answer she could give him saddened her. She could not give him the answers he might reasonable expect from a woman he asked, the woman he thought might want to be with him. Angela fought back an overpowering sense of loss, of its inevitability. Where would she want to travel with him? Absolutely anywhere!

"It all sounds lovely, of course," she began. Her chest felt heavy, her mouth dry. She wondered that she could still breathe. "There are one or two things I need to wrap up..." she said.

Jeremy frowned, shifted in his chair.

Places to go, things to do, she could tell him...as if she didn't care, or understand he wanted to be with her. Is that how she wanted him to remember the woman he thought of as Silke? When he found out she wasn't the wealthy sophisticated Silke, wouldn't he feel blindsided, feel she'd made a fool of him? No, she cared too much to do that to him, and about herself.

She needed to end this somehow and all she could do is tell another lie, pretend she would consider his suggestions.

Angela kept her voice light. "Sounds like fun. I've read the coast is quite lovely".

Jeremy smiled, leaned closer. "If you can wrap up your business within a couple of weeks after the cruise. It would be a bit early to enjoy the beaches, but if the drive north appeals to you, we could visit the wine country. Napa and Sonoma Valleys are lovely even in April." He paused. "You might even decide to stay longer, maybe visit San Francisco."

"What date did you have in mind?"

Chapter Twenty

Thirty minutes after breakfast, Angela opened the door to a Japanese rock garden complete with a tiny carp pool and miniature waterfall back-lit with a rainbow of lights. At the end of a short path beneath a simulated Torah gate, a woman, who could easily be the winner of a Miss Universe contest, smiled at Angela.

"A pleasure meeting you Lady Von Chassen."

Angela managed to hide her surprise at being so quickly identified.

The woman whose uniform badge identified her as spa hostess "Zoe" checked an appointment book on her desk and said, "I see you are early for hair and nail appointments. May I assume you also plan to enjoy more of our spa facilities?"

"Yes, you may. With all the delicious food the ship offers, I need an hour on a treadmill before I eat one more cream puff," Angela said.

The hostess nodded, looked her up and down, then

apparently satisfied with what she saw, said, "May I ask if you've toured our spa?"

"No, this is my first visit."

"Then perhaps you might take a moment to consult with our spa director and spell out the kind of experience you would like during your visit with us."

Angela hesitated and the receptionist waved her hand at a nearby room. "Naturally, if you simply wish to utilize the exercise machines, I'm certain you will find our gym acceptable."

From where Angela stood she could see into the room beyond. It held all the state of the art exercise equipment anyone could want.

"However," she went on, "we are a full service spa and like to provide our guests with all the benefits one might find at any of the world's outstanding resorts."

Aside from the fact that as a physical therapist Angela knew the benefits of exercise, she also knew a bit of pampering would relieve some of the stress she'd been dealing with since she boarded the Q.C. Self-indulgent sure, but hadn't Carstairs made it clear that she might use any service she chose while on the cruise?

"But, what about the appointments I've scheduled?"

"I'm certain we will be able to work those in for you. If you will be seated, I'll notify Deanna, the spa director, of your arrival."

After a brief interview with the spa director, Angela found herself on a treadmill dressed in the Q.C.'s signature spa outfit, a pair of turquoise leotards and a sleeveless tee shirt embossed with the Pryce Cruise lines Celtic emblem: a multiple branched tree encircled by its own leaves. An assigned personal trainer directed her from one machine to the next, while busily entering physical data into a handheld tablet and occasionally pausing to suggest Angela increase or decrease the intensity of her workout. By the end of the morning's exercise when she slid into the warm, lightly perfumed water of a Jacuzzi, she knew where every muscle in her body was located—and they all ached.

Partially submerged and lulled by hypnotic music from a hidden sound system, Angela completely relaxed for what seemed like the first time since she'd walked off the set of the game show. She slid down into the warmth, and let her mind wander. Through the floor to ceiling windows of the spa she could see part of Old San Juan. Jeremy would be expecting her to meet him for dinner. Perhaps she was making a mistake avoiding him. No one had connected her with the contest. What difference would it make if she met him at the Marmalade, if she spent one more evening, one more night with him? But... she was so close to winning.

"If?"

When she said it out loud, that tiny word made such a small sound, yet it carried so much hope, far too much hope. If she remained unrecognized for the next four days the one million would be hers. Of course, Jeremy would be out of her life and...and somehow she would deal with that. Wouldn't she?

"Are we feeling all relaxed now?" The personal trainer stood at the edge of the pool with a fluffy white robe draped over her arm. "Lunch time," she announced, extending the robe. A few minutes later, Angela joined three other passengers for a vegetarian lunch served in the spa's glass topped, private dining room.

Obviously acquainted with each other, three women sat close together and talked quietly while Angela's mind continued to wander. Heather might be trying to reach her by now. She'd left a message on her telephone that she'd return calls, not when. Surely Heather would be on her way to San Juan. As for Jeremy...? She had time to decide if she would keep her dinner engagement at the Marmalade. The massage, facial, shampoo, cut and style she'd scheduled should take—a shrill voice carried across the room, interrupted Angela's thoughts.

"I'm sure you must have heard of her, she..." one of the women at the table in the corner began.

"Famous, yes, I saw a special about her on PBS," a second, quieter voice chimed in.

"Barbaric!" the first voice announced and added "She..."

But the woman lowered her voice, and Angela couldn't hear what she said.

She checked her watch and signaled the waiter, time for her next appointment. The conversation from the corner continued and before the door completely closed she heard the third woman ask, "Did they say who found her?"

After an hour long massage, Angela was lying on a table with something warm and refreshing on her face. A ginger mask, the esthetician said. A facial was one of the pluses of being Silke, she thought, and she'd almost fallen asleep, when a door opened and closed nosily somewhere.

"Barbaric!"

It took her a second to recall where she'd heard that shrill voice, that word.

Yes, she remembered, in the dining room.

"He'd been waiting for Ackerman in her suite?"

A second, quieter voice asked. "How do you know?"

"My steward told me. And if you'd listened, you'd know I didn't say he took things. I said he moved things," the shrill voice said, "except for her bath powder. He took the bath powder."

"Maybe it was mislaid?" the second voice suggested.

"On her body? He sprinkled bath powder all over her lifeless body."

"Bath powder? Surely you're exaggerating? The man who told you—he wasn't her steward?"

"So what if he wasn't. He should know," the shrill voice insisted. "He had to help clean up the mess. He said there was blood everywhere and the head steward..."

"Oh, I'm so sorry Lady von Chassen, the noise." The esthetician rushed into the room, closed the door, and the voices disappeared. "I didn't realize I'd left the door open. How does the mask feel?"

Suffocating. The word unsaid, surfaced in her chaotic thoughts. Ackerman, surely not Irene Ackerman the historian. Dead? Angela removed the hot towel from her face and sat up abruptly. "Sorry," she said to the startled esthetician. "I'm afraid I won't have time to finish the facial. I have to move on to the hairdressers."

Shortly after three p.m. and six decks below the spa and

beauty salon, cruise security personnel helped impatient and sometimes fearful Q.C. passengers climb into or down out of ship tenders. A small fleet of motorized launches pulled up beside the ship to transport passengers across a harbor to and from San Juan. At the moment an incoming storm set the boats rocking. And, MacDonald, head of the Q.C.'s security found it necessary to enlist most of the ship's security personnel to safely load and unload passengers into the launches.

Fairly certain the killer they wanted would not likely be roaming the ships corridors until well after dark, Mac as he was known, hadn't checked with Johnson in the surveillance cabin and Johnson hadn't called, yet. The perp might not even be on board, Mac reasoned. He and his boss Burt Chaney thought it likely the killer may have left the ship in St. Thomas before or soon after Ackerman's body had been discovered. And at the moment, he felt supervising the safe loading and unloading of passengers demanded his attention.

At three p.m. that afternoon, while many passengers were on their way to San Juan and Mardi Gras, a man wearing a bright red wig made his way down a deserted executive suite corridor. The man in the wig paused, grinned, and gave the camera near the ceiling the finger. The surveillance camera blinked steadily, recording nothing. Earlier in the day on the crew deck, he'd heard two guards talk about seeing someone roaming the executive suite corridors the night he'd had his little party with the

Ackerman woman. Today he'd taken care of that. He'd also been careful to let his bunk-mate know he'd be napping that afternoon.

Around one p.m. he'd lured the officer manning the surveillance equipment to the employee dining room with a false fire alarm. That gave him just enough time to sneak into the cabin and disable the camera leading to the executive suites corridor. Unfortunately, he knew it wouldn't take the guard more than a couple of hours to discover the problem with the camera.

"Plenty of time, plenty of time," he muttered. Before he discovered the ship would be dropping anchor in the harbor, he'd planned his party for midnight when most Mardi Gras parties would still be going on in San Juan. With a little careful questioning of her butler, he'd learned the von Chassen woman would be going ashore around five to meet Pryce. By three, that afternoon, even if security spotted someone on their cameras wearing a wig, they would find more than one person wearing one while roaming the corridors. That was why he knew he'd be smart to start his party early. Naturally he preferred the early morning hours, less opportunity of being interrupted. But, he shrugged, it didn't pay to be predictable.

He smiled when he recalled how well unpredictable worked in Venice, when he'd followed the British journalist off the ship. Although he'd discovered that loser guy sharing her suite had passed out in one of the bars, he couldn't take a chance Mr. Loser might return to the suite and interrupt the party. Drunks were so unpredictable. Because he knew the journalist and her boyfriend were on the outs, it was a lucky break for him to offer to escort her when he "accidently" encountered her near the Bridge of Sorrows. She, like most of the passengers, would only have seen the uniform, not the man in it. The ruse worked well. He'd taken a chance going after her in port, and not being predictable had paid off.

Even if someone asked about him this evening, he didn't need to worry about being interrupted. Should his cabin mate return from his post early, he'd see him asleep in the upper bunk.

In the spa Angela hung up the telephone. She'd used up the last ounce of her patience, she decided. Heather had already left the ship. She probably went shopping, or perhaps to meet Burt, Angela thought. She was sure of it when she couldn't reach him or Jeremy. Both of them had left word they could be contacted in San Juan at the Marmalade restaurant.

She looked at her watch, a little past two o'clock. After her stay in the Sauna, her hair was a mess. But, there were advantages to having short hair. It wouldn't take long to have it washed and dried, not more than thirty minutes.

When she left the hairdressers, the sun was sliding down the sky toward three fifteen. In the elevator, she mentally surveyed her closet. The ball gown was out, too long, too heavy. One of the less glamorous cocktail dresses would work, one with a short skirt to make climbing in and out of a launch easier, but attractive enough for an evening in a posh restaurant or a casino. She reached the door of her suite about three fifteen.

Queen of Charades

Chapter Twenty-One

The long corridor on the executive deck was deserted when Angela stepped off of the elevator. She always seemed to pass someone on her way to her suite, at least a steward doing something, going somewhere. When she reached the door of her suite she hesitated. She did not reach for her keycard. Heather must already be off the ship, she'd concluded. Would Burt be with her? Shouldn't he still be on board? A killer was on the loose. Wasn't it his job to protect the passengers on the ship? Did any of the women she'd overheard in the spas dining room say if they knew how or when the murderer entered Irene's suite? Irene, intelligent, charming, an internationally known historian, a celebrity. Why would anyone attack Irene? Incomprehensible. Yet it had happened. Someone on the ship killed her. With close to two thousand people on board, would it have been someone she knew or might have met, someone who appeared harmless, who was polite even helpful, a maniac, a sociopath? Why? How would she know? A smiling face could just as easily mask a killer. Questions, no answers. Could the killer still be on board? She checked the corridor behind her once more. Empty. According to her watch, it wasn't quite four. If she wanted to catch up with Heather, she should hurry. Open the door silly. It's still daylight. Did I tell Anastasia I wouldn't be going to the ball, wouldn't need her help? I can wait, or locate a steward. You're being paranoid, Angela. Open the door. And reaching into the pocket of her leotards, she pulled out her keycard, inserted it into the door and turned the knob.

The opaque drapes across the two sliding glass balcony doors were closed against the Caribbean sun; the room ahead in partial darkness. She'd started down the short hallway, past the door off the entrance area that led to the guest bathroom, and was about to enter the living room when she noticed a sweet odor. It seemed to be emanating from the hallway. She stepped back into the hall. Juicy Couture. She'd recognize the heady perfume of her bath powder anywhere. Had the steward located it? She reached for the bathroom door but before touching the handle she jerked her hand back. Bath powder?

"He sprinkled her body with bath powder." The penetrating voice of the woman in the spa's dining room echoed in her ear.

A warning screamed through her limbs, but the muscles of her legs tightened. For what seemed an eternity she remained rooted to the spot. She had to move. Where? There was no turning back. To reach the door of the suite, she would have to pass the guest bathroom. If he was waiting for her behind the bathroom door he would surely hear her pass by, hear her opening the door to the corridor. Even if she made it out the door of the suite and into the corridor, what about the corridor? Would it still be empty? Would he follow? Was it a he, was anyone in the bathroom, was it her imagination? She moved into the living room, looked across the room to her bedroom door, she'd go into the bedroom...lock the door, telephone for help.

She didn't see it until she turned to the bedroom door. The living room telephone, on the floor, the receiver off the hook, its cord ripped from the wall.

No, not the bedroom. You'll be trapped. She chanced a look toward the entry hall. No one there, no sounds from the bathroom. Was he waiting for her to go into the bedroom? Frantically, her gaze scoured the spacious room, no place to hide no way out. Except? She saw them. The two balcony doors, one on either side of the living room. If she only had time to reach those doors. Throughout the cruise the residents of the luxury suites had gathered in early evening for pre-prandial drinks and conversation at the exclusive executive deck bar and private dining room some ten feet below her suite. If she could get out onto the deck, the opaque drapes might shield her long enough for her to get the attention of someone below.

Commanding herself to move slowly, she crossed the living room on tip toes, and slid open the door of the balcony on the right side of the television wall between the two doors. She stepped out and closed it silently behind her.

The drapes on the inside of the door no sooner settled than she saw the dim outline of a figure with what appeared to be an enormous head emerge from the bathroom and move toward the center of the living room. She stifled a scream and flattened herself against the steel divider separating the two balconies, and held her breath. The shadowy figure moved to the middle of the living room and stopped. The grotesque head turned left and right until apparently satisfied she wasn't concealed behind a couch or a chair. He turned to the bedroom and disappeared through the door. Angela moved away from the divider to the railing, gripped it with clammy hands and looked over. The deck below was deserted. Where was everyone? Not even one of the ship's ubiquitous waiters was in sight. She glanced over her shoulder in time to see the door to her bedroom begin to open. She stepped back from the railing and with arms pressed tightly against her body, once more flattened herself against the hot metal of the divider.

Inside the suite she could see the dim outline of that grotesque head turn again, first left then right. She held her breath when he began to move across the living room toward the balconies. If she was spotted, could she get over the rail before he could open the door? Then before she could move, the grotesque figure veered to the left toward the other set of balcony doors. He hadn't seen her, not yet. She heard the door slide open. She licked beads of sweat from her upper lip, listened. Something crashed to the floor, probably a deck chair, a low curse, followed by a gentle sigh, the sound of the sliding door opening. She stepped away from the wall, moved to the edge of the balcony, grasped the rail and looked down. Out of the corner of her eye she saw the drape behind her flutter against the unopened glass door. Time had run out. She put one leg then the other over the balcony rail and, gripping the balustrades, lowered her body until she could grasp the floor of the deck. For a second she hung dangling below the balcony. Then a foot in a blue canvas shoe appeared at the edge of the deck above her. Angela let go.

"Bitch."

The word, hardly more than a whisper, propelled her to her feet. Not even the painted face could disguise the domed forehead, the prominent nose of the man leaning over her balcony rail. Did he realize she recognized him? She had to get help.

She had twisted her right ankle when she dropped from her balcony to the executive deck. It still throbbed, but afraid to wait for an elevator Angela painfully made her way down six flights of steps, then one more below the numbered decks. Passenger's intent on leaving the ship filled the corridor, their lines stretching to where security was busily loading them onto launches. She didn't see the man, Mac something she recalled, a security supervisor, the one she'd overheard Jeremy's friend Burt talking with. Heather mentioned he had an office somewhere on board. This Mac...MacDonald wasn't it? He should know where she could find Burt.

Across the harbor in Old San Juan, Jeremy found Burt and Heather seated at the Marmalade's luxurious leather bar, oblivious to the people around them and with eyes only for each other, they didn't notice him come in. For a moment he stood watching them. Anyone who saw them together would be a fool not to recognize the way they felt about each other. Yet, he thought, Burt was proud, and pride worn too long often became a mask someone wears to avoid seeing their own need. Would Burt's unexamined ego allow him to ask Heather to marry him? But he was realistic. Burt's parents had divorced over money. Heather might never convince Burt her love for him meant more to her than family money. Because she knew what lasting love looked like. When they'd lost their own parents, they'd been raised by their father's parents. John and Samantha Pryce, two people from profoundly different backgrounds, who often said because of the money that stood between them they might never have married without the storm that brought them together. Given the love they shared, Jeremy didn't believe anything other than death could have permanently kept them apart. And he didn't believe Heather was a quitter. Crossing the floor he joined them at the bar.

A few minutes later, the hostess escorted them to their table and handed out menus. Silke still hadn't appeared by the time the waiter arrived to take their orders. He noted their selections, collected the menus and left.

Their wine arrived first, followed shortly with the appetizers. When Angela still hadn't arrived by the time dinner was served, Heather suggested, "Perhaps she forgot we were meeting for dinner. She'll be at the ball."

Jeremy wasn't sure about that. His gaze kept drifting to the dining room entrance while Heather recited the pleasures of Mardi Gras past for Burt's benefit,

Where was the illusive Silke?

"I could call MacDonald. He's supervising the launches," Burt said after he caught Jeremy checking the door for the fourth time. "He'll know when she left the ship, if she left."

Jeremy shrugged and said, "Maybe she changed her mind." He couldn't shake the feeling her absence was deliberate. At breakfast, he'd noted a certain reluctance to commit to any of his suggestions of when and where they'd meet after the cruise. And while he wanted to believe he meant something to her, he hadn't forgotten that the celebrity news media consistently labeled Silke von Chassen "the first lady of one night stands."

Yet none of the popular news gossip fit the woman who'd lain in his arms last night. Or, maybe his ego would not allow him to believe her reputation.

He reached for his glass. "Perhaps she found something more interesting to do?"

"Not necessarily," Heather suggested. "There are always delays when everyone on a ship is trying to disembark at the same time," Heather said, adding, "and you've forgotten, during Mardi Gras, once they arrive, there are so many of them, I'm amazed when anyone finds a taxi."

"You're probably right," Jeremy said, and raised his glass. "A toast to Mardi Gras. To all who dressed up tonight to live their unfulfilled dreams behind a mask."

Burt looked at his friend closely, hesitated, then raised

his glass. "Especially to those who can accept the good times."

"To Mardi Gras," Heather repeated. But before her glass reached her lips, a waiter with an agitated look approached their table.

At their table the waiter hesitated, "Mr. Chaney?" he asked looking from one man to the other.

"I'm Chaney," Burt said.

"Sorry to interrupt, but the maître d' wishes to inform you there is a call for you at his desk."

"His desk?" Burt reached for his iPhone where he'd placed it on the table. It appeared to be working.

"Are you certain you have the right Chaney?"

The waiter reread the note in his hand then looked from Burt to Jeremy and back again. "I believe the message is from your ship." He hesitated, squinted, at the hastily written note again. "A message from a Mr. MacDonald on the Q.C.?"

Burt rose, reached for the note, scanned it quickly. "They think they got the perp," he said, "and Silke has left the ship."

Burt handed the note to Jeremy who read it and handed it back to Burt.

"So where is she?"

"The note's not clear. He doesn't say they have someone in custody, and he thinks Silke's looking for us. I'm heading back. Why don't you and Heather check out the hotel? She might be looking for us there. But if she's still on board, we'll find her."

⤳

The maître d' did his best not to appear rude, but from her tennis shoes to her sweat stained tee shirt, the woman in front of him looked and sounded as if she'd accidentally veered off the course of a Marathon run. Her hair was disheveled, and she spoke in a rush the words stuttering out as if she couldn't get her breath. It took him a minute or two to understand what she wanted.

"Mr. Pryce, Mr. Chaney and a woman?"

"Yes, I believe that was Mr. and Ms. Pryce. The reservation, let me see, yes, it was for four, but there were only three people at the table and," he paused as once more his gaze traveled from her feet to her hair. "...and you say you were supposed to meet them here? Are you certain you have the correct venue, perhaps a costume ball...?" His voice trailed off.

Angela voiced an emphatic "No!" and "You're sure they're not here now?"

The maître d' nodded.

"When did they leave, how long ago?"

"There was a telephone message," he began.

Her voice rose. "How long ago?"

Whoever she was, he decided, it was best to get her out of the restaurant. Scenes were not appreciated by Marmalade's customers.

"Ten minutes, perhaps. There was a telephone call," he began again.

But Angela wasn't listening. "Get me a taxi," she demanded.

Angela had just enough cash with her to pay the taxi driver. She didn't know if Jeremy and Heather had gone on to the ball at the casino. She certainly wasn't dressed for the ball. She didn't have a choice now. The maître'd said Burt was returning to the ship. When she got back to the ship. She would wait in Burt's office until Jeremy got back, or until security found the man with the wig.

The taxi let her off at the harbor gate. She cleared security in time to see one of the white launches leave the Q.C. It appeared insubstantial in the early dusk, a misty shadow above the choppy water. After the launch arrived and unloaded, Angela joined the end of a line of passengers that stretched ahead of her until it curled out of sight. From where she stood, she could hear the cacophony of the boat's engines settling into a thumping rhythm. A broad-backed man ahead of her moved a step forward. She fought back panic. It would be dark soon. Where was the man in the wig?

She knew from something she'd overheard Burt saying that there were senior security officers at the head of the line. They would recheck the identification of every person before clearing them to board the launch for the return trip. But once they saw Silke's I.D. name, would they believe a celebrity-seeking "poor little rich girl" that she had been attacked by someone who might have followed her? Could she trust them? Irene was dead. She probably should have listened to security on the ship before she boarded the launch heading for San Juan. But, she'd been certain she could find Jeremy, Burt and Heather at the Marmalade. And, surely the security guards on the pier also knew about the murder and would listen to her story, Angela told herself. Although, even now it seemed hysterical to her, like a front page on a grocery store magazine, so unbelievable, the red wig, the painted face.

What was taking so long? With all the Mardi Gras parties and parades going on in San Juan, there should be more tenders carrying passengers to and from the ship. She leaned to the side in an attempt to see around the man in front of her. Only six more people ahead.

"Looking for something?" His grin said he knew what. She stepped back and bumped into the woman behind her. "Sorry," she said.

The woman stared at her, "Haven't we met?"

Angela felt herself shrink. "I, I'm sorry, I don't believe so."

The line moved forward and stopped. The woman behind her also moved forward, so close she thought she could almost feel the heat of her body on her back.

When she tapped her on her shoulder, Angela stifled an almost overpowering urge to scream, to yell at her to go away. Summoning up all the control she could manage, she took a deep breath, told herself she was being paranoid, forced a smile and turned around to face the attractive fortyish something woman wearing a ballerina costume.

"It was Barcelona. Wasn't it?" the woman insisted. "I just this minute remembered," she added. "Short term memory is so annoying, isn't it?"

Angela dug her fingernails into the palm of her hands. "Is it?"

The woman colored. "Well, of course, someone so young wouldn't...I'm almost positive it was Barcelona," she repeated.

Don't be rude, Angela thought, "Sorry, I've never visited Spain."

"Yes, it was in Harper's...let me see...yes the December issue. You know the one, the Christmas edition."

Angela shook her head.

The woman frowned. "A special. They had pictures of your villa."

Angela shrugged, forced a smile. "We just can't trust the media anymore, can we?" she said. Then she turned back around in time to join the line moving forward again.

This line now curved left and seemed shorter. If she leaned that way slightly, she could see the pier and the launch ahead. Relieved, she watched while one by one the ship's crew and the guards took an arm of each passenger and steadied them when they stepped cautiously from the pier down into the rocking boat.

The line inched forward. The boat already looked crowded, too crowded, Angela thought, while ahead of her the big man moved one more step forward. Now she could also see the bow of the launch. She still could not identify individual passengers. Perhaps when she got closer. On her way into San Juan her boat had passed another tender headed for the ship. Had they all gone back to the ship? Did she miss them? No, the maître d' said they'd been at the restaurant earlier, and that he understood at least one of them was returning to the ship. Probably Burt, she realized. She had to calm down, her panic was distorting her reason. Once he received the call, of course Burt would return to the ship. But, what about Jeremy and Heather? Where were they?

At the harbor gate, about a hundred feet behind Angela, a man costumed like a deep sea diver climbed out of the taxi he'd hailed outside the Marmalade. He'd have gotten here sooner if the stupid taxi driver had stepped on it like he'd told him. Lazy like all islanders, he thought. They lived the good life, food on trees, great weather, no need to hurry. Yeah, time to check out that good life. Time enough after he'd taken care of the bitch. He slammed the door, rattling the taxi window. The taxi driver swore.

The security guard stopped him when he attempted to walk through the gate at the harbor. He recognized the guard as the new kid who'd joined the ship at St. Thomas.

"Boarding Pass?" the young man said.

An angry blue vein began to pulse in Henry's forehead. The bitch is getting away, the pompous little man at the restaurant desk, the stupid taxi driver. He'd had it. "You know who I am!" His hand tightened on the knife in his pocket.

"Rules. Rules." The guard grinned and added, "Guess some tight ass in management thinks Jack the Ripper's on board or might board."

He released his grip on the knife and laughed.

"No kidding, the Ripper?"

"Yeah, I heard some woman on board got herself murdered, probably by her boyfriend."

Figures, he thought, security would be looking for some no class lover. That was enough to make him laugh again. So they thought they were dealing with someone so rich and so bored by his wife he took down whores.

Henry grinned. "You got it kid." He reached for his I.D. and waved it at the guard.

On the other side of the gate he joined the line leading to the pier. Stupid kid, bastard couldn't have guessed who he was. A man like him, one who never paid for it, always went after class. When they found out he'd gotten past security at the gate. They'd probably fire the kid. Too bad. We all have to learn.

That British TV anchor he'd done, now there was class. He'd never forget how she begged him for it. Not that she meant she really wanted him, lying bitch. He'd bet that smart ass Chaney and pretty boy Pryce never connected her death to the one on the *Lyre*, either. Another class act. The daughter of a congressman. Maybe the two dumb heads would get it when he caught up with the von Chassen woman. Once he was back on board he had time, plenty of time. She hadn't seen his face. And she had to sleep, didn't she?

"Got the time?" A gray haired man ahead of him turned back to him and asked.

"Yeah, late, but not too late. See!" He laughed and held up his arm with the plastic replica of a diving watch.

The man tensed, stared at him, turned away and hurried forward.

~

After the big man ahead of her moved forward one step, Angela could see the bow of the boat. She still could not identify individual passengers on board, but in front of the man ahead of her she recognized the boy Luis and his nurse. Perhaps by the time they boarded she'd be close enough to see who was already on the launch. What was it the maître d' said? Burt received a message from his ship? Did he return to the Q.C.? If he did, what about Jeremy and Heather? Maybe they were on the launch. If they were, it didn't mean she'd see them before boarding. Some of the launches carried as many as fifty passengers. Of course, they might have gone on to the ball. According to Heather, Jeremy would be seeing important business associates there.

At the head of the line, the nurse, Kettering, in charge of the boy Luis, hesitated. When she'd heard about the Mardi Gras parade in San Juan she'd thought it would be fun to see it, something the boy might like. The water in the harbor had been reasonably calm when they left the ship in early afternoon. The trip across pleasant, the parade colorful. She hadn't counted on getting the boy out of his portable wheel chair and into a rocking boat on the way back. Who knew a storm would come up while they were at the parade? Next to the pier she watched while the boat rolled and heaved. The two guards stepped forward to help her board. When she stiffened the guard on her right said, "It's easier than it looks. If you want, one of us can take the kid." Kettering nodded, but when the guard reached for the boy, Luis awoke. He lifted his head, took one look at the security guard, then twisted away and buried his face in the nurse's shoulder.

"It's okay, Luis," the nurse said, but the child only tightened his arms around her neck.

"You can't wait, lady. There's a storm coming in," one of the men said. "It's only going to get worse. If you want to hold him we can get you on board together. We won't let you fall."

The boy began to cry. The nurse shook her head, stepped back, "No, I can't—he won't—we'll wait."

Angela watched the scene unfold from where she stood. He's terrified, she thought. She'll never be able to board with the boy in her arms.

The nurse stepped away and the guard proceeded to help the man in front of Angela. Luis raised his head from the nurse's shoulder, saw Angela and smiled.

"I saw a dragon," he said.

"Really," Angela said, "Was he a purple dragon?"

Luis laughed. "Dragon's aren't purple. Dragons are green."

Again, the security guard signaled to Angela to move forward, but she shook her head and joined Kettering and the boy.

"What about the dragon we saw in your dragon book?" she said, "He was purple?"

"Nooo. He was a green dragon."

"Oh," said Angela, moving closer. "Are you sure?"

Luis nodded, "Green."

"I've never seen a green dragon,"Angela said, "Do you have the book?"

"No." Luis pointed at the ship. "Bed."

"Oh, in your bed. I guess you'll have to show me when we get back."

Luis looked at the boat. Then back at Angela. "Green."

"Let's go. We'll read it before bed time." The boy reached out his arms to Angela. She took him from the nurse and moved to the front of the line. With a crew member steadying her from the pier and carrying Luis she stepped down into the rocking boat. The nurse followed immediately. They found two seats at the stern. Once on board, Luis seemed to settle down. Within minutes he fell asleep. Angela smiled at the sleeping boy in her arms. Perhaps one day she would have a child of her own.

In the meantime they would all be back on board the ship in a few minutes. If Jeremy or Burt weren't there, what then? One thing she promised herself is that she would not go near her suite, not until they found the man with the red hair.

～

Earlier, when MacDonald messaged Burt at the Marmalade, he reported that Lady von Chassen had said a man wearing a wig and makeup was in her suite, a man she recognized, and then she left the ship.

Heather and Jeremy who had decided to stay in San Juan after Burt left for the ship headed for the Radisson. When they arrived at the hotel, it wasn't yet six o'clock. The manager confirmed what they already guessed, the invitation-only cocktail party scheduled to launch the ball from the casino would not be held until after dark. And

"No," he assured them, if Lady von Chassen had approached any hotel employee, he "personally, would have been promptly informed."

While Jeremy and Heather were looking for her at the hotel, back on board the Q.C. MacDonald met Burt as he stepped off the launch and brought him up to date on their search for Silke. "According to the suite's butler, a woman named Anastasia, Silke expected her around four to help her don a heavy ball gown she'd be wearing to a ball. Ms. von Chassen, she said, had told her she might be in the shower and to come in if she didn't respond to the doorbell."

Burt nodded as Mac continued. "When the butler arrived at three forty-five she'd found the living room empty. Both sliding glass doors to the double balconies stood open and the drapes from the balcony door on the right was on the floor. That seemed odd, but she thought the wind might have blown it down. When she didn't hear any noise in the suite, she knocked on the bedroom door and went in. That's when she freaked and called security."

Burt frowned.

"This was on the bed." MacDonald held up a shredded ball gown.

"Odd maybe. But, could it have been some kind of Mardi Gras costume?"

"Not according to the butler. She claimed she's seen it in Lady von Chassen's closet. Said it was some fancy New York designer outfit. Said it must have cost the von Chassen woman a fortune, and she liked it."

"No doubt," Burt agreed. "So where does that leave us? Where is she?"

"Cuzak claims she left the ship. I double checked the passenger files before I telephoned you," MacDonald said. "Computer data has her boarding a launch before five."

"Mr. Pryce's sister Heather said she'd planned to meet her and Mr. Pryce and me at the Marmalade for dinner. If she went there after five, we were no longer there."

"Too bad you missed her," MacDonald said. "She may know more than she thinks she does. At least she told us she recognized the guy in the wig. Although she admitted she'd only seen him once when she boarded in Fort Lauderdale,"

Burt scowled and said, "I was in the lobby when she boarded. I recall the guy at the gate did have some questions, so she was probably right. But, you know what I think about witness identification. Anyway, how did her assertion she recognized him square with our request from the head office for photo ID confirmation?"

Mac was ready. "Personnel in New York ran the entire crew through our facial recognition program, matched it to the sketch Johnson did of the guy in the wig. They were pretty sure they got the right man. If so, he's the one she identified. He's worked for the line for about four years. This morning headquarters asked for a recent photograph. We got the results back about an hour ago. I sure as hell recognized him."

MacDonald handed Burt a photo. "Here. And Pete Cuzak rounded up his cabin mate. The guy claimed he'd seen him asleep in the top bunk."

"And?" Burt said

"Clever, but not clever enough. A dummy facing the wall."

"What are the chances he followed her off the ship, Mac?"

"Fair," MacDonald said. "We weren't looking for him then. He could have been standing around watching the passengers leave, I suppose. When we got his photo we spread it around. One of our guys remembers seeing him near the crew exit. I put another copy of that photograph I just gave you on your desk along with an interesting message we got from the Romance in the Adriatic after they'd seen the photograph."

"Let's go," Burt said.

~

Chapter Twenty-Two

Earlier, convinced Silke hadn't gotten to the Radisson, Jeremy and Heather decided to return to the ship. Beyond the gate, they joined the line to the pier behind a couple of teenagers. By the time they reached the front of the line, the launch appeared almost loaded. Only four passengers remained waiting to board. Ahead of the teens, a man costumed like a scuba driver, complete with goggles, stood looking straight ahead. Something about his rigid stance caught Jeremy's attention. On some level of consciousness he knew what he was seeing, an angry man, the anger barely controlled.

That's when Jeremy spotted Angela in the stern. Relief flooded over him, and he drew in a deep breath and completely forgot the angry man in the wet suit until he heard one of the security guards tell him he'd have to wait for the next launch. Ignoring the security guards order to stand back, the man in the wet suit shoved the guard aside and jump from the pier into boat, eluding a second guard in the launch who tried to grab his arm. But he stormed past him and headed for the stern. By that time the first guard regained his balance and followed the man on board. In the stern the big man who'd been ahead of Angela in line saw him coming with the guard behind him. He stood up, blocked the aisle. But the man in the wetsuit belly punched him and he fell back and barely missed landing on woman in a seat. She screamed.

Angela, who'd been quietly talking to the nurse, still held the boy in her lap. When she saw the man in the wet suit coming, she knew instantly who he was, but before she could hand the sleeping boy over to the nurse, the costumed man grabbed the child out of her arms, threw him overboard and reached for Angela. Behind him the big man had regained his feet and once more he charged. While the two men struggled, Angela climbed up on the seat in the stern of the boat. From the corner of her eyes, she saw Jeremy moving rapidly down the center aisle toward her. She kicked off her shoes, climbed over the low rail and dove, launching herself as far as she could away from the boat. She hit the water in a shallow dive, surfaced, then struck out powerfully for the last place she'd seen the small blond head. She felt rather than saw a lean muscular form enter the water behind her. She couldn't look back.   .

An inexperienced swimmer, Angela knew, much less a frightened child, could not last in stormy water. Fear drove her through the darkening, wind whipped waves.

With her head down and her eyes scanning the waves, she propelled her body forward. Seconds seemed like hours since she'd first hit the water.

Phosphorescent-tipped waves fell into black trenches then rose again to block her view. She didn't dare raise her head or slow her pace until she was certain she was close to him. Luis could be hidden anywhere in those trenches. A heavy ball of fear formed in her belly—threatened to overpower her concentration. She'd been certain she had noted the place in the wake of the boat where he went into the water. Then almost before the thought was completed, in a brief glimpse between waves, she caught sight of his head a second before he sank. Dear god...she prayed, let him surface again. Then, just as she wondered if she'd gotten off course, the blond head surfaced only a couple of feet to her right. She struck out, but before she could reach him, he went down.

If only he'd surface once more. Her eyes searched the darkening waves. She swam forward until again she spotted the bright head bob up between the pulsing waves. For less than a few seconds, he seemed to hang there in the water and look in her direction. Had he seen her coming for him? He couldn't last much longer, if he went down again, could she find him? With darkness closing in time was everything.

"Dog-paddle, Luis!" she shouted, "dog-paddle!" He seemed to hear her and began paddling as hard as his small arms would allow, barely staying afloat, his eyes wild with fear. Then he saw her. When she reached out to grab him he slipped beneath the waves. Jackknifing, she dove into the blackened water. She held her breath searching for him in the murky depth. Seconds passed in the darkness with no sign of him. Hope and her breath drained from her bursting lungs. She knew she'd have to surface soon but she turned around and looked behind her one more time.

And this time she saw something sparkle and realized instantly what it had to be. Blindly reaching down, she caught the child by his upraised arm, pulled him to her breast and with one powerful kick propelled herself and the boy upward. As they surfaced she looked down at the child in her arms. The gaudy metal symbol of the cruise line Jeremy had given Luis the morning they'd played ball in the pool hung on a chain around his neck. Holding the choking boy close her, Angela shook her hair out of her face and treaded water. She didn't see Jeremy until he was beside her.

"That was some impressive performance for a non-swimmer," Jeremy shouted to be heard above the sound of the approaching launch. "Did it occur to you to yell 'man over board' before you dove in? If I hadn't seen you go in, you both might have..."

Luis sputtered and began to cry. Angela shook her head, glared at Jeremy.

"Look over your shoulder." He turned in time to catch a tow rope hanging from a small inflatable raft the launch crew had thrown overboard.

"Hey Luis, buddy," Jeremy said, "Want to ride on the raft with me?"

Luis raised his head from Angela's breast, smiled at Jeremy, but continued to cling to Angela.

"It's okay, Luis. You go with Jeremy now," she whispered to the boy. "He's going to take you to the boat, to your nurse. I'll come later."

"Read my book?"

"Wouldn't miss it," she said, and passed the child over to Jeremy. The storm was moving in faster, but she continued to tread water while Jeremy settled the boy on the raft. Holding him there he guided the raft to the prow of the boat, far enough away from the idling motor to prevent the raft from being swamped. At the launch, voices and hands reached out to help lift the boy into the launch.

Once she saw he was safely on board, Angela turned and struck out for shore, her slender figure almost invisible in the wind-whipped waves.

After helping to get the Luis into the launch Jeremy continued to tread water and stare at the retreating figure expertly plowing through the heavy sea, heading for the pier.

~

Chapter Twenty-Three

O ne of the security guards offered Angela a hand up
when she swam back to the pier.

Yes, the guard told her, Jeremy and the boy were back
on board the Q.C. The fight ended when the guy in the
scuba outfit was knocked overboard. The last time anyone
saw him was when the harbor police spotted him in the
water. No one had heard if they got him.

In the distance the Q.C., ablaze with lights, rode the
turbulent water of the harbor. Angela's hands shook as she
raised them and pressed her palms against her eyes. It
seemed every muscle in her body ached, including the
muscles that kept that organ pumping life into her in spite
of the emotional pain. What could she possible say to
Jeremy except that when she'd boarded that magic castle
he called a ship, she'd fallen in love with the prince and
lied about who she was. What else could she do when she
knew he could only love a princess?

While she waited for a launch to carry her back to the

ship, the oncoming storm carried Angela back to another night, another storm, another dock.

The tragedy of that night played over again in her mind as it had for so many years. The night her father drowned. She hadn't known he'd recently discovered he'd be spending the rest of his life in a wheel chair. He'd been a swimming coach and he'd spent his best years training her and others for the Olympics. It had always been his dream for her.

And after she graduated from high school she told him weeks before the finals meet in Nebraska that she didn't want to go, that even if she'd qualified she didn't want to swim in the Olympics. He was devastated.

Later, she couldn't recall the source of her rebellious mood swing, but her rebellion only lasted a few days. Years of pleasing her father won out, and when they'd gone sailing to Catalina a few days later, she had relented and agreed to go to the national meet in Nebraska and compete for selection to the summer Olympics.

That night in Catalina he went overboard. If she'd known he was drinking...?

"You could not have saved him," his friends insisted. "He wouldn't have let you. He knew alcohol and deep water don't mix. He's been walking dead for a long time."

As for the present, it shouldn't take Jeremy long to decide she'd used him for her own ends. And wasn't she a phony? Living as Silke von Chassen made her question herself. Who was she really?

Perhaps when Luis was thrown overboard, she reverted to who she was. When she'd seen the child safely on the launch, all the years she'd punished herself because she couldn't save her father vanished. His friends had been right. When the time came she would swim because she had to, because she could not have saved her father.

And now, if it had been possible, she would have given up her dream of a new clinic to be with Jeremy. But she knew now that could never work—couldn't change who she was, neither could he. And their relationship would have failed ultimately, as it just had. He had only known her as Silke. And it was Silke he'd fallen in love with.

But her name was Angela and Angela was a caregiver, a person who'd dedicated her life to relieving pain. She also understood now that she didn't need a new clinic to be who she was. It didn't matter where she worked, anywhere she was needed would do.

By the time the launch reached the ship, the towel Angela she'd wrapped around her for the ride back from the pier was soaked through. Anastasia met her in the lobby and wordlessly offered her a dry towel. Still trailing salt water behind her, she ignored the curious stares of her fellow passengers while she followed her butler. She wasn't surprised by her butler's appearance. Naturally, she thought, Jeremy would have sent her.

And Angela wasn't surprised when, at the elevator bank, Anastasia said. "Mr. Pryce asked me to tell you he'd come and see you as soon as he's changed. Would you like the kitchen to send up some coffee?"

"Yes, thank you, strong and black. And my telephone needs..."

"I've notified maintenance. I'll see to the coffee, now."

Back in her suite, Angela went straight to the master bath and dropped the soaked beach towel on the floor. Bone cold, she wanted nothing more than a hot shower. When she'd finally struggled out of the wet clothes she heard an impatient knock on the door. Anastasia with the coffee could not possibly have arrived. Let him knock, she thought, and stepped into the shower.

Several minutes later, warmed and wrapped in a thick terry cloth robe, she emerged from the master bath to find Jeremy in her bedroom. Of course, she thought, what else? He'd used a master key.

"At the risk of sounding clichéd, when did I invite you into my bedroom?"

Jeremy, ignoring the question, rose from where he was sitting on the bed. "That was some stunt for a non-swimmer. Why did you tell me you couldn't swim?"

She tightened the belt of her robe and crossed her arms under her breasts. "I don't recall telling you I couldn't swim"

"You didn't tell me you could. Do you know how you terrified me when I saw you go into the water?" he demanded. "What in the hell did you think you were doing?"

"I was attempting to pull a small boy out of a harbor before he drowned. If it's any of your business, and I can't see why it is."

"You know damn well there are plenty of reasons it's

my business. Starting with I'm not in the habit of allowing children to be thrown off one of my boats."

"Right. It's all about business."

Jeremy reached for her, but she avoided him and marched out of the bedroom door. When he followed her, she stopped in the middle of the living room and turned on him. "Why are you here? You got what you wanted from me."

She could almost see his orderly mind scrambling to understand.

He stared at her, slowly shook his head.

Her heart stuttered. But, she lifted her chin and said, "You seem surprised Jeremy. I don't know why you should be, going in you knew I was a player."

Pain laced his eyes.

She looked away. For a second she felt the mask slip, but she cared about him too much to let him see her now. Everything and nothing had changed since the day he walked onto the set of the game show. She knew then what she could not deny now. Independent women, the kind she was, didn't get involved with men like Jeremy Pryce. She thought she'd understood that when she broke her engagement to Edward Fournier. Men like him, like Jeremy, married women like Monica. "Eye candy" her father had called them. Women who didn't have to think for themselves, women like Silke, who wouldn't dream of pursuing a career. "Money marries money," her grandmother warned. She could never be part of his life.

Jeremy looked away. His eyes seemed to focus on the wall behind her. He blinked, grimaced and said, "A game,

Silke? Or whatever your name is. A game?" His eyes narrowed, he looked down at her.

She watched his lips part, but he did not speak. Seconds passed, He seemed to wait for her to deny his words.

When she did not respond, he took a step toward her, stopped inches from her. She could almost feel the heat of his body when he lowered his voice to a whisper. "What now, now that you've had your fun?" Angela saw his jaw tighten, saw dismay replace the pain.

"Will the Enquirer be at the dock when you disembark, cameras at the ready, salivating while the woman masquerading as Lady von Chassen describes her latest escapade, warning other single women to stay off our ships?"

Angela paled. The band in her chest tightened.

"No, no!" The words burst from her. "I won't be the one to tell them...if that's what you're worried about. And I won't share Silke's latest conquest for the Paparazzi to chew on either."

Fighting back tears she moved past him to the door of the suite, opened it and stood waiting. When he walked out she closed the door behind him and leaned against it her face pressed to the cold, hard wooden surface. "Goodbye, Jeremy. No more lies."

~

Chapter Twenty-Four

L ater that night, the authorities questioned her in the captain's quarters. Angela explained her presence on the cruise, provided them with her real identification, and explained how she had escaped the killer.

The captain verified her story and said the purser had access to information about the passengers and may have known she was a Charades game show contestant

During that interview the authorities told her how the battle on the launch ended with a well-placed punch by "the big man" that sent Henry Boyle, the purser, overboard.

The harbor patrol representative also said, they located Boyle's body shortly after the fight on the launch. Although the results of the autopsy wouldn't be available immediately they said they believed, based on the police surgeon's initial examination of the body, that Boyle had drowned. "That seems likely," the captain said, "as his employment records indicated he couldn't swim." Angela did not miss the irony.

The interview was brief. The captain and the local authorities thanked her for her cooperation, congratulated her on saving the boy.

The following morning Burt came to see her before the ship sailed. Angela wasn't surprised to hear he and Heather would not be finishing the cruise. "She sent a message to wish you good luck," he said, adding that Heather was on her way to Los Angeles to begin her job with the company, He didn't mention Jeremy by name, but did say "top executives" of Pryce Line would remain in Puerto Rico, to cooperate with local law enforcement. Angela's face remained neutral, but her insides were far from indifferent.

Burt didn't go into detail, but he said there was little doubt Boyle had killed Irene Ackerman and probably three other women on Pryce Line cruise ships. He was continuing to help with the investigation. He asked if Boyle said anything at all during his encounter with her.

Angela told Burt she later realized that Boyle seemed to be questioning her identity on her passport the day she boarded the ship. Burt nodded, obviously recalling the scene he, too, had witnessed. When Angela saw that Burt was not pursuing the identity subject with her, she continued.

"I heard nothing when he was searching for me in my suite, but..." She hesitated before continuing. "But after I climbed over the balcony and dropped to the executive desk below, I heard him mumble something about 'that Irish bitch.'" When she thought about it later, she said, she felt he wasn't talking about her or about Irene. Names like Ackerman and von Chassen, certainly weren't Irish names.

Burt didn't seem surprised and asked only a couple more questions. After praising her for rescuing the boy, he left.

At no time during the interview did he mention he knew she wasn't Silke von Chassen, but she could tell by the questions he asked, and by the one he didn't, that he might not know who she was, but she was sure he knew who she wasn't.

For Angela, the four days it took the Q.C. to sail to Fort Lauderdale slid by in a haze, followed by a five hour flight from Miami International back to Los Angeles.

Charlie and his fiancé Liza met her at LAX and drove her to her apartment above The Raven's bookstore facing the Venice Beach boardwalk. They said they'd been watching the game show every day and so far no one seemed to have identified her, or as Liza suggested, maybe someone did, but they had to wait until the contestant returned. The news of the murder on the Q.C. had appeared on the local television stations and in the Los Angeles Times. The media wanted to identify the unnamed person involved in the investigation someone, a passenger or crew member who supposedly could name Irene Ackerman's killer.

Angela didn't tell Charlie and Liza she knew the media wanted to identify her, or rather Silke. Not that it mattered, she thought, who knew the person they were seeking was an imposter. However, some news agency discovered the authorities in San Juan had been in touch with a reporter in St. Thomas who claimed a ship's officer told him there'd been multiple murders on Pryce Cruise Line ships. Any self-respecting journalist, Angela decided, would not find it difficult to identify the woman passenger named Silke as the person the police questioned. Some investigative reporter might have checked the passenger list and determine Silke von Chassen had never been on board the Q.C., but someone pretending to be Silke von Chassen had been.

Once identified all they had to do was put two and two together, contact the game show and claim she'd been the contestant on board. With that information the game would have ended, and she wouldn't know who had revealed her identity. While Angela had accepted she couldn't win if identified, and although she hated to lose and hated to disappoint Charlie, who'd been such a staunch supporter, she knew what she had to do next.

Dawn slept somewhere behind the range of the Santa Ana Mountains. The damp gray morning mist of Venice Beach blanketed the shoreline, smothering the sound of the waves. On the second floor above The Raven's bookshop, Angela awoke on her first day home. She pulled on a pair of worn sweatpants, and an old tee shirt, emblazoned with *Love—a Curable Psychosis*, and a windbreaker. With her running shoes in her left hand, she slipped down the back stairs. At the bottom she unlocked the heavy stairwell door, paused and checked the alley for vagrants. Most of the year she could be certain she would see at least one person curled up beneath the eaves that shielded the back entrance of the neighboring shops. Winter and early spring sent most of them inland to Arizona or Nevada. Angela had lived above the shop on the boardwalk since her father died. She'd always felt safe, but after her experience on the cruise, she didn't want any confrontations. She needed time alone—time to think, to plan, time to...what? Make a decision? Wasn't it already made? Jeremy would never forgive her for deceiving him. For her, a chance to choose love, real love, went overboard with Luis. She'd cheated the killer of two deaths and revealed him and herself as imposters.

She stepped off the concrete bicycle path that ran along the front of the shops and into the sand. She stopped once more, looked over her shoulder. No one appeared in the lingering mist behind her.

By the time she'd plowed through the deep sand and reached the hard packed shingle at the water's edge, the sun had begun its ascent behind the Santa Anna's. Only the sound of the waves disturbed the silence. For several moments Angela stood on the shore, mesmerized by the sea—until she saw, far out on the edge of her visible world, a cruise ship emerge from the morning fog and glide majestically along the rim of the Pacific. She stood riveted, entranced with its majestic progress until it disappeared again into the mist. Then, fighting back the tears, she turned her back on the reality of her home on the boardwalk and began to run, gradually picking up speed until her heartbeat rose to match the drumming rhythm of the sea against the shore.

Hurry, hurry, the voice inside her head warned, you'll "be late." Late for what she wondered? Like Alice in Wonderland, it didn't matter anymore, she'd already fallen down the rabbit hole into a fantasy called true love. Marooned in her real world now, there would be no more adventures.

The day after she arrived home, determined to get on with her life, to forget Jeremy and her dreams of another clinic, Angela contacted Pete the owner of Metro Therapy Center. It would take the rest of the week, she told him, to finish closing down the clinic before handing over the keys to the building's owner.

When she hadn't heard from Carstairs she scheduled the following week to take care of personal business. And later when Pete telephoned, they agreed on a time and date for the job interview.

For the rest of the week Angela fell into a routine. Each morning she ran at least a mile on beach in front of the boardwalk, then left for the clinic. With that deadline for turning over the keys to the clinic hovering, she worked steadily until noon each day. She sorted and packed all remaining personal property that must be disposed of or stored for a future she no longer dreamed of. Afternoons she stopped work long enough to swim in the clinic's pool, gradually rebuilding the skills she'd denied herself for almost five years. Nights were difficult.

During her first two nights at home Angela tried to watch television, but couldn't find a program she liked. The third night she attended a movie she thought she wanted to see, but the lead actor, much too handsome and much too blond, reminded her of Jeremy. She didn't stay.

~

The fourth day Angela reached home early to find the blue Mercedes limousine parked in the space reserved for her apartment above the book store.

Samantha sent her chauffeur for a walk after she'd convinced a reluctant Angela to join her in the back seat, for what she described as a "girl's chat."

They sat next to each other as they had several weeks before outside the clinic. A ballad on the car radio drifted out the open door. Neither of the women heard the music.

"You love him," Samantha said without preamble.

"I didn't want too." Angela's words were just above a whisper.

"It happens. I believe I've lived long enough to say how unpredictable love is."

"I could have walked away. It wasn't fair to Jeremy. He didn't know me, and I knew who he was. He would not have looked at me twice if he'd thought I wasn't the woman I was pretending to be."

"Nonsense. I'll admit my grandson wanted to believe he had to marry a woman he considered his social and financial equal. Like most young people, he thought he could control all of his emotions, order a tailor made wife the way he could order a new suit." Her eyes twinkled. "Typical man," she said.

Angela turned to face Samantha, "Is it so terrible for a man in his position? Wouldn't it be reasonable for him to marry someone with a similar history, someone he could be sure would share his values?"

Samantha tilted her head. "I can't say I believe in arranged marriages. Jeremy wouldn't approve of my interference any more than I suspect you will or I did when my parents tried to convince me to marry Colin Boyle. But it's not your fault or Jeremy's that you met on the Queen. For that I'm culpable. When you won a chance to compete for the Grand Prize, I'll admit I encouraged the advertising agency to choose the Q.C. for your trip."

Angela stiffened, her lips parted.

Before she could reply Samantha said, "You told the police something the purser said when you got away from him that afternoon. I thought you should also be told I am the 'Irish bitch' he referred to. I know the killer as Carin Boyle, not Henry Boyle. He was born two generations later than I in Kenmare, County Kerry, Ireland, but he was the grandson of the man my family expected me to marry."

"But why..." Angela began, but Samantha continued.

"Why did he hate me? He believed he should. His grandfather convinced him of that. My parents thought they knew the man they'd promised me to, but he was a misogynist. He only wanted to marry me to gain control of my father's small business. My friends and I knew him to be a bully and too much like his own father and grandfather, both wife abusers."

Samantha shifted in her seat. "I was terrified of Colin Boyle, Carin's grandfather and in love with an American who had visited in my home town, Kenmare, since he was a boy. The year I turned seventeen, I eloped with my American, John Pryce."

Samantha hesitated a fraction of a second as a cloud of wistfulness crossed her face. "Angela, somehow in Carin's twisted mind he believed he could revenge his grandfather, satisfy his sickness, and destroy me by destroying the cruise line."

She looked directly at Angela. "His determination to destroy the line has nothing to do with the fact that my grandson is in love with you." The two women looked at one another. "According to his sister who is quite fond of you, by the way, he is not likely to forget you. I'll admit to putting you in his path, but I can't imagine Jeremy being a lesser man than his grandfather who loved me and married me, a poor Irish girl. I thought you should know."

For an hour after Samantha left, Angela walked the beach. She appreciated knowing Samantha had nothing to do with her competing for the Grand Prize other than having Monsieur Jacque, a friend, do her makeup. She obviously thought she understood her grandson, but she was from a different generation. She didn't want to believe today's women would allow their parents to dictate to them who they would marry. How sad it must be for Samantha to know her love story led to so much tragedy.

But that didn't change the fact that she'd lied about who she was, and Jeremy, even if he discovered her real identity, had every reason not to trust the woman he knew as Silke von Chassen.

Later that afternoon, Charlie and his fiancée Liza met Angela at the Santa Monica pier for beer, and sandwiches. During the evening she told them an abbreviated version of her ten days on the Q.C. Then Charlie told her about his new job at Pete's clinic, and although he liked and respected Pete, he professed he would still prefer to work with her.

By the fifth night, when she couldn't find anything else to keep her busy Angela drove to Santa Monica Place, an upscale shopping mall, where she wandered through the stores she couldn't afford, and thought of Heather. Did she finally buy a dress for the Mardi Gras ball? They'd become friends so easily. She'd never forget their visit to Coles in Nassau and how people stared at them when they couldn't stop laughing. Whatever the future held she'd always cherish their brief friendship and that day in Nassau.

By Friday Angela knew she had spent too many sleepless nights. Over-tired, she was unprepared to hear Carstairs' voice when she answered the telephone that morning.

"That was some trip," Carstairs said. "I'd apologize if I thought my having you masquerade as von Chassen almost got you killed. From what I've read, the perp was after celebrities, any celebrities."

"That's what I was told," Angela said.

"Actually I called to congratulate you."

Angela pulled in a deep breath. Did she win?

Carstairs continued. "I know I probably don't have to remind you to be at the studio Monday. I thought you might want to know the cruise line and the shows advertising agency wants to publicly reward you for saving the life of that boy."

Angela's hand tightened on the receiver. The cruise line? The last person she wanted to see was Jeremy. She hoped Carstairs didn't mean Jeremy. "That isn't necessary," she said. "I'd rather forget the whole affair. I just happened to be able to go in after the child. Anyone would have done the same."

"I wish that were true," Carstairs said, "but I'm too much of a realist to agree with you. And, I doubt if the agency or the line would care whether or not you wanted a reward. If you insist I'll speak with them. No promises they'll listen though."

"I'd appreciate it. And thank you for the information. You've been very kind. Whatever you find out, I'll be there Monday."

～

Chapter Twenty-Five

Several miles north of Venice beach, and less than a week after Jeremy's return from San Juan, he arrived at his childhood home in Malibu. Samantha had invited him to dinner that Sunday evening. Her purpose, she claimed, was for him, to fill in any details of the murders not in Burt's report.

Samantha neglected to mention Heather's extensive recital of the cruise events the day she flew back from Puerto Rico. Heather had said that, in her opinion, Jeremy had fallen in love with the woman on the cruise she now knew to be masquerading as Silke von Chassen.

Samantha agreed with Heather, saying, "If it is truly love..." she knew Jeremy had to be the one to make that decision to find that woman and tell her he didn't care what her name was. What Samantha didn't suggest was that Jeremy, like so many men, could be obstinate if accepting they'd made a mistake that potentially threatened their ego. Admitting he was in love with the woman who tricked him might not be possible.

What she also did not add was that creating the opportunity for the two to meet might allow both of them to reconsider what they stood to lose. And without confiding in Heather, the following day Samantha telephoned her old friend, Jacque, in the makeup department of KCBT.

During dinner that Sunday, she also asked Jeremy to visit the game show the next day reminding him the recent Grand Prize contestant would appear on the show and either receive a check for one million dollars or lose the fifty thousand they'd gambled for. She claimed she wanted his opinion of the audience's reaction to the winner.

As a favor to his grandmother, Jeremy agreed he would go to the show if he could squeeze in the time.

Monday morning, he arrived in his Century City office before his secretary. Outside the thirty story office building, the Los Angeles basin remained submerged in late spring fog. No doubt his secretary would be late, he decided.

He turned on an oversized television set on the wall next to the door of his office. Then, moving to his desk, he powered up his computer and began scanning company computer files for the name of a detective agency Burt had used and recommended. It had been over two weeks since he returned from San Juan, and he was determined to find the woman masquerading as Silke von Chassen. When his search for the agency failed he made a note to telephone Burt. He'd find the agency for him.

His secretary arrived with a list of appointments and temporarily distracted him. He turned down the sound on the television while he reviewed the list and marked out two appointments. Then, looking up from his desk to hand them back to her, he noticed the news show he was watching had segued into a commercial break announcing the next show, "America's Favorite Game Show, Charades."

"Charade!"

A jeweled mask, long blonde hair back then, a green scoop-necked sweater, legs that went on forever.

"Idiot!" he exclaimed, startling his secretary. He still didn't know the masked woman's name. In fact he knew nothing about her except that she was the one woman on the planet meant for him.

Abruptly dismissing his confused secretary, he checked the time on the television screen, compared it to the Apple watch on his wrist, opened his desk drawer and removed a small white box. He shoved the box into the pocket of his suit jacket. Then punched an intercom button. When his secretary answered, he told her to cancel all his appointments for the day—"No," he added to the clearly baffled secretary, "for two weeks."

Fairfax was about five miles from his office. He might make it before the show ended. If not, he'd get her name if he had to shake it out of that toothy M.C.

Across town, Carstairs' secretary Mary Ann had just met Angela in the reception room on the second floor of KCBT and escorted her to the producer's office.

"Welcome back." Carstairs rose from her chair, came around her paper laden desk and offered Angela her hand.

"Please sit down," she said with a wave in the direction of two deeply cushioned chairs in front of her desk. "I'll be with you in a minute." She turned her attention to her secretary. "Please advise Mr. Martin, Ms. Hamilton has arrived. She'll be waiting in the Green Room with me until we're wanted on the set."

After the door closed behind her secretary, Carstairs returned to the chair behind her desk. "Nice tan," she said to Angela. "Must be plenty of sun in the Caribbean."

"On a cruise ship you'd have to be a recluse to avoid a tan," Angela suggested. "I think it's the first tan I've managed since I graduated from college."

Carstairs smiled, nodded thoughtfully, "How's that going? When we spoke Sunday, you said you might be considering a new position."

"I believe I'll be working in a clinic owned by a friend and colleague. In Santa Monica."

"You like your work, like the beach area, the ocean, all that?"

"Less smog."

Why the questions, Angela wondered. Why weren't they going directly to the set? It almost seem as if Carstairs stalling for time? Surely a woman in her position had better things to do than question a former contestant about where they lived and where they worked. She decided to ask a few of her own questions...had someone contacted the show, identified her as a fake? But before she could speak a soft rap sounded at the door.

"Enter," Carstairs said.

"Sorry to interrupt." Her secretary crossed the room once more and handed Carstairs a note.

The producer read it, then handed it back. "Please tell him it will be taken care of, and I'll be with him in a moment."

The woman smiled at Angela and left.

Then, before Angela could ask who won, and if she'd lost, and what she was expected to say or do during the show, the door opened again. And the little small man with a smile she remembered thinking was as wide as an Arizona canyon, stepped into the room.

Carstairs stood. "I'm sure you'll remember meeting Monsieur Jacque. If you will accompany him to the Green Room, I'll join you there in a few minutes."

"A pleasure to see you again, Mademoiselle. You will please to follow me."

Nothing had changed in the Green Room. Although it appeared to be clean, Angela could identify its recent history with its odors of stale coffee, cheap perfume and fear that hung in the air. Had someone come forward and identified her? Surely they had or Carstairs would have told her, she decided.

The television in the corner was on. It pictured a sweeping view of an audience. Today's audience. Waiting like the ancient Romans in the Coliseum for the Gladiators, for the kill.

Monsieur Jacque didn't look pleased. He immediately hurried across the room and turned it off.

"If you will please be seated at la table?" He indicated the well-lit tables at the back of the room. "We will proceed."

For the next ten minutes, he kept busy with his brushes and jars until at last he stepped back and reaching beneath his cart full of makeup withdrew a mask. Angela eyes widened. The same mask, the beautiful mask she'd worn the last day of the contest.

"I am told, Mademoiselle, that for you there has been an adventure, and perhaps amour?"

Angela flinched. Color rose in her cheeks.

The little man continued speaking, his tone gentle. "Today you see only a mask covered with artificial gems. But they tell us many things. La Emerald promises rebirth and is the rarest of gems and green reminds us to cherish our planet. The Ruby is the king, the most valuable of gems. Wearing a fine Ruby bestows good fortune love, health and wisdom. Look closely you will see Diamonds, they symbolize love, the ability to foresee the future and your spiritual destiny. And on this special masque we also see aquamarines. They reflect the color of the sea; they protect those who sail."

He held out the beautiful, jeweled mask. "Masks, Mademoiselle, like gems, make many promises, but we must have courage to lift the mask and accept our future."

Carstairs entered the Green Room seconds after

Monsieur Jacque wished Angela good luck with a "Bon Chance, Mademoiselle" and left.

"This won't take long," Carstairs said. Please take a seat on the couch. "Coffee?" she suggested, and without waiting for a reply she went directly to the machine and poured two cups.

On the set of the game show fifteen minutes later three chairs stood as before behind a curtain.

At the front of the stage, Mad Martin reminded the studio audience of the rules of the game: to win the Grand Prize the contestant must successfully masquerade for ten days without being identified as an impostor. A person who claims to know the name of the person being impersonated cannot be an employee, family member or associate of Pryce Cruise Line, Pryce Merchant Ships or anyone associated with producing the game show or its advertising agency.

"Ladies and Gentlemen," Mad Martin continued, in his sonorous voice, "the first person to identify the name of the celebrity the contestant is impersonating will win the fifty-thousand dollars—the same fifty-thousand dollars the contestant chose to gamble for an opportunity to win the Grand Prize. Then, if the impersonator is revealed, the winner will be escorted on stage to receive a check for fifty-thousand dollars from a representative of Pryce Cruise Line. If, however, the contestant escorted onto the stage has successfully impersonated a celebrity for ten days, as promised, she will win one million dollars."

The audience applauded when a Pryce Cruise Line vacation advertisement on the wall of the set followed

Martin's recitation of the rules. Behind the curtain at the back of the stage Carstairs escorted Angela to the dais. "Please take your seat." She gestured to the middle chair.

Angela offered Carstairs a brief smile and a curt nod. Then she stepped up onto the dais, sat down, put on the mask she'd worn for the final show, then lifted her chin.

"Good luck," Carstairs mouthed the words and left the set.

Almost before Angela could tuck her skirt under her hips, the show's opening music swelled. The dais began to turn and once more Mad Martin stepped out of the wings. In rapid order, he smiled his toothy grin, greeted the audience, completed his opening spiel, walked across the stage, and reached out his hand to Angela who took it and stepped down from the dais.

With her right hand held tightly, he escorted her to the center of the stage. The audience applauded wildly when he introduced her.

"And now Ladies and Gentlemen, the moment we've all be waiting for is here." Behind them a huge white cruise ship flying the American flag and a smaller Pryce cruise line flag of orange and green appeared to sail through an impossibly blue sea disappearing in a distance.

Mad Martin paused smiled, squeezed Angela's hand and, turning, addressed the audience. "First a word from our sponsor."

Then, instead of the disembodied voice of an announcer describing the joys of cruising, Martin gestured to the tall, blond man in the wings. "Ladies and gentlemen, please welcome Mr. Jeremy Pryce, CEO of Pryce Cruise Line."

Across greater Los Angeles on Malibu's shore, Samantha, Heather and Burt, stood before the small television in Samantha's office and watched Jeremy walk to the center of the stage.

In the studio, a television camera moved in closer and focused on his face when he bowed to the audience and shook hands with the host. The audience applauded enthusiastically. While the nearest television camera rolled back to film the entire stage.

Beside Mad Martin, Angela closed her eyes and opened them slowly before turning to face Jeremy. Hands clenched, chin up, adrenaline coursed through her limbs. This time she would not run.

"Hello, Jeremy." Angela spoke first.

Jeremy's smile curled up from the corner of his mouth. "It's Angela, then. Right? Perfect name. Fits."

Between them Martin appeared confused. He opened his mouth as if to speak hesitated, looked from Angela to Jeremy.

In front of the stage the audience seemed to lean forward. Then someone coughed and one of the television camera caught a shot of an obviously surprised Martin looking from Jeremy to Angela before continuing his spiel.

"Ladies and Gentlemen at home and in the studio audience," he paused, hesitated, and began again. "You know the rules of the game. It's time now to introduce our contestant." He stepped back from between the couple then looking at Angela and said, "Please remove your mask Ms. Hamilton."

Angela reached up behind her head where her fingers

found the elastic band, lifted the mask and then facing Jeremy she slid it up and off exposing her face.

Jeremy's smiled broadened. Then he stepped forward erasing the distance between them. In his left hand he held out a manila envelope.

"Ms. Hamilton, please take the envelope Mr. Pryce is holding and please open it."

Angela took the envelope, tore open and withdrew a check for one million dollars, which she held up for the television cameras and approving, applauding audience to see.

When the applause ended, Martin turned to Jeremy. "Mr. Pryce, unless I am sorely mistaken, I believe you also have something else for Ms. Hamilton."

Determined not to cry, Angela turned to face Jeremy. What she saw written there, startled her. His eyes, overly bright, questioning, seemed to search hers.

And reaching into his coat pocket, he pulled out small white box. "My grandmother made me promise that the ring my grandfather gave her one stormy night in Ireland would only belong to the woman I knew in my heart would live there for the rest of my life. Marry me, Angela."

Tears gathered, spilled over, and when she brushed them away, she raised her head, her answer written on her face.

"Yes," she whispered, "yes Jeremy." And his arms gathered her in while the audience roared and the television cameras moved closer and closer as they kissed.

When the kiss ended, the couple turned to the audience.

Mad Martin recovering his poise, grinned, coughed, moved to the front of the stage and said, into the camera. "Please repeat your answer a bit louder, Ms. Hamilton?"

The audience leaned forward, rustled and waited.

Angela, once more brushing the tears from her eyes, lifted her head from where she'd placed it on Jeremy's shoulder and facing him repeated in a clear voice. "Yes! Jeremy Pryce, Yes, I'll marry you."

In front of the stage, the audience, now stood, laughed, shouted, and applauded wildly.

"Please open the box, Angela," Jeremy said.

Martin signaled the audience to wait.

Inside the box, a ruby ring nestled in blue velvet and the tiny jeweled mask she had admired in St. Thomas sparkled and shone.

Angela caught her breath, while Jeremy pinned the mask to her dress and slid the ring onto the finger of her left hand.

At Malibu Beach, Samantha noticed Burt reach out his hand to Heather. I've always liked weddings, she thought, perhaps a double wedding. That would be far more efficient. Then after two or three weeks for honeymoons, everyone could get back to work.

Samantha turned away from the two beside her to stifle the laugh she recognized was for herself. Always running things, she thought with a grin.

Then, lowering the volume on the small television set, she walked to the French doors of her office, opened them and stepped out onto her veranda. The fog had lifted.

Close to the water's edge, two children and a dog came into sight. Samantha smiled.

The End

About Donna Benedict

The author has been a reporter, a radio announcer, a communications analyst, an English, journalism and creative writing teacher for 28 years, and now a short story author and novelist.

Benedict's short story "Hot Box" was chosen for the Capitol Crimes chapter of Sisters In Crime 2021 Anthology, Cemetery Plots of Northern California.

Queen of Charades is Benedict's first full-length Romantic Suspense novel. The mother of six is currently working on her second novel. She resides in Northern California.

Made in the USA
Las Vegas, NV
19 August 2021